THE
CALL

BOOKS BY KERRY WILKINSON

THRILLER NOVELS

Two Sisters

The Girl Who Came Back

Last Night

The Death and Life of Eleanor Parker

The Wife's Secret

A Face in the Crowd

Close to You

After the Accident

The Child Across the Street

What My Husband Did

The Blame

The Child in the Photo

The Perfect Daughter

The Party at Number 12

The Boyfriend

The Night of the Sleepover

After the Sleepover

ROMANCE NOVELS

Ten Birthdays

Truly, Madly, Amy

THE JESSICA DANIEL SERIES

The Killer Inside (also published as *Locked In*)

Vigilante

The Woman in Black

Think of the Children

Playing With Fire

The Missing Dead (also published as *Thicker than Water*)

Behind Closed Doors

Crossing the Line

Scarred for Life

For Richer, For Poorer

Nothing But Trouble

Eye for an Eye

Silent Suspect

The Unlucky Ones

A Cry in the Night

THE ANDREW HUNTER SERIES

Something Wicked

Something Hidden

Something Buried

WHITECLIFF BAY SERIES

The One Who Fell

The One Who Was Taken

The Ones Who Are Buried

The Ones Who Are Hidden

SILVER BLACKTHORN

Reckoning

Renegade

Resurgence

OTHER

Down Among the Dead Men

No Place Like Home

Watched

THE
CALL

KERRY WILKINSON

Bookouture

Published by Bookouture in 2024

An imprint of Storyfire Ltd.
Carmelite House
50 Victoria Embankment
London EC4Y 0DZ

www.bookouture.com

ISBN: 978-1-83525-469-1
eBook ISBN: 978-1-83525-468-4

ONE

SUNDAY

Melody Bryant pressed into the reclining chair on the deck and stared across the rippling lake, to where the sun had disappeared over the distant trees.

'Red sky at night,' Nina replied whimsically, seemingly thinking the same thing as Melody.

'Something's on fire,' Melody replied, flatly.

The sisters laughed to each other, because that was what their dad would say every time a hint of orange whispered its way into the evening sky. Melody was into her teens before she had realised there was another version of the saying that actually rhymed, and made much more sense.

There was red in the sky now, creeping over the treetops as a purply-black started to spread from the other side of the lake. The warmth of the day had held and Melody knew that if she could stay awake for another hour or so, then the rest of the holiday should be broadly jet lag-free.

The thought of jet lag signalled the beginning of a yawn, as Melody wafted a hand in front of her mouth, failing to flap it away. Her eyes watered as the infection of tiredness jumped from her, across the small table, leading to a back-and-forth ping-pong of yawns with her sister.

'What time is it at home?' Nina managed through teary eyes.

Melody blinked away the remnants of the successive yawns, before checking her phone's lock screen. 'Half four in England. I think it's Monday there.'

It was a little after half past eight the previous evening on Vancouver Island, just off the west coast of Canada. Saturday had been a long day and a half or so of waiting in an airport, waiting for a plane to cross the Atlantic, waiting in a different airport, waiting for a different plane, waiting for luggage, waiting for a hire car, and then a final hour and a bit up the highway to the lake house in which they were staying.

Today had been largely spent around the house and sitting on the bank of the lake. For now – basics such as a time to eat, or a time to sleep, had been replaced by barely knowing which day it was. They'd first landed at roughly the time they had taken off, which was thrilling for Melody's nine-year-old son. Real-life time travel existed – but for Melody it was more exhausting than thrilling.

'It's so quiet,' Nina added, taking her glass of wine from the table. She sipped and then replaced the glass, before returning to gaze across the water.

Nina was five years older than Melody, although insistent that mid-forties was the new thirties. It had been a long time since the sisters had been able to sit together to enjoy such calm.

Melody didn't reply. There was a faint buzz of a boat some-where out of sight, maybe a distant chirp of some birds – but the peace was undeniable. It was a far cry from the housing estate on which Melody lived. There were parked cars up both sides of the street there. Everyone lived on top of everyone else and life never really stopped. There was always somebody getting up for work in the early hours, other people getting home from nights out.

Melody had done plenty of reading about Shawnigan Lake before the trip. It was long and narrow, like a capital letter Y. The Airbnb she had found was a holiday house, built at the back end of a large plot, away from the main property. There was a mini beach and a boat launch, as the water stretched far into the distance. The house was on the north shore and it was four miles or so to the furthest tip.

Two weeks of lounging on the water's edge was going to be heavenly.

'Is Sam asleep?' Nina asked.

'He was when I last checked,' Melody replied. Her nine-year-old hadn't stirred when she'd poked her head into his room. He was the only one of them who had managed to sleep on the plane the day before. He had been entirely unaffected by anything that could be called jet lag, which meant he would likely be up as the sun rose.

'What about Dad?' Nina added. 'Is he back yet?'

'I don't think so. He said his back was sore, so he was going to walk it off.'

The women exchanged a micro glance, not needing words. Their father was of the generation who'd try to walk off a broken leg if it meant avoiding the doctor.

They sat and watched the water together as the sky continued to darken. A minute passed. More.

'Not much has changed, has it?' Nina said, although the sentence drifted to nothing, because it wasn't true.

Nina had another sip from her glass as the silent acknowledgement settled that one huge thing *had* changed. The last time they'd seen this lake, their mother had been with them. It had been a lifetime ago.

Well, thirty years.

It had been a long wait to return – too long for their mother to be able to make it – but it was going to be worth it.

Nina picked up her phone from the table and glanced at the screen. 'What time is Evan getting here?' she asked.

Melody grabbed her own device to check the time, then jumped as it began to buzz in her hand. 'Evan' flashed on the screen and Melody pressed the green button to answer.

'We've opened the wine,' Melody told him, as she reached for her own glass.

There was a chuckle from the other end. 'I've got you on speaker,' her fiancé replied. 'I turned off the highway about ten minutes ago. I'm maybe another ten or fifteen minutes away, so leave enough for me.'

'We're on the deck – but Nina's already gone through half a bottle, so you better hurry.'

That got a middle finger and a smile from Melody's sister, who was again holding her glass.

'Is Sam still up?' Evan asked.

'Dad took him to the park earlier, so he's tired from that. He didn't complain about going to bed. He's excited for tomorrow.'

There was a distracted-sounding 'uh-huh' from the other end and then: 'There are a lot of potholes around here.'

'What car did you get?' she asked.

'Something silver. It's automatic but I think everything is here.' He paused for a moment. 'Have you got my Garmin? I couldn't find it in my bag.'

'It was in mine,' Melody replied. 'I left it on the stand at your side of the bed.'

'Oh! Great! I thought I'd lost it.' She could feel the relief through the phone. 'If we do hire those bikes, I can record it. There's also those walks we talked about.'

Melody bit her lip, suppressing the smile that her fiancé wouldn't have been able to see anyway. Even though he wore something he called 'more professional' to work, the running device was used to record every last step, walk, run, ride, hop, jump, or journey up the stairs. He kept spreadsheets chronicling how far he'd travelled every twelve months – and liked nothing more than explaining that he'd have made it two-thirds of the way up Everest based on the number of times he'd gone up the stairs in their house over a year.

'Do we need anything from a supermarket?' Evan asked.

'I don't think so,' Melody replied. 'There aren't really any shops close to here but we all went to the big supermarket earlier.' Melody glanced to her sister and then added, 'Nina and Thomas stopped off at a vineyard on the way back.'

She expected interest at that, though all she got was a low hum. 'Hang on,' Evan said, sounding hurried. There was a fuzz of activity from the other end of the line and then: 'There's someone in the road.'

It took Melody a moment to realise what he meant. 'Someone walking?'

She'd noticed the day before that there was little in the way of pavements around the lake. Most people seemed to drive everywhere, though there had been the odd person walking on the verge.

There was no reply at first, but Evan's voice sounded confused when he next spoke. 'I think it's a little girl. Hang on.'

Melody realised she'd sat up straighter as her sister turned to take her in, suddenly interested. From the other end of the phone, there were muffled scratchings of what sounded like tyres on gravel – and then the unmistakeable *thunk* of an opening car door.

'Are you OK?' Evan said, although his voice wasn't as clear as it had been seconds before.

'Are you talking to me?' Melody asked.

'There's a girl here,' Evan replied, and the phone was seemingly back to his mouth. 'I don't think there's anyone else around. She's covered in mud, or...' he tailed off, before adding a whispered: 'blood...?'

'Blood?' Melody repeated, which had Nina sitting up straighter.

'Whose blood?' Nina asked, just as Evan said something that Melody didn't catch.

'Where are you?' Melody said.

'What's wrong?' Nina asked, which again cut over what Evan was trying to say.

'I didn't catch that...?' Melody added, though there was no reply. Instead, Evan was talking to somebody.

'What's your name?' he asked, his voice distant; phone likely away from his face. 'Are you OK? Do you live around here?'

There was quiet, with only muffled breathing coming from the other end.

'Evan...?'

Melody's question was unanswered, though jilted by a sudden muted huff and a crackle of... something. She winced at the sound of an echoing bang. When she looked at the screen, her fiancé's name was still there.

'Evan...?' she said.

The breeze murmured, a board on the deck creaked, the water drifted.

But there was no answer.

TWO

Melody was watching the map on her phone as Thomas drove the darkened route along the lake. Nina's husband was the only adult at the house who hadn't been drinking, though he was seemingly not understanding the gravity of the situation.

'Where did Evan say he was?'

'He didn't,' Melody replied. 'Just that he had turned off the highway and was on the way.'

Thomas grumbled an unconvinced 'huh' to himself that went without reply. He'd been in bed, watching something on his laptop, when Nina had gone to find him.

They'd had to transport five people and luggage from the airport – and, though the SUV they'd hired had suited its purpose on the Saturday, it now felt big as they rumbled along.

'There's only one road,' Thomas said. 'I dunno how he's got lost.'

Melody ignored her brother-in-law as her gaze flicked between the map on her phone and the gloomy road ahead. Night was closing in and, as the trembling trees rattled overhead, the day was slipping.

Thomas eased to take a bend, as they passed someone's

driveway. There were intermittent houses on both sides as flashes of the lake appeared through gaps in the trees. Orange lights sparkled somewhere across the water, there and gone as the car bumped over a pothole.

'Why's he coming a day late anyway?' Thomas asked, even though he'd been told at least twice. Melody wondered if he was making small talk, or if he'd not been listening the other times.

'He couldn't get the extra day off work,' Melody said, through a clenched jaw.

She swiped away from the map and tried calling Evan again. They'd been cut off at some point, even though he hadn't spoken since she'd heard him asking someone whether they lived locally. As Thomas continued to drive, Melody's reception wavered between two bars and none. She couldn't get a call to connect.

They'd been driving for around five minutes and hadn't seen another vehicle since taking the turn onto the route that ran along the west side of the lake. The road itself looped around the water, though they were staying on the north-west side, in what the Airbnb listing had promised was 'unparalleled peace'.

A moment passed as Melody pinched in and out of the map screen, trying to figure out where Evan might've been when he called. Assuming he was following the shortest route offered by his phone – which he would've been – there was only one road.

'I lent your dad two-hundred dollars at the airport,' Thomas said.

It was so unconnected to what was going on that Melody needed a moment to take it in.

'You... what?'

'He told me not to tell Nina but didn't say anything about you.'

'Why'd he borrow that?'

'Something about his card not working out here.'

Melody thought for a moment. It wasn't the first time Thomas had told her something he wanted passed onto her sister. Before they'd been married, Thomas had asked Melody what she thought Nina might say if he proposed. Melody had told her sister, who said she wanted to get married – and then the official proposal had happened. It took Melody a few years to realise it was Thomas's way of asking without actually doing it.

Except she had bigger concerns now.

The houses on each side had become more sporadic, giving way to a narrow road with no street lights. It would be drab, even on a bright day, let alone as night approached.

'Is that it?' Thomas said. He was already slowing as the headlights illuminated a silver car on the other side of the road.

He didn't wait for a reply, as he passed the vehicle and then indicated. Melody twisted in her seat, trying to get a view of the car as her brother-in-law performed a three-point turn in the middle of the road. Moments later, he rolled to a stop, half on the verge, as the headlights beamed across a silver car.

Stars were beginning to blip into view overhead as a creeping draught zipped through the rustling trees, interrupting the crippling silence.

The world felt empty.

Melody didn't remember getting out of the vehicle but found herself at the side of the silver car. She crouched to look through the driver's door, momentarily wondering where the steering wheel was, before remembering it was on the other side. The glare of the headlights fizzed off the glass.

Thomas was on the other side of the car, looking out of place in the loose pyjama-like shorts and T-shirt he'd been wearing when Nina had gone to find him. There was a click as he opened the driver's side, which made Melody realise the car was unlocked. She opened the other door and then hunched to look inside.

There was nobody in the car.

Thomas had already ducked out of the vehicle, though his voice sounded from the back. 'There's a Budget sticker on the bumper,' he said. 'This must be his car, right?'

It felt too final for Melody to admit it likely was. Evan said he had a silver car – and their booking had been with Budget. She wasn't sure what she'd expected when she'd set off with Thomas to find out what had happened, though it wasn't this. She wondered if her fiancé had slipped and hurt his leg. That he'd dropped his phone, something like that. She hadn't expected... nothing.

There was no sign of Evan.

Melody stretched across and pulled the keys from the ignition. Leaving them in the car didn't feel like the sort of thing Evan would do. He wasn't the forgetful or careless sort.

As she edged out of the car, there was a clunk from the back as Thomas opened the boot. Melody joined him, as they stared into the open space.

'If this is his car, he took his luggage,' Thomas said.

An enveloping sense of dread was beginning to worm its way through Melody.

'He had a blue case,' Melody said, picturing it, and needing to say something out loud.

'Everton fan...' Thomas replied.

That was true. Evan would never wear red, a quirk Melody had found hilarious when they first met.

She stepped to the side, where the verge disappeared into a clutch of trees. There were places in which the road almost kissed the lake, others where it arced away, leaving room for houses or – in this case – the woods. There were more trees on the other side, too, the branches hanging low, swishing in the lingering remains of the day.

'There was a girl,' Melody said, reminding herself.

'What girl?' Thomas asked, fighting a yawn.

Melody didn't answer. There was a gap in the trees a short distance along the road, on the other side, and she found herself heading towards it. Her shoes crunched on the mix of gravel and dry dirt. There was no give to the verge, as if it hadn't rained in a while. In the distance, something buzzed: a boat or maybe someone's car.

The headlights flared along the road as Melody stepped over the verge into the gap. She squinted towards what looked like a field on the other side. Tall grass rustled, though it was hard to see much else.

No Evan.

No anyone.

When Melody turned back to the cars, Thomas had an arm raised, as if trying to tell a teacher he knew the answer. It was only as Melody reached him that she realised he was holding something.

'Found this by the front wheel,' he said, handing her a phone.

It was easy to recognise from its perfect condition, as if brand new.

'It's Evan's,' Melody said.

THREE

Night had swept across the lake, leaving a blanket of stars above, and the hint of a moon somewhere through the trees.

Thomas had turned off the headlights, saying something about not wanting the battery to go flat. Melody hadn't really been listening. She'd spent some time trying to unlock Evan's phone, before giving up. She didn't know the code. After that, she'd paced up and down the road, calling her fiancé's name. Her voice had echoed through the trees, boomeranging back without reply.

A few vehicles passed, though nobody stopped. They'd have likely assumed it was just a pair of parked cars, unaware of Melody's mounting terror at what could've happened.

Thomas wasn't helping. He'd called Nina to tell her there was no sign of Evan and that they were waiting for the police. He'd then spent the rest of the time repeating, 'I just don't know what could've happened to him.'

It felt like an age for the spinning red and blue lights to flash through the murk. Melody checked her phone. It had been almost two hours since Evan had called to tell her he was ten or fifteen minutes away. Close to ninety minutes since Melody and Thomas had found the abandoned car.

They had been so close to their dream holiday properly beginning.

The police vehicle pulled in across the road, leaving the lights spinning. Thomas had been sitting in the car, pretending he wasn't cold. But Melody could only take so much of him repeating himself. 'What did Evan mean by "girl"?' had been annoying the first time. She'd been leaning on the back of Evan's car, feeling lost and fighting away her darkest thoughts. There had to be an innocent explanation.

It took a few seconds for the officer to emerge from his car. He flashed a torchlight across the ground, then up until it was focused on Melody's midriff. From what she could tell, he was wearing dark pants and what looked like a stab-proof vest over a lighter shirt.

'Are you Melody?' he asked.

'That's me.'

He sounded unsure as he added: 'I'm Constable Burgess. I'm here for a missing person...?'

A missing person. Is that what Evan was now?

Melody explained that they were on holiday and staying at a house further around the lake. She had arrived the day before with her son, her dad, her sister and her brother-in-law. Her fiancé was due to arrive – and she'd been speaking to him on the phone when he said he'd seen a girl in the road. There had been some sort of bang, the call had cut out – and then they had driven to find the abandoned car, with Evan's phone at the side.

The officer's light shifted as he shone it along the length of the silver vehicle. He let out a long 'Hmmmm', which didn't sound promising. What Melody wanted was some sort of 'Oh, this happens all the time', followed by an obvious explanation and a triumphant reunion.

Instead, as the light returned to her, there was a frown on

the officer's face. It felt as if he'd been told this wasn't as complicated as it was. He scratched his head with his free hand, apparently searching for the right question.

'Are these both your cars?' he asked.

'Rentals,' Melody said.

'Hmmmm.'

The officer bobbed from foot to foot for a moment, probably debating what to do. When he decided, he strode around to the other side of the silver car and opened the door. Melody was about to tell him that she had the keys, though he wasn't looking for those. Instead, he emerged with a handful of papers, taken from the glovebox. Melody wondered why she hadn't thought of that.

Burgess flattened the pages on the bonnet and shone his light across them. 'Is your husband Evan Gallagher?' he asked.

'Fiancé – but yes. We're getting married at Christmas.'

It was hard to see the officer, though it felt like he was probably frowning again.

'You're Melody Bryant?' he asked.

'Right.'

The officer moved around the car and handed Melody the papers. 'You're named on this,' he said.

'I had to leave them scans of my licence yesterday,' Melody explained. It had been complex trying to book two cars across two days, with various people needing to be named on each policy. Not that the officer needed to know any of that.

He had crouched and was shining his light under the car. After that, he did a lap of the vehicle, before opening the boot.

'Can you tell me what your hus—*fiancé* said about seeing a girl?' he asked, when he returned to Melody.

'I don't really know. We were on the phone. Evan said he was ten or fifteen minutes away, then that there was a girl in the road. He said she was covered in mud, or maybe blood. I think he stopped to make sure she was all right.'

'Blood...?'

'That's what he said.'

There was another, longer, 'Hmmmm' – and then Burgess told her to wait. He crossed to his car and got in, closing the door behind him.

When Melody turned back to the other vehicle, Thomas had switched on the inner light, and was looking to her expectantly. Melody turned away, not wanting to explain her minimal conversation to somebody else.

She had been telling herself it was all going to be fine, but Burgess's unease had fed her own. There was a lake on one side, trees on the other – and, despite the smattering of houses along the road, they were more or less in the middle of nowhere. If the local police didn't know what was going on, who would?

Canada suddenly felt very alien. Very big. A lot of space in which Evan could be.

Time passed. Maybe a minute, maybe more. Melody jumped back to the present as the officer reopened his door and crossed the road. 'There are no reports of missing children in the area,' he said. 'You don't really get kids out by themselves around here.'

Melody was too scared to ask what that meant in reality.

'Did you try turning it on?' Burgess asked, suddenly sounding like a bored IT worker at the end of a long day.

'Turning what on?' Melody asked.

'The car. Does it start? I'm just wondering if it broke down and he started walking.'

Melody figured she should have thought of that, though handed the officer the keys. He opened the driver's door, before perching on the seat. He stretched to the ignition and started the vehicle first time, before turning it off again.

When he got back out, he passed Melody the keys.

'Not that,' he said.

Burgess tapped his foot for a moment, let out another

'Hmmmm', and then started walking along the road. Unsure what to do, Melody followed a pace behind as he shone the light from side to side. The white clipped quickly across the dusty verges, glimmering through the littering of trees. Burgess halted as he reached a vaguely human-sized bush, before continuing to shine it across the other side. There were more bushes, the patch of long grass, and then what looked like an endless stretch of trees.

When he stopped with the light pointing at the road, Melody knew what was coming.

'There's not a lot we can do tonight,' Burgess said. 'There'll be more officers around in the morning. What I can do now is write up everything you've told me. We can put a missing person report into the system and then, hopefully, by morning, there's a clearer picture.'

He said the final bit with a forced optimism, as if Evan would magically show up.

It didn't help that he was so much taller than Melody. Through no fault of his own, he was literally talking down to her.

'I can give you an email address and you can send us a photo of him. That will help us get it out there.' He paused a moment, perhaps realising it didn't sound like much. 'I'm sure he's just lost. He'll be on his way to wherever you're staying.'

'But why would he leave his phone and the car? He didn't even take the keys.'

That was baffling and the officer didn't reply.

Melody fumbled for a moment, not quite able to believe this was it. Shouldn't there be officers to search through the woods, or across the lake? She was just going to have to head back to the house without Evan?

'Are there cameras on the road?' Melody asked.

That got a shake of the head. 'Not here. Some of the property owners might have their own.'

'Can you, um, I dunno… go door to door, or something?' she added.

It felt like the kind of thing Burgess should be suggesting.

The officer's awkward pause was probably accidental, though it left Melody feeling like she had confidently announced that two and two made five.

'There's only really me on at the moment,' Burgess said. 'It's Sunday and a bit late. People will be in bed, plus there aren't a lot of houses out here. Everything is spaced out.' The time thing was true, but only because he'd taken so long to get there. Either way, the officer didn't wait for a reply, before clapping his hands and quickly adding: 'There's a public dock back that way.' He pointed in the direction from which Melody and Thomas had come. 'I know you're worried but I'll drive back and pull in. You can follow. There's a bit of a shore, so we'll see if there's anyone around. There are only trees around here.'

'Do we leave this car?' Melody indicated the silver vehicle her fiancé had apparently been driving. It wasn't the sort of road on which people left their vehicles. There was little room to pass.

The officer thought for a moment. 'You're on the document, so you're free to drive it if you feel comfortable. Your brother-in-law can follow. We'll stop at the boat launch.'

He spoke with such certainty that Melody started to believe Evan would be sitting at the dock waiting for them. Evan had mistaken something for the girl he spoke about, then he'd somehow got injured and limped off to the dock, ready to be found. Unlikely, yes – but what were the other options?

By the time she thought about telling Burgess she'd had half a glass of wine, he had already disappeared to speak to Thomas in the vehicle behind.

Melody got into the silver car and waited. She doubted half a glass of wine would put her over any sort of limit anyway, let alone when she'd finished it a couple of hours before. It still didn't feel quite right being behind the wheel of a car.

Despite being on the rental agreement for both vehicles, Melody had never driven on the right side of the road – and didn't particularly enjoy driving at all. Evan would do much of the shuttling back and forth for their household. It took her a few seconds to figure out where everything was in the strange vehicle. Not only was the steering wheel on the wrong side – but so were all the various buttons and levers.

By the time Burgess had turned his police car around, Melody had found the headlights and realised the gearstick was also the brake. With the doors closed, everything had that artificial air freshener smell. Part-dodgy salesman, part-airplane toilet: definitely nothing good.

The three vehicles headed back the way they'd come in convoy as moonlight dappled through the swaying trees. The police car no longer had its lights spinning on top and it all felt like more of a leisurely cruise.

It was only a couple of minutes until the car in front indicated towards the lake, and then pulled onto a narrow gravel path. Stones skittled as Melody bumped down the lane until she emerged in a wider car park. The officer had left his headlights on, as he pulled to a stop facing the water. Melody parked to the side of him and then got out, heading towards the small wooden ramp at the front.

A part of her expected to see Evan sitting on the dock, staring across the lake. He'd turn to take her in, then grin. 'Found me then!' There would be a simple explanation and they would have to apologise to the officer for wasting his time.

The fantasy lasted less than a second as Melody took in the empty launch area. There were lights across the water, another up on the hill beyond, but only a bobbing rowboat at the water's edge. As Thomas's headlights swept across the space, the tyres sending a *tick-tick-tick* of stones scattering, Burgess peered into the boat and then shook his head.

Melody waited as the water lapped the pebbles. Thomas and the constable soon joined her as the three of them spent a moment watching the black waves babbling.

'He's not here,' Melody found herself saying. She was desperate for someone to tell her she was wrong, that she was missing something obvious. Except nobody did.

Evan was gone.

FOUR

It was almost midnight as the adults assembled on the lake house deck. Melody's dad – Michael – had returned from his walk, while Nina had sobered up from the wine she'd put away. Thomas had found a proper pair of trousers and they sat watching the light from the house glimmering across the rippling water's edge.

'Sam's still asleep,' Melody said, as she took a place in one of the reclining chairs. It didn't feel right to relax, so she hunched forward, staring at the lights of other houses on the far side of the water.

She waited for somebody to speak, anybody, but felt her family exchanging glances around her.

'What did the police actually say?' her dad managed.

'Not a lot. He said to wait 'til morning, when there will be more officers around. There are no reports of missing children, or anything like that, so it's hard to know what Evan saw.'

Melody sensed her father swapping another look with her sister. It felt like they'd had a long conversation while they were waiting for her to get back.

'I was looking on the map,' Nina said, hesitantly. 'There's

the lake on one side of the road and then it's just forest on the other. It goes on for miles, all the way out to the Pacific.' A short pause. 'There's nothing there. There are all these towns up the east coast and then nothing inland.'

It wasn't what Melody wanted to hear, even though she knew it was true. The officer had implied as much when she'd asked about going door to door. There weren't tightly packed streets to check in with anyone who had a light on, only houses on the lake, spaced acres from one another. After leaving the highway, there was one road that looped around the lake. Evan had been driving up the west edge, so there was the lake on one side, the woods on the other, and a smattering of houses along a single route. There wasn't a long list of places he could have gone – and, seemingly, there were very few officers who worked in the area and could do something.

Melody had seen news footage, had watched documentaries and dramas, in which someone went missing. Hundreds of officers would appear from nowhere to start combing forests and fields. A part of her expected that, certainly wanted it. How else was somebody supposed to be found? She'd got one bloke, who'd taken an age to arrive, and then not done a lot of finding.

'Could he have broken down?' Melody's father asked. 'Maybe he started walking?'

'The car works,' Melody replied. 'The keys were in it. We drove down the road he would've been walking on.'

Her dad thought on that for a moment and then nodded towards the front of the house and the two vehicles beyond. 'Don't the police need that for evidence?'

It was the first time Melody had considered the vehicle could've been left for someone in authority to look through. They had found Evan's phone, the keys, and the rental agreement – but his luggage was missing. Maybe there were finger-prints, that sort of thing?

'It's a bit late now,' she replied, figuring the officer who told her to drive it probably knew best. She didn't want to admit to herself that Constable Burgess seemed as bemused as she was.

They sat quietly for a while, nobody quite knowing what to say. This sort of thing happened to *other* people.

'I knew we shouldn't have come here,' Melody's dad muttered – and it was true that he'd said as much before they left the UK. He had slowly been getting more negative since retiring, and it had become much more noticeable since Melody's mum had passed. His 'What's wrong with the lakes closer to home?' had been said at a time when Melody had been planning the trip for only her, Evan and Sam. The inclusion of her wider family had happened later. 'What did Evan *actually* say to you?' Melody's father added. He had always been rational, wanting an explanation for everything.

Melody was trying to remember what he'd said but the conversation already felt distant. 'He said he was ten to fifteen minutes away,' Melody replied. 'Then he saw a girl on the road and I think he stopped to help her.'

'Did you hear the girl?'

A chill crept along Melody's arm and she brushed the goosebumps away. 'No...'

She sensed yet another glance between her sister and her father. What had they been talking about while she was gone?

Melody looked to the pair of phones on the table. They had found Evan's by the front wheel, so he must've been in that car. Had to have been on that road.

'Where would he go?' Melody's father asked, though it was unclear to whom he was speaking.

'I'm sure he'll turn up,' Nina added.

Melody took a breath and wondered if this was what it was like when something bad happened. Out would come the clichés and meaningless small talk. What was she supposed to say in response?

Then a real question came: 'What are you going to tell Sam?' Thomas asked.

Melody's brother-in-law had been quiet since they got back. He and Evan had always got on and it had only been a few months before that they'd spent a weekend at Twickenham for the rugby. All bootcut jeans and brown shoes. They went out for drinks semi-regularly – and Melody had already resigned herself to being without her fiancé for a few evenings as he and Thomas went off to do 'man things', whatever that entailed.

Everyone was looking to her but Melody couldn't meet their stares. She was used to sharing parenting decisions with Evan but this was one she'd have to make herself.

'Doesn't he start camp tomorrow?' Thomas added.

Melody couldn't reply because, yes he *did* start camp in the morning, but *no* she didn't know what to do. She could tell her son that his father had disappeared – and ruin whatever holiday they had in front of them, or she could try to keep it from him.

Not much of a choice.

'I'm sure he'll turn up,' Nina repeated.

'He probably broke down,' their father added, despite having been told the car was working fine.

Melody knew she couldn't take any more of this.

'I'm going to bed,' she said.

FIVE

MONDAY

Melody was already awake as the sun crept over the tops of the trees. It was a little after six and she'd spent the night dozing, while jumping awake at the merest of sounds. Thomas and Nina were sharing the room next door and she had listened to her brother-in-law use the toilet at 3 a.m. on the other side of a wall that was unquestionably too thin. Every other creak had left her awake, wondering if Evan was at the front door.

He never was.

She mooched into the kitchen and filled the well of the coffee machine, before setting it burbling. Melody leaned on the island in the middle of a kitchen that was much nicer than hers at home. Twice as big, as well. The Airbnb ad said the house had been custom built a few years before, specifically for tourists. It was part-IKEA showroom, part-TV advert with a grinning family eating breakfast together. The appliances were gleaming chrome, the countertops spotless and solid. All very nice but nothing in the way of character. A kitchen wasn't a kitchen unless there were toast crumbs across the surfaces, with a grubby sponge abandoned in the sink, spreading E. coli.

Melody unlocked the door and headed onto the deck, first

taking in the lake, then the main house in the opposite direction. It was the sort of thing that didn't exist where Melody came from. Big and detached, all decks and porches. It might be Canadian but it felt intrinsically American. She stared for a while, a part of her still believing Evan would be standing on the driveway, saying he'd been knocking, but nobody had heard.

He wasn't.

The smell of brewing coffee filled the kitchen as Melody returned inside. She poured herself a mug and was about to head back to the deck when the stairs began creaking. Melody knew her son's gentle footsteps and it was only as his grinning face appeared that she made her mind up. An instant decision that had been nine hours in the making.

'Is Dad up yet?' Sam asked.

'He missed his flight,' Melody replied. Sam had been on the way to the cupboards but he stopped and turned, features crinkling with confusion. 'The airline booked too many people on the plane, so he had to wait. Then a few things came up at work, so he's going to get here when he can.'

The lie came so easily. Melody hoped it was vague enough, though she saw the cogs whirring in Sam's mind.

'Can he call?'

'He would but the times are all mixed up. When it's evening for him, you'll be at camp; then, when it's evening for you, he'll be asleep.'

Melody hoped that mentioning camp would switch her son's attention back to the excitement he'd had building the day before. Besides, Sam was used to his dad having to prioritise work at times. She wanted her son to move on from the questions and, though he wavered for a second, he quickly turned back to the cupboard. He'd been allowed to choose one cereal at the supermarket – and had, somewhat unsurprisingly, gone for something that was essentially a box of chocolate-chip cookies.

Melody had almost said 'no', before figuring he was on holiday too – and would run it off anyway.

Camp was the best place for Sam. A day of chasing around with people his own age and having adventures. By the time he got back, his dad would have shown up, laughing about how lost he'd got.

Sam filled a bowl and then sloshed milk from a giant container as Melody watched. He looked up half a dozen times, wanting that silent approval that it actually *was* OK to eat such forbidden food this early in the morning.

'What time are we leaving?' he asked.

Melody glanced to the camp schedule that was fixed to the front of the fridge with a magnet – and it was impossible not to remember why they were there.

It had been three decades before that Melody and Nina had last visited Vancouver Island. Melody had been nine, Nina fourteen, when their parents had won some sort of competition at the local travel agent. They were the days when everyone picked holidays from a brochure and paid in cash instalments over the counter. They'd been given free flights, a choice of cars, and a cabin to themselves on the bank of Shawnigan Lake.

Melody and Nina had spent three weeks at camp, mixing with the local children, who were off school for the summer. Because of her accent, Melody had ended up as something of a mini celebrity. The time at the lake was one of her clearest childhood memories. That sense of being popular and desperately wanting the next day to roll around.

She wasn't naïve. In some ways, Melody knew she had spent thirty years chasing the high of those three weeks. But life happened. College, jobs, a partner, buying a house, having Sam. Other things, too. She'd wanted to return to the lake, but never had.

Finally, so many years on, she had found an incredible Airbnb, then booked Sam into a camp a little down the road.

She wanted him to have the same memories she had and, though she knew times had changed, it couldn't be *that* different.

She also wanted to enjoy the area as an adult, which was partly why she'd convinced Evan that they could turn it into a wider family holiday. His parents had already booked their own cruise, as they did every year, but camp was a joint memory for both her and Nina.

Once Nina and Thomas were in, neither of the sisters wanted to leave their father at home by himself – and the idea of the holiday had a sense of inevitability to it.

'…Mum?'

Melody blinked back into the kitchen. She'd been drifting to the time in which she didn't have to make tough decisions.

'It's drop-off from half seven, so still another hour,' Melody told him. 'Did you check your kit list?'

'Yes.'

'Did you double-check it?'

That got a grin as Sam continued eating his cereal.

They had been emailed a daily camp schedule, along with everything the children would need. It was mainly towels and a change of clothes for lake swimming. Melody remembered the warmth of the water when she'd last swam in the lake – but it wasn't long until thoughts of Evan returned.

Constable Burgess had left a card, though Melody worried it was too early to call. Would he be back in the office? Would somebody else know what was going on? Would someone call her? How did it work when a person went missing?

Nina soon joined them in the kitchen. Sam eagerly told his aunt what he was looking forward to at camp, as a silent glance between the sisters explained that he didn't know his father was missing.

When Sam had finished, Melody sent him upstairs to brush his teeth and triple-check his kit list for the day. He returned not long after with a small backpack – and his granddad behind him. For a moment, Melody feared her father had spilled the news about Evan – but, instead, he was asking Sam what he was up to. Melody's son didn't need another invitation to list the things he was looking forward to.

It would have been a normal morning at the beginning of a holiday, if not for her missing fiancé. Melody kept checking her phone, expecting him to have messaged to explain, before remembering she had Evan's phone in the drawer next to her bed.

As Melody bundled her excited son into the silver car, Nina followed her onto the gravel outside the front of the lake house.

'Can I have a word?' she asked.

Melody told Sam to put on his seatbelt and then left him in the car, before joining her sister at the back of the vehicle. Nina was squirming, avoiding eye contact, in the way she did when she'd rather not be doing the talking.

'Thomas and I were wondering if you minded us taking the other car today?' she asked. 'Obviously we can stay at the house to help if you need us around but we sort of had plans and I, um...' She tailed off, finishing by eyeing the house in a way that made it clear Thomas had asked her to talk to her sister.

'Where are you going?' Melody asked.

'Thomas wanted to walk out to that wooden bridge thing we talked about. It's not far, so if you need us, we can come back.'

When they'd been looking for things to do in the area, checking out the old railway bridge hidden in the middle of the woods was something on which she, Evan, Nina, and Thomas had all agreed. It was an activity they were supposed to be doing as a foursome.

Melody stared blankly for a moment, unsure what to say. She hadn't thought much past taking Sam to camp and then trying to talk to someone from the police. Except Nina was already fidgeting, anticipating an answer. Melody found herself going along with the sentiment, saying it was fine.

Nina thanked her and then headed back to the house as Melody watched her sister go. Should she expect everyone to sit around, waiting for her missing fiancé to show up? What were people supposed to do?

Sam was squirming in the car, so Melody clambered in. According to Apple Maps, it was only a seven-minute journey around the lake to Sam's campsite. Melody bumped the car over the gravel drive, around the main house. She passed a beaten-up white car parked at the side of the house, next to a newer silver vehicle, and then continued onto the road.

The area had felt empty the night before, though there were a few more vehicles in the morning as Melody followed a dusty white truck towards the camp. She still wasn't quite comfortable driving on the other side of the road – but at least the vehicle was an automatic. Like driving a giant go-kart.

Sam was craning to look through the window on Melody's side, taking in the brief glimpses of water.

'Do you think everyone else will be Canadian?' he asked.

'Probably.'

'Do Canadians sound like Americans?'

'I guess they kind of do.'

Sam thought on that for a moment. 'Do you know there's a Vancouver *and* a Vancouver Island?'

'Is that right?'

Melody played dumb as he continued to list some of the facts he'd been reading, many about how large Canada was compared to the UK.

They had only been driving a couple of minutes when they passed what looked like a mottled, weathered, red dress hanging from a tree. Sam angled to look at it, asking what it was. Melody had to admit she didn't know. It was there and gone, not that his attention was held for long. He pointed out the fire station and the big truck at its side, then said 'There!' as they reached a sign for the camp.

A short line of vehicles snaked its way through the trees, following what turned out to be a one-way system. There was a drop-off point at the edge of a green, with the lake beyond. Each vehicle stopped long enough for a child to jump out and head towards the picnic tables.

'Is this it?' Sam asked, and there was a sudden creep of nervousness to his tone. With that, instead of using the drop-off spot, Melody pulled into the small car park, next to a sand volleyball court.

Sam was angling around her, looking towards the gathering of boys by the tables.

'You're going to have a great day,' Melody told him, as he gulped.

Sam opened his mouth and it felt as if he was about to say something before he closed it again.

Melody tried to recall her first morning at camp all those years before – but the memory wasn't there. She knew the faces of the girls with whom she'd made friends. She knew some of the activities they'd enjoyed, yet much of her enduring enjoyment from then was how important everything made her feel.

It was only as Melody checked over her shoulder that she realised a police car was parked near the exit. Parents were still pulling into the drop-off spot to leave their children, before looping around the one-way system. Melody unclipped her belt and twisted to see what was going on.

Which is when she spotted Constable Burgess talking to a woman, pointing across the lake, a grim look on his face.

SIX

Sam reached for the door handle.

'Can you take me?' he asked – and the vulnerable twinge in his tone almost made Melody offer to take him back to England. They'd call off this shambles of a holiday and find something better to do.

She checked the rear-view mirror, watching Constable Burgess continue to talk to the woman.

'Come on then,' Melody replied, opening her own door and waiting for Sam to join her. She glanced across to the police car but then headed in the opposite direction, to where a girl was standing by a picnic bench with a clipboard. She was wearing a light blue T-shirt with 'Camp Cowichan' stencilled on the front, and looked up with a large grin to take in Melody and Sam.

'Who have we got here?' she asked, talking to Sam.

She seemed so young to Melody, maybe eighteen at the absolute oldest.

'Sam,' he replied.

The girl scanned her clipboard quickly, before looking back up. 'Samuel Gallagher?'

The fact she was speaking to him immediately had Sam perking up. He stood a fraction taller. 'Yeah.'

'Do you prefer "Sam" or "Samuel"?'

Melody watched as her son thought it over. She wasn't sure he'd ever been asked. 'Um... Sam, I think?' He phrased it as a question, which got a smile from the girl.

'Did you bring a towel?' she asked. 'We do have spares if you forgot.'

Sam hoisted his bag and the 'That's great' had him smiling wider.

The girl pointed him across to a set of tables closer to the water. 'Everyone's gathering by the lifeguard chair,' she said. 'You can wait there, we'll go through rules for the lake – and then we can get on with the day. It's great to have you here.'

Sam beamed, his nervousness gone as he started towards the lake without looking back. Melody watched him go, somewhat amazed at how quickly his confidence had returned.

'Are you his mom?' the girl asked.

'Yes. I'm Melody.'

The girl flipped a page on her clipboard and seemingly ticked a box. 'I've got you down as the emergency contact,' she said. 'You're also on the pickup list along with an Evan Gallagher. Is that right?'

Melody winced slightly at the mention of her fiancé's name. It didn't feel as if he'd be picking up their son any time soon.

'Yes,' she replied.

'Do you need to add any other names to the pickup list? We can't release Sam to anyone not listed. It's just in case you can't get here.'

Melody thought for a moment. It was a question she hadn't expected. 'My sister might come. She's called Nina. Or her husband, Thomas.'

The girl wrote on her clipboard and then said 'thank you',

before smiling amiably past Melody towards the next boy making his way down the bank.

Melody turned to where Constable Burgess was still standing next to his vehicle. The woman to whom he'd been speaking had disappeared, only to be replaced by somebody new.

There was no more avoiding it as Melody waited to cross the road and then headed to where the officer was standing. He had his arms folded, body language making it look as if he craved any conversation other than the one he was having.

When he spotted Melody, he nodded to her, welcoming her into what became a triangle. Burgess seemed even taller than the night before, his broad chest bulked by the oversized dark vest. His eyes said bad news as they wandered across her, stopping to linger as she got closer.

Something lurched in Melody's stomach. This was it. She had pushed away the needling thoughts throughout the night that something truly awful had happened to Evan – but now she would have to face the truth.

'Any news?' Burgess asked.

Melody froze for a second, having expected something much more serious.

'I was about to ask you the same,' she replied.

The other woman took a half-step back. She was around Melody's age, wearing shorts and a jacket over some sort of vest.

'Did your husband get to where you're staying?' he asked.

Melody bristled at the word 'husband', not because she wasn't looking forward to being married – but because it felt as if Burgess hadn't been properly listening the previous night.

'No,' Melody told him. 'Have *you* heard anything...?'

She already knew the answer based on his questions to her – but the shake of the head still felt devastating. Evan had been gone for eleven hours now.

'I was on my way over to yours,' Burgess said. 'I came here

to check in with a few parents who live in the area, see if they'd seen or heard anything. The place I met you last night is only a kilometre down the road.'

The woman at Melody's side shuffled a little, though said nothing. Melody had known the site of Evan's disappearance was close – but not *that* close.

'Did you find anything?' Melody asked, again knowing the answer.

Another shake of the head. 'We've checked again but there are definitely no reports of missing children in the area. I also spoke to the owner of the house nearest to where your husband disappeared—'

'Fiancé,' Melody corrected.

Burgess took a second, though didn't appear particularly flustered. '*Fiancé*,' he replied. 'Anyway, the owner of that house says there are no children at the address. I figured I'd ask some questions here, before stopping off with you.' He paused a moment. 'Do you have a child at this camp?'

Melody told him she did, as the officer nodded along. He was looking over her head, towards the lake. The babble of young voices had been steadily increasing as more children arrived.

'Nobody has turned up to our station and reported themselves as lost,' he added. 'We've also not had any calls overnight of strangers in yards, that sort of thing.'

Melody suddenly had an image of Evan climbing over fences, trying to figure out where he was. She hadn't considered that as an option before.

'What now?' she asked. 'He was definitely here ten or eleven hours ago. I've got his phone. He can't have just disappeared.'

Burgess was unmoved. He had hooked his thumbs into his vest and was nodding along. 'The report has already been filed and I've got the photos you sent through. Things will be filtering onto our website and social channels later.'

It sounded like some sort of automated phone memo. A recorded message that didn't mean an awful lot. Were any of those things actually going to find Evan? Did people pay any attention to a police force's website? She knew she'd never looked at one.

'Surely you can search the woods?' Melody asked.

There was a momentary meeting of eyes between the officer and the woman. Something unsaid that made Melody feel as if she was missing something huge.

'I've been down there this morning to check the immediate area – and we'll have more people in later to do the same. We'll also be looking at the lake as best we can. I've already asked our neighbouring district for some help, but haven't heard back whether they can spare anyone. The forest is huge and too dense to see much with drones. We'd have to go in at ground level. The best we can do for now is ask if anyone saw or heard anything – which is what I'll be doing this morning.'

Melody thought on that for a moment. She'd not been in the area long but knew it was a small community. The lake, the forest, a smattering of houses. It was one of the reasons why they'd chosen the area for a break. It was something different from the endless hum where they lived. The people all on top of one another. All that, yet she'd not considered the down sides of when something went wrong. Fewer people meant less of everything else.

All the space, all the trees, all the endless miles of wilderness. No easy way to search, no obvious solution. No way of knowing where Evan was.

She suddenly felt so small. So hopelessly, insignificantly, *tiny*. A dot.

Burgess unhooked a thumb and angled it across the water. 'You could ask around the village. I'll be over there later but

there are some shops on the other side of the lake. They'll probably put up missing posters if you ask. Folks are pretty friendly
around here. If you get posters, you could also try up the road in
Duncan.'

There was a twinge of anger, as it seemed to Melody that he
wanted her to do his job for him.

'What about the girl Evan saw?' she asked. Her tone was
louder than she meant. Harsher. The words snapped and
Burgess's eye twitched a fraction.

'There's nobody reported missing. I'll be checking in with
the local houses in case someone's child was out. That's also
why I'm here now. I promise I'm doing all I can.'

He nodded past her kindly, towards the children, as Melody
realised – reluctantly – he had a point. The girl on the side of
the road might well have been a camper. In fact, that was the
most likely scenario. Where else was he supposed to ask
around? It was a better solution than going door to door,
because so many youngsters were in the same place, along with
their parents.

Melody deflated slightly. 'What's Duncan?' she asked.

Burgess and the woman swapped another brief glance,
before he replied: 'It's the next town up. Not huge but a few
thousand people. Bigger than here.' He patted his vest, before
reaching for the cardboard coffee cup that was sitting on the top
of the car. 'I've got your details and will be in touch if anything
comes up.'

He hovered for a few moments, though Melody didn't know
what else to say. She wasn't quite sure what she expected him to
do, though it felt like more than sitting in a car park and talking
to parents on the way out.

'I'll be in touch,' he repeated, before clambering into his car.

Melody stepped out the way, giving him space to turn
around, before he edged onto the path that led back to the road.

The woman who'd been standing to the side was now

watching Melody – and didn't turn away when Melody looked to her.

'That's all you get round here,' she said, with something of a shrug.

'With the police?'

'There's hardly any of them, especially at the lake. The only ones you usually see are up in Duncan, dealing with the overdoses. I'm surprised he's down here, asking questions.'

'What overdoses?' Melody asked, somewhat surprised at the word.

'There's a big homeless community up there,' the woman replied, which felt like the only reply Melody was going to get.

'I'm Lori,' the woman added.

'Melody.'

A beat passed and it seemed like Lori was weighing up whether to say something. She had angled towards the lake, where the camp counsellor had joined the children near the lifeguard chair. The stream of vehicles dropping off had dwindled to nothing, leaving only a handful of cars in the parking spaces. The sun shimmered off the water's surface, as Melody's arms prickled with the heat. It was the first time she'd noticed the warmth of the morning.

'Did I hear your husband disappeared last night?' Lori asked.

'Fiancé – but yes. He was driving from the airport to meet us and never made it. We found his car abandoned, just down the road.'

Melody had been pointing in the direction it had happened and, when she looked back to Lori, the other woman's face drained.

'My husband disappeared too,' she said.

SEVEN

One thing shared by Canada and England was an overabundance of options in a coffee shop. The poor young woman in the small café across the lake flitted around the counter, patiently frothing different types of milk, to pour into various quantities of coffee, all while smiling in a way Melody knew she herself couldn't force in the same situation. That was a difference between the two nations. Canadians at least pretended to care.

Melody and Lori stood in line as a pair of women ahead of them chatted about some sort of nightmare wait for a ferry trip.

It had been a fifteen-minute drive around the lake, with Melody following Lori's rusting car until they parked on the street outside the café. After ordering, they carried their drinks to a table on the kerb outside.

'This is the village centre,' Lori said. Melody looked past her, towards the crossroads. 'This is where that officer was saying you could put up posters. There's also a park about two minutes that way, on the edge of the water.' Lori pointed across the crossroads, towards a slope.

'Is this it?' Melody asked.

'What do you mean?'

'It's just very... small. Is this the whole village?'

Lori laughed at that.

From where Melody was sitting, she could see a general store with a Coca-Cola sign on top, a sushi takeaway, a Subway, petrol station, pizza place, pharmacy, and a shop that looked like it sold bedding.

'We passed a police station by the crossroads,' Lori added. 'There's a community centre at the back of it. This is basically it, though.'

Melody hadn't seen the police station, so they took a moment to walk thirty seconds to the corner and peer back to a small red-brick building. A maple leaf flag was flying above a white sign that read 'RCMP'. Lori had left her bag on the table – and it was untouched as they returned. Melody didn't come from a crime-ridden place, but she wouldn't have turned her back on her bag, let alone left it. Everything felt so alien.

'Are the lake *and* the village both called Shawnigan Lake?' Melody asked.

Lori seemed confused by the question. 'What else would they be called?'

'I dunno. Isn't that confusing? You don't know if someone's talking about the lake or the village?'

Lori pursed a lip. 'I've never thought of it like that.'

Melody felt a little silly as she sipped her second coffee of the morning. She hadn't thought it was an odd question – not that Lori appeared to mind. She was stirring a packet of sugar into her mug and then wedged the paper under a mug that was holding cutlery.

'There's not much on the west side of the lake,' she said. 'Houses, obviously – plus the camp. The fire hall's over there, but that's about it. The village is on this side, then there's some vineyards and orchards between here and the highway.' She nodded over the top of the café. 'I live up the road in Cobble

Hill. It's about five, ten minutes away.' Lori paused to sip her drink, then added: 'What happened with your fiancé?'

Melody told her about Evan coming a day late, the phone call, the girl in the road, and then... she didn't know. The car was abandoned with the keys inside and Evan's phone on the floor. It was beginning to feel increasingly like a dream.

Melody had expected more in the way of shock or surprise but Lori simply nodded along. She was a third of the way through the coffee when she stirred a second sugar into it. 'This was last night?' she asked.

'About twelve hours ago.'

It felt strange to be sipping coffee with a stranger while her fiancé was missing – but Melody didn't know the area. Didn't know what to do. There was an urge to search herself – but search where? She couldn't walk aimlessly into the forest, or drag a lake. It was this or wait at the lake house.

'You said your husband disappeared a few years ago...?' Melody asked.

Lori paused a moment, staring aimlessly over at the cross-roads. There were stop signs on each of the four sides, with vehicles rolling to something close to a stop, before continuing. As with the main house where Melody was staying, it was something from an old-time American movie.

'Brent,' Lori said solemnly. 'He was my husband. He was training for the Victoria Marathon and went out on one of his training runs. At the start of his training he would be gone for an hour or so. The closer he got to the race the longer he would be gone. But then one day he didn't come back. I went out looking for him in the car.' She waited a moment, picking up her mug but not drinking from it. 'You've probably noticed we don't have sidewalks around here.'

Melody had. When her father had said he was going for a walk the night before, she had asked *where* he was going, because there was no obvious route to anywhere.

'Does everyone walk in the road?' Melody asked.

'Everyone drives – there's not really anywhere you can walk to.' Lori put down her mug and raised a hand to indicate the area around them. 'Unless you live near the village – but, even then, you need to drive to the supermarket, or get a bus.'

Lori waited a moment, scrunching up her lips, probably trying to remember what she was saying.

'Anyway, Brent would run at the side of the road. He'd always wear this yellow vest thing, and would sometimes go up onto the trails if it wasn't too muddy. I was always worried he'd get hit by a truck, something like that. When he didn't come back...' She tailed off, though the implication was clear.

It was such a different life to Melody's. She and Evan lived on the back end of a housing estate, where Sam could walk to school, or get the bus if it was raining. Within ten minutes' walk, there were two smaller supermarkets, a chippy, pizza place, curry house, florist, bike shop, pub and bakery. Bigger supermarkets were barely ten minutes in the car, or fifteen on the bus. Everything was on their doorstep – and the idea of needing to drive everywhere was baffling.

A waitress appeared around them, checking everything was all right, before clearing plates and mugs from the table at their side. She was humming gently to herself, then slipped them a smile, before expertly balancing everything on a tray and heading inside.

'There's been the odd hit-and-run over the years,' Lori said when it was back to just them.

'Don't you have cameras on the roads?' That got something of a blank look, so Melody added: 'There are cameras everywhere back home. People's numberplates are recorded.'

Lori was still staring, eyebrows dipped with confusion. Melody turned away, suddenly wondering whether she was the crazy one. Was it better to have roads monitored to help with this sort of thing, or was that the surveillance culture others were always so angry about? Melody hadn't thought about it too much – but now it felt important.

'We don't really have cameras,' Lori said. 'I think there's a few on the highway, but nothing like that on the roads around here.'

Melody was slowly beginning to understand that Constable Burgess wasn't deliberately being unhelpful – it was that policing was very different between the two countries. Back home, officers would have been checking the traffic cameras to identify vehicles that had been in the area at the same time as Evan disappeared. There was none of that here.

'People drink-drive around here,' Lori said, sounding far too matter-of-fact for Melody's understanding. As if it was normal. 'They smoke weed and drive after that, too. There's never anybody to stop them, so as long as they don't crash, nobody knows. Occasionally, you'll see a car in a verge and figure someone's coming back to get it the next day. But that's why you get the odd hit-and-run. It's not worth stopping.'

She let that sit – and, though it seemed callous, Melody didn't think it was meant as such. It sounded more like a resigned fact of someone who'd lived it.

'So when Brent didn't come back, you figured it was some sort of hit-and-run?'

A nod. 'I called the police, obviously – but had conversations a lot like the one you did. It feels like they're not doing anything. They put out a media release thing with his photo, and there were some Facebook posts. I did my own posters – but nothing came of it. He was gone. That was eight years ago.' Lori waited a beat and counted on her fingers. 'Almost nine.'

She stopped to finish her drink but she had spoken so directly again. Not callously, more accepting this was her life now. Melody felt a chill ripple through her, despite the heat of the day. Is this how things would be? It had been less than a day since Evan had disappeared but she was already sitting down for coffee with someone she'd just met. How quickly would this be a new normal?

'Have you noticed any red dresses hanging from the trees?' Lori asked.

Melody needed a second to adjust to the subject switch. 'I think I saw one this morning. I was driving,' she said.

'You'll see it in a few places around here, mainly up island. People put them out to represent the women who've gone missing over the years.'

Melody had picked up her own mug but froze with it part-way to her mouth. 'That makes it sound like lots of women have gone missing...?'

There was a moment in which Melody wondered quite where she'd ended up. They had spent much of the previous evening sitting on a sun-kissed deck, watching the enticingly gentle waves of the lake lapping. Bad things surely didn't happen in a place like this.

Lori's short nod didn't provide much in the way of assurance. 'It's usually First Nations women.' When it was clear Melody didn't know what that meant, Lori added: 'The natives.'

'How many are missing?'

That got a gentle shrug: 'Too many to count. Hundreds.'

The coffee was bitter as Melody swallowed. She found herself twisting on the chair, taking in the gentle life of the village centre around her. A truck had stopped for a couple to cross at the corner, heading in the direction of the park. Meanwhile, a trio of women had entered the café, each dressed in walking boots and shorts. It felt so serene and yet...

'I don't mean all those women have disappeared right *here*,' Lori added – which was some comfort. 'Almost all of them are on the mainland – but you'll still see posters in places like Duncan when you drive around.'

Melody needed a moment to remember that Duncan was a town. To her, the name Duncan was synonymous with some sort of dim middle-manager who talked about golf a lot, then ended up having a heart attack in his fifties.

'Why would so many women go missing? What do you think happened to them?' Melody asked.

Lori pressed back in her chair, opening her palms. 'The province is a big place – and most of it is forest. In the middle of all that are bears, and cougars. You hear about the odd wolf now and then.' She stopped a moment and chewed on her lip, before adding: 'I guess there are predators among the people, too...'

Melody was still holding her mug, which she couldn't quite lift. There were a lot of people out there, hoping and waiting in the way she was. Things suddenly felt very dangerous.

When she looked up, Lori was smiling gently.

'I suppose talking about all this is why I got fired from the department of tourism.'

Melody got it a half-second before Lori added: 'That's a joke.'

Neither of them laughed, though Melody had some degree of relief that they shared a similar humour. She wasn't sure what to say. Those perfect memories of her youth, that thirty-year craving to return. It now seemed so naïve.

'Is it dangerous here?' Melody asked, not necessarily wanting an answer. It was a bit late now. She pictured Sam at camp, unaware that bears and wolves were hiding in the trees. It was impossible not to imagine Evan on the side of the road. Could he have somehow confused a girl with a bear cub? It was unlikely – but so was everything that had happened since he'd called. Even if he had, what then? Melody was beginning to feel under-prepared and under-researched for what she thought would be a relaxing time at a lake.

'Not really,' Lori replied. 'If you're heading into the woods, you should probably have bear spray.' She clocked the confusion on Melody's face, adding: 'It's a sort of mace. Pepper spray. You'd only need it as a last resort – but, for the most part, animals leave people alone. I know it's a cliché but they're more scared of us.'

'Have you ever seen a bear?' Melody asked.

'Now and then. You have to be careful what you put in your bins because the bears will come and look through overnight. Sometimes people are careless. There was a bear on our road last fall, picking through someone's bin. He ended up going back into the woods, no harm done.'

It was such a difference to where Melody lived. There was an occasional fox sighting – but that was about it.

'Do you want another?' Lori asked, nodding to Melody's now empty mug.

Melody didn't, not really, though she wasn't sure what else to do. At least Lori was someone on her side. A person who would listen and might have some ideas. She wasn't ready to leave that quite yet.

'Not a coffee,' Melody replied. 'Maybe a tea, or something?'

Lori picked up their cups and moved them to a trolley next to the door, before disappearing into the café. Melody watched as the trio of women in walking boots scooched around her new friend, passing through the door and settling on one of the other outdoor tables.

Vehicles drifted through the crossroads with kayaks strapped to the top, as a skinny lad in a wetsuit appeared at the top of the slope, his wet hair leaving a dripped trail behind. Life was carrying on, even though Melody's fiancé had disappeared from the other side of the lake hours before. She thought of Sam again, hopefully enjoying himself across the water. How could she possibly tell him his dad was missing?

When Lori reappeared, she had a tray. She dropped three sachets of sugar onto the table, along with a Twinings packet that had 'English Breakfast' on the side – plus two more mugs.

'I figured English tea?' Lori said.

Melody said it was fine, feeling unable to explain that, back home, there was just tea which didn't need a time of day assigned. There were bigger things to think about anyway.

She waited for Lori to settle and then leaned in, not wanting to be overheard by the trio of women. 'Were there ever any leads on your husband?'

Melody needed to hear that there were.

'Sort of,' Lori replied. 'There were a few sightings but nothing that came to anything. Either innocent mistakes, or cranks. Brent was six foot, with dark hair, no distinctive features. If you didn't know him, it could be easy to confuse him with someone else. Someone found footprints on one of the trails that could've been his – but things like his sneakers, watch, or phone were never found.'

It sounded as if she'd come to terms with that, which Melody guessed was what happened when almost nine years had passed.

'It doesn't feel real,' Melody said, finally able to tell another person. 'Evan was only ten minutes away. We were supposed to be going to the wooden bridge thing today.'

'The Kinsol Trestle?'

'I think so. We'd been looking through Tripadvisor for things to do. Cowichan Bay looks nice and there's a lookout point off the highway that Evan wanted to see. I was going to go whale watching with my sister...' The sentence drifted and a part of Melody still believed it would happen. 'We're getting married at Christmas,' Melody added.

Lori nodded along as she stirred a sugar into her coffee. Melody probably appreciated the lack of blind optimism of which her father and sister had been full. Lori had lived through it herself and wasn't about to say everything was going to be all right in the end. It hadn't been for her.

Melody liked that but she didn't. In truth, she didn't know what she wanted to hear from others – she simply wanted Evan to turn up.

'Why did you choose to come here?' Lori asked.

'Is that another question from your department of tourism days?'

Lori laughed and Melody managed a smile. It had come out without her thinking about it.

'I visited when I was little,' Melody added. 'Mum and Dad won a holiday at a cabin here – and I went to camp during the days with my sister.'

'Sounds like it made quite an impression...?'

'I always wanted to come back. Mum and Dad couldn't afford it after that first time and then I had work, and Sam came along.' A pause. 'He's my boy. He's the same age now as I was then. I thought he'd be able to have the same experience I did.'

She faltered a little, knowing the time would come – probably soon – when she had to tell Sam his dad was missing. It would be hard to enjoy much after that.

'Evan, my fiancé, works a lot. We weren't going to have time for a honeymoon in the new year, so I suggested this. It turned into a bit of a family thing. My dad and sister are here – plus her husband. We've got an Airbnb on the lake.'

Lori nodded along. She was a good listener. 'Is Sam your only child?' she asked.

'Yes.'

'I've got a daughter – Alice. She was starting daycare when Brent disappeared. I think that's what helped at the beginning, because I had to be there for her. I did all the drop-offs and pick-ups, that sort of thing. Plus I still had a mortgage to pay. Life carries on. There's this huge thing that's happened – and a big part of you kind of expects everyone else to stop. But then your daughter needs dropping off at soccer, plus you've got bills, and the car needs gas, and there's no milk. Everything keeps going.' She gulped and then added: 'Alice is twelve now. They grow up so fast.'

'She's at camp?'

'She goes every year because most of her friends from school are there. I think she's got a crush on one of the counsellors, too.' Lori gave a *we've-all-been-there* grin that Melody struggled to match. She was still thinking of what Lori had previously said. Children needing dropping off, bills to pay, petrol to put in a car, milk to buy. Her fiancé was gone and yet life hadn't stopped. It wasn't going to.

Melody's mind was drifting to the mundanity of day-to-day life. Evan would fill the dishwasher and she'd empty it. Without him, somebody would still need to fill it.

'I'm assuming you don't have a printer where you are,' Lori said. 'I can make posters if you want. I've got some time. You can email me a picture and I'll do the rest.'

It was something Melody hadn't thought about. There definitely wasn't a printer at the lake house. Lori spoke with the efficiency of someone who'd done it all before and Melody wondered if she'd simply load up her old posters of Brent and just change the photo and name.

'I've not told Sam yet,' Melody said. 'I guess I'm still kinda hoping Evan turns up and I don't have to.'

Lori didn't reply, though she smiled kindly. They were a similar age, yet, in that moment, Melody felt so naïve. So inexperienced.

'What if Sam sees one of the posters before I've told him?' Melody asked.

'You could just put them up here? Probably in Duncan, too? If he's only going from camp to yours and back, it'll probably be all right for a day or two...?'

Melody wanted to believe that was true. Evan would appear within that day or two anyway. He had to.

'I'm in a few missing people groups on Facebook,' Lori said. 'It's not only people on the island but, if I'm honest, I don't think anyone's ever had a result from a poster. I'm sorry if that's not what you want to hear. It still doesn't do any harm.'

Melody sank in her chair and glanced over Lori's shoulder towards the trio of women who were gathering their things. One of them had walking poles that Melody had failed to notice before and they manoeuvred around the tables before heading towards the slope and the park beyond. Melody watched them go, thinking it was the sort of carefree break which she'd been looking forward to. A morning coffee with Evan and then off for a wander in the forest. It felt incomprehensible he wasn't there.

'I thought the police would do more,' Melody found herself saying.

'We don't get a lot of help out here,' Lori replied. 'And if someone's not on the main road, or in the town, they could be anywhere. You walk five minutes into the trees and, before you know it, you're in the middle of nowhere. So much of it is rocky and impassable, or there's been a mudslide in the winter, something like that. Then it's not long until you're in the mountains. If every person who lived here went into the woods to help search, it would still take weeks, months, to get very far.'

Melody's sense of feeling tiny was back. A minuscule being, lost among miles and miles of earth. She just about stopped herself from sighing. It had been a useful conversation – and a part of her appreciated the honesty. Except, in the moment, what she *really* wanted was the false confidence of her sister.

EIGHT

It was a short drive for Melody around the top of the lake, until she pulled off the road. She drove around the main house and headed down the gravel drive before stopping at the side of the lake house. The air con from inside the vehicle was in sharp contrast to the searing morning sun that stung as Melody got out of the car. It was hotter near the water than at the café. The lone shade was underneath the umbrella on the deck – and Melody had only been outside for a few seconds when she felt dots of sweat prickling her forehead.

Before leaving the café, Melody had swapped phone numbers and email addresses with Lori. She had also replied to Nina's message, asking if she was 'OK'. How was she supposed to reply? What counted as 'OK'?

There was no sign of the other vehicle as Melody parked, meaning Nina and Thomas had gone out for their day of being tourists. Melody didn't blame them, except, now some time had passed and she was by herself, a part of her did. She wanted them to walk through the woods with her and look for clues. Or endlessly drive around the lake in case Evan was sitting on a wall somewhere, waiting. Or even just sit on the deck together, so she had company.

She wanted all that but she didn't.

Melody was on her way to the deck when gravel crunched behind. She turned to see two men making their way out of what looked like a barn that was nestled off to the side between the lake house and the main house. There were two huge doors at the front, one of which was open.

The older man was in his seventies, with a ponytail, though was largely bald on top. His scruffy white beard matched what was left of his hair and he had the look of a man who'd sit on the porch with his dog in a western, drinking whisky.

The other man was probably in his early forties, beefy across his tanned shoulders but bigger in the gut. A walking advert for lager, gout, or possibly both. He stopped a couple of paces away.

'How are you getting on?' the older man asked. He had that flat Canadian accent that was so hard to place. Not quite American.

Melody couldn't remember his last name – but it was Harrison who'd answered her messages when she was booking the house. She'd met him for the first time properly when they had checked in on Saturday. He owned the property and, at least according to the listing, had built the lake house himself.

'The house is lovely,' Melody said, on autopilot.

'Thank you. This is my son, Rick,' Harrison indicated the younger man at his side.

As soon as he said it, Melody noticed how similar they looked. Rick must surely look at his dad and see his balding future.

Harrison was still going, poking a thumb towards the barn structure: 'Rick helps out. Sorry if there are fumes around. I've got a bit of painting to do. There's a workshop in there but it shouldn't be too disruptive.' He stopped to point at some trees on the furthest side of the house. 'I'm going to trim those later in the week, too. Probably Saturday. It might be a bit noisy but I'll haul everything off, so it won't get in your way.'

Melody eyed the trees, where the branches arced low towards the ground. She'd barely noticed them – and they were so far off to the side that she didn't realise they were on the same property. It was a world away from their boxy back yard at home. Half the garden was given over to uneven paving slabs, with moss growing through the gaps. The other half was grass that sat in permanent shade, and was often a bog, even when it had been dry. Here, there was so much space.

'I'm sure it'll be fine,' Melody replied.

'Have you been enjoying the view?'

'It's lovely,' Melody said, immediately realising she was repeating herself. 'So quiet...'

Rick angled towards the main house, arms crossed, seemingly bored of the conversation.

'If you need anything, you know where I am,' Harrison said, nodding towards the main house, and repeating what he'd told her when they arrived.

'My fiancé disappeared last night,' Melody said, suddenly unable to stop herself. The words all came out at once and were met by a confused silence.

'Disappeared from the house...?' Harrison replied, curiously.

'He didn't make it this far. He was driving from the airport. I was talking to him on the phone and he stopped for a girl in the road. I think he was going to see if she needed help – and that was it. The car was left with the keys in it. His phone was there – but he was gone.'

Rick looked towards his dad, then back to Melody. He frowned. 'Gone where?'

'No idea. The police are looking for him.'

The mention of authorities had Rick's eyes narrowing. 'You've had the police round here?'

The sudden urgency had Melody taking half a step backwards. The *not now* stare from father to son was impossible to miss.

'Don't you have somewhere else to be?' Harrison said forcefully, talking to Rick. He sounded calm, though there was an edge.

Rick mumbled something that sounded like 'nice meeting you', before trudging off towards the main house.

Harrison relaxed slightly with his son gone. 'Rick's had a few run-ins with the police over the years. He's also split from his wife not long back – and their son is at her house this week. He doesn't even live here.' He waited a moment and it felt as if he was weighing up whether to say something. In the end, he added: 'He should probably grow up.'

There was a grumble of an engine and the sound of tyres on gravel, which Melody assumed was Rick leaving.

They waited until the grumble had gone.

'What have the police said?' Harrison asked.

'Not a lot.'

A nod. 'You get a lot of complaints around here about them. People saying it's not worth reporting thefts, that sort of thing. It's worse in the winter, when it snows.'

Harrison glanced towards the road, where everything had gone quiet.

'You won't get a lot of sympathy for the police around here,' he added. 'Rick's sister was killed by a driver who didn't stop back when they were kids. I don't think he's ever quite forgotten that they took a while to find her.'

Harrison was rubbing his hands, apparently ready to get back to whatever he was working on, and Melody took a second to realise he was seemingly talking about his own daughter.

'How old was she?' Melody asked.

'Grace? She was ten.' He pointed over the lake, in the vague direction of the camp. 'She was riding her bike. They left her on the side of the road and kept going.'

Lori had said something about drink-driving being a problem in the community, and Melody wondered if this was what she was talking about.

'I'm really sorry to hear that,' Melody said.

Harrison nodded blankly as Melody struggled to know what else to say.

'How long have you lived here?' Melody added.

Harrison blinked and puffed out a long breath. He nodded towards the main house. 'I was born right here – but the house didn't look like that then. We put a second storey on it and built the deck at the front. I was born on the kitchen table... or at least that's what my dad used to say.'

'I hope they didn't cook dinner on it afterwards...' Melody smiled and Harrison laughed generously at the joke.

It was a momentary distraction from thinking of Evan. Was his fate similar to Grace's? Was he in a bush somewhere, waiting to be found? Surely the police had been looking? Wouldn't there have been blood on the road?

'It was all a long time ago now,' Harrison added. 'With Grace.' He cleared his throat and, when he next spoke, the tone was lighter. 'Anyway, I was telling your sister when she was leaving earlier – but I forgot to tell you the other day. Feel free to pick any fruit you see.' He indicated towards the dangling trees on the far side of the land. 'There are blackberries over there, plus apples, blueberries, and a plum tree.' He switched to point towards an area of shade in the other corner. 'Mushrooms there, if that's your thing.'

There was something about the way he said it that made it sound as if he didn't mean the sort of mushrooms to go in a risotto. He spoke so casually that Melody didn't want to sound prudish in querying exactly what he meant. Instead, she thanked him for all the help, in the way British people did when feeling somewhat awkward. *Thank you for the offer of magic mushrooms, I'm sure they're lovely.*

'I hope your husband turns up,' Harrison said. 'I'll ask around.'

She didn't correct him to fiancé, but thanked him for that as well, before they each turned to head in opposite directions.

Melody was almost past the car when she noticed the dark speck. She stopped and stared, first wondering if it was a trick of the light, before slowly approaching. As she crouched, it became clear there was no trick. The mark had been missed in the gloom of the previous night, and the rush of the morning. It was obvious now, though – a crusty blob of crimson-black encrusted on the bottom of the driver's door.

Blood.

NINE

A tow truck came a little over an hour later. The driver explained that he did subcontracting for the police, then loaded the silver car onto the back of his vehicle, before heading off with a splutter of gravel. Melody wasn't sure which officer she'd spoken to on the phone but the woman had said they would test the substance and see what came up. It all felt like a bit of a mess in that they probably should have done that in the first place. She had wanted to say that to someone, in much stronger terms, but hadn't expected a random guy with a tow truck. Everything felt so slapped together.

Melody had spent much of that hour peering at the mark on the car door, trying to convince herself it wasn't blood. Perhaps there was a lot of local clay in the soil, and it was actually mud? Maybe Sam had spilled some sort of juice on it that morning?

She knew it was blood, though. Probably Evan's.

Melody wanted to visit the part of the road from which he'd disappeared – except she no longer had a car. She could walk around that way, except it would take an hour in the searing heat, and there was no pavement. She'd be walking on the road, which Lori and Harrison had already warned about.

Lori had emailed a potential version of a missing poster for Evan. She'd asked if Melody wanted her to put them up in the village, adding that she was driving up to Duncan to go shopping, and could place some there as well. Melody had thanked her, saying that would be great, and then had a lengthy phone call with the car hire place. Lori's kindly advice that life continued regardless was never truer than when Melody found herself trying to explain to someone that the car wasn't damaged, but that the police had taken it to look at whether the blood on the driver's door matched that of her missing fiancé.

As she waited on hold, the horrifying idea occurred that there would be so many more conversations of a similar nature. Not only the dreaded ones with Sam, or Evan's parents – but the mundane ones with his boss, their bank, people like that. The council tax was in his name, so she'd have to get onto them. What if a parcel arrived in his name, and she had to get it from the sorting office? They'd want ID, and she'd end up having a breakdown trying to explain to someone behind a counter that, actually, her fiancé was missing in a foreign country.

It hadn't even been twenty-four hours.

Melody sat on the deck and stared across the lake. A handful of boats were drifting in the open water, though it was unclear if the people within were fishing, or simply relaxing in the early-afternoon sun.

She had no idea what to do.

It was a little after one that Melody's dad appeared. He sat in the reclining chair across from her, iPad on his lap, with the *New York Times* crossword app open, though untouched for now. It had become part of his routine, since he'd gone down the same pandemic Wordle wormhole as the rest of the world. He now spent a few hours every day working his way through various puzzles.

'Any news?' he asked.

'The police have taken the car.'

'I thought they'd have done that last night. Hopefully they'll find something.'

Melody couldn't quite bring herself to mention the blood. She asked what he'd been up to, and it sounded like he'd been out walking. Melody wanted to say that the side of the road wasn't safe – but it wasn't as if he'd listen.

They sat quietly for a while, Melody's father occasionally typing a word into his app. He'd never been the sort to talk about his feelings. When Melody's mother had died, her dad had barely spoken for a month, which more or less summed up his approach to grief.

Which was probably why it was such a surprise when Melody realised he was looking over his reading glasses towards her.

'You're going to have to tell him sometime,' he said.

Melody pictured Sam at camp, hopefully with new friends, having a fantastic time. 'I know,' she said, not quite able to meet her father's eye. She turned to watch a man on a paddleboard instead. He was balancing effortlessly, gently propelling himself across the surface of the water. 'I want him to enjoy himself for a day or two first.'

Her father seemed to think on that for a moment, before tapping something more into the iPad.

'Have you told Evan's mum and dad?' he asked, almost certainly unable to remember their names.

'Not yet. They're still on the cruise. I know they've got Wi-Fi but it's not like they can do much until they get back to land.'

It was largely the truth, but Melody could've probably got in touch if she really wanted to – which she didn't. No point in spoiling two sets of holidays, let alone having to navigate a minefield of questions to which she didn't have answers.

Melody's dad clicked his tongue into his cheek and she wasn't sure whether it was some sort of tic, or a disapproval.

'What's it like being back at the lake?' Melody asked,

changing the subject. The paddleboarder was now lying on the board, legs in the water as his torso baked in the sun.

She didn't see it, though she sensed her father's finger falter as he was about to type something into his app.

'I don't remember much of it,' he said.

It sounded like a lie, although Melody wasn't overly surprised at him pushing those thoughts to the back of his mind. The last time they'd been here, his wife – Melody's mum – had been alive. In the couple of years since she'd passed, he'd slipped into a routine of walks, his crossword app, and twice weekly games at the lawn bowling club. He'd hate the description but the truth was that he pottered around. It had taken a real push to get him out of the rut, and on holiday with them.

Melody didn't push further on those past memories, though there was one thing she didn't want to let go.

'Are you OK for money?' she asked.

Melody felt her father frowning. Finances were another topic of which her dad would keep to himself.

'What do you mean?' he asked.

'Thomas said you borrowed some money at the airport.'

'Why'd he say that?'

Melody knew the reason: Thomas wanted to make sure he got it back at some point. He wasn't going to ask his wife to talk to her dad, so he'd gone to Melody instead.

'It was just conversation,' Melody said. 'He didn't mean anything by it.'

Melody often wondered how far her dad's 'pension and investments' went each month, though never brought it up. She'd even asked Evan to raise it with her dad at one point, although that hadn't got much of an answer. She'd witnessed things like her dad putting four quid's worth of petrol in his car, wondering if it was because he was stressed and didn't want to admit it. His cupboards didn't have much food in them but what was there tended to be own brands, or items on sale. He'd always been frugal but she hated the idea of him struggling in silence.

'I'm fine,' he said, clipped to end the conversation.

He returned his attention to the puzzle for a moment, although his fingers never touched the screen. Melody knew she'd annoyed him. He had never been the type to ask for help. She often thought it must have been exhausting growing up in his generation.

'Why were you so keen to come back?' he said after a while.

The paddleboarder had turned over, lying face down on his board, exposing his back to the sun. Paddleboarding was one of the things Evan had suggested they do during the day while Sam was at camp. He'd even found a place that hired them out. Melody had vague memories of kayaking when she had been at camp all those years before – and it had been something she was most looking forward to. Now, it felt distant and impossible.

'I told you,' Melody said. 'I really enjoyed it the last time I was here.'

'You were a kid then.'

'Exactly. I wanted to see what it was like as an adult. I wanted Sam to have a chance of experiencing what I did.'

Her dad didn't reply to that and she couldn't tell whether he thought it was a good idea. Evan hadn't questioned any of it, telling her over the years that it sounded like a great place to visit. He'd encouraged her to try to find some of the girls with whom she'd been at camp – except Melody could only remember the name 'Heather'. Without a last name, it was impossible to find out whether that person lived locally. When Melody had last visited, email wasn't a thing. She was fairly sure she and Heather had swapped addresses, with the intention of becoming pen friends. Melody couldn't remember why she hadn't written, though no letters had ever arrived for her.

Even though Evan had been supportive, it was hard for Melody not to feel a childish pang at times. When people at work asked where she was going on holiday and why, Melody found herself saying things like she'd always wanted to visit, as if she hadn't been before. The idea that her thirty-nine-year-old self was chasing a feeling she'd had as a nine-year-old didn't feel as joyous when said out loud.

'What else do you remember about the trip?' Melody's dad asked.

'I remember the yellow car you got from the airport,' Melody replied. 'Nina was saying you should get a convertible, so we could ride around with the top down. But then you got—'

'A Corvette,' her dad said. 'Like the one in *Cannonball Run*.'

That got a roll of the eyes from her and a hint of a grin from him. Burt Reynolds movies and cars were two of the things Melody remembered her dad enjoying when they were younger. She didn't remember the car itself, only that it was bright yellow. She could imagine her mum trying to talk her dad out of getting such a vehicle, based on practicalities alone, only to give in as he told her it was the *Cannonball Run* car.

'I remember telling people at school that you'd won a competition for a holiday,' Melody said. 'Everyone was so jealous.'

'It was your mother who won,' he replied. 'She used to enter everything. She'd fill in the backs of cereal packets, or write in to TV shows. I'd always say there was no chance of winning and—'

'She'd say that someone had to win...' The memory had appeared from nowhere. Melody's mum would save crisp packets and send them off to claim free toys, or footballs – even though neither of her daughters were into sport. She'd fill up with petrol at the same station, because they were giving away collectible coins. 'What sort of things did she win?' Melody asked, suddenly wanting to remember the rest.

'Vouchers for the butcher was a big one. She probably won

about a hundred quid's worth in total. Plus she got a Christmas hamper one time. That kept us going for a month. She won a bunch of mugs from the radio. Then the holiday, of course. Three weeks with a private cabin, flights, spending money. I thought there must be a catch at first, like it was the sort of thing other people might get. Your mum took me into town to talk to someone at the travel agent, because I thought she must've missed something. Turned out the agent had lived out here, so recommended camp for you and your sister. We had to get you both passports but everything else was legit.'

Melody had forgotten that the trip was her first time abroad. They had barely had holidays before that, let alone anything overseas. Some of her school friends would talk about ski trips at Christmas, or they'd head off to France in the summer. Such decadence was a dream back then – which was likely another reason Melody had immortalised the trip so much. It was the first time she had felt special.

'I don't remember much more than camp,' Melody said.

'You were always so tired when you got back,' her father replied. 'What were you? Nine?'

'Right.'

Her dad unexpectedly pushed himself up from the chair and stepped off the deck, moving towards the water. Melody picked up her phone and found herself following until they were at the edge. The paddleboarder had disappeared, likely off to one of the private docks that lined the shore.

'We had a cabin somewhere that way,' he said, pointing in the vague direction of the village centre, across the water from the camp. It was too far to see anything specific.

'Do you want to go round there one day?' Melody asked. 'See what it looks like now?'

Melody pictured Evan being back and they could all visit together. Her dad would tell stories and it would be the trip she imagined.

The suggestion got a shake of the head regardless. 'We didn't all have the same holiday back then.'

Melody was about to ask what he meant when her phone buzzed. She glanced to the screen, expecting some sort of junk email – except it wasn't that. The subject 'Missing man' burned enticingly, until Melody swiped to open the message. Someone had seen one of Evan's missing posters.

I'm looking at your husband right now.

TEN

Melody had called Nina first, though her phone hadn't rung and the WhatsApp message had gone undelivered. She was probably in the woods somewhere. With no car, and unsure what else to do, Melody had contacted the only other person she knew with a vehicle.

Lori took barely fifteen minutes to get to the lake house. Melody was waiting on the side of the road and apologised her way into the passenger seat, as the other woman U-turned on the empty road. Melody could have asked her dad but Lori offered a kinship of their shared experience. She also knew the area.

Melody repeated her sorrys, saying she didn't know who else to call. She explained about the blood on the car, plus her sister having the other one. Lori batted everything away, saying it wasn't a problem, as she drove along the crumbling lanes. As they turned away from the lake, heading up a hill, they passed small blue house numbers jammed into the verges, as driveways banked down to out-of-sight houses. It was only then that Melody thought she could have called Constable Burgess to ask what he thought of the email.

Bit late now.

Lori was focusing on the road as Melody tried to contain her excitement. One of the posters Lori had put out had apparently worked. Evan would have some explaining to do – but he was twenty minutes away.

Melody strained against the seatbelt, watching the roadside flower stalls zip past. There were other stands as well, selling eggs and berries.

'How do people pay?' Melody asked, after spying the third egg stand.

'What do you mean?' Lori replied.

'For the eggs and stuff. It says six dollars a carton – but there's nobody there.'

'There'll be an honesty box somewhere. You just put in the money and take change if you need it.'

Around the next bend and they passed another wooden stand at the end of someone's drive. There were punnets of various berries stacked next to a cardboard sign, on which someone had written $5.

Melody didn't live in a particularly high-crime area – but she knew for a fact that anyone who'd left a money box on a wall outside their house wouldn't expect to see it again. She doubted it would last ten minutes. Here, there was some sort of roadside economy, seemingly all done on honesty alone.

They passed a bus stop with a plastic, once-white, lawn chair sitting underneath, and then Lori pointed off to a street that ran to the side of a sign advertising a drive-in coffee place.

'I live through there,' she said.

It was blink-and-you'll-miss-it as they zipped around a corner, towards a lengthy stretch of overgrown trees.

'Do you work from home?' Melody asked, quickly adding: 'You're not missing work for this, are you?' Melody felt the urge to add another apology on top of the others but Lori was unbothered.

'I gave up my job about a year ago, when Brent's life insurance came through.'

The 'Oh' slipped out without Melody meaning it, though Lori brushed it off.

'It takes seven years for someone to be declared dead once they're registered as missing. Can you believe that?'

Melody wasn't sure how to reply. Seven years felt like a long time. Evan had been gone for less than a day but at least someone had now seen him. She wouldn't have to tell Sam his father was missing.

'I'd been working the whole time since he disappeared,' Lori added. 'I had a job at the government office in Duncan. Alice would finish school before I was done at work, so she'd be at the house by herself for about an hour and a half. Then, if she wanted to play soccer, or something like that, I'd be relying on other mums to drop her off. It was always a rush to get up the highway and back. So, when Brent's money landed, I figured I'd have a bit of a stop and rethink.'

Melody was still somewhat stuck on 'life insurance'. She thought Evan had a policy through his work, though it wasn't something they'd ever talked about too deeply.

Still, she was glad she wouldn't have to think about that now he'd been found.

'Alice goes to high school next month,' Lori added. 'I was going to give it until the end of the year and see how everything's going with her, then make a decision about what to do next. I don't think I can face another twenty years working behind a desk.'

It sounded as if Lori had already put a fair bit of thought into her future – even if she hadn't yet told anybody else. Her throwaway 'what does Evan do?' was almost lost as Melody drifted to thoughts of what she'd say to her fiancé when she saw him. A part of her felt anger at everything he'd put her through

– but what if he was hurt? The emailer hadn't mentioned an injury.

'He works in finance,' Melody replied.

'What does that mean?'

Melody laughed, mainly because it was the question she asked herself, even as she parroted the line 'he works in finance' to others. None of her friends or family ever bothered to be as bold as Lori and actually ask.

'I don't really know,' Melody replied. 'Something to do with corporate banking but the moment he starts talking about work, I switch off. I don't know how anyone's interested in that stuff.'

It felt something of a relief to actually speak with such honesty. Melody had never admitted such a thing.

'What about you?' Lori asked.

'I was an office manager when I took some time off to have Sam. I never quite went back and ended up helping out as a nursery assistant. I was looking to get back into things when Covid happened, which made it basically impossible to get a job for two years. Then the four-year CV gap was a six-year gap.' Melody wafted a hand to cover a sigh. 'I've been working in a coffee shop,' she added.

'Nothing wrong with that,' Lori replied, although Melody had spent the best part of a year trying to convince herself of the same.

'Is that why you ordered a flat white earlier?' Lori asked. 'I saw your dirty little look at those women ordering oat milk mocha, frappe, chocca, whatevers.'

Melody laughed at that. Properly laughed for the first time since Evan had called her the day before. 'You can always tell those who work in shops like that,' Melody said. 'We look out for each other.'

The spaced-out houses had given way to long rows of hedges. As they crested a slope, Melody saw a stretch of fields disappearing towards a mountain in the distance. The sky was cloudless but hazy, as if the windscreen was smeared with a gentle film of grease.

'Evan must earn quite a bit more than you,' Lori said – which was true, albeit blunt. Perhaps it was a Canadian thing? Melody's friends would've never mentioned such a thing to her face.

Melody mumbled a 'right', though didn't explain her discomfort at such a thing. Of her café wages, she had been putting a little into a savings account each month. Evan knew nothing about it and she wasn't quite sure why she did it, other than that her mother had once told her that women needed to make sure they had emergency money just in case. Melody had been a teenager then and hadn't thought too much of it – even if she'd never forgotten.

Lori must have sensed Melody's unease, because she moved on seamlessly. 'How did you and Evan meet?' she asked.

'At a crazy golf place,' Melody replied – even though it wasn't completely true.

'Is that like mini golf?'

'I suppose. We ended up hitting it off and things went from there.'

'How long have you been together?'

'About thirteen years.'

For a moment, she thought Lori might have a series of follow-ups but, instead, she went for the jugular.

'How come you're not married?'

It made Melody snort. 'You sound like my mum, before she died,' Melody said. 'She was old-fashioned. Didn't like the grandchild before marriage part.'

'Sorry,' Lori replied.

'It's fine. Evan and I didn't think it was for us. Then we had Sam and there was all the stuff with the school about different last names and all that. We didn't want to do the double-barrelled thing, so decided maybe it would be better to get married.'

Lori's deadpan 'sounds romantic' had Melody laughing again. There was something about the way she took everything unseriously that was so appealing. Is that how life became once the worst had already happened?

There were a few moments of quiet as they reached the main intersection with the highway. A large supermarket sat on the other side of the junction, along with a gym and liquor store. It was the plaza Melody had visited on Saturday, when she'd realised supermarkets didn't sell alcohol on Vancouver Island. Instead, there were entirely separate shops – a fact they had all found utterly bewildering.

'It's about fifteen minutes from here,' Lori said, as she took the left turn to head north.

'What's Duncan like?' Melody asked, still unable to get over the image of a middle-aged man. It was such an odd name for a town.

'It's the biggest town in the area,' Lori said. 'There's a Walmart and a Superstore, which are cheaper than most places. There's loads of traffic, though. They built the highway through the middle of it for some reason. Once you turn into Duncan itself, there's an abandoned train line that runs through the centre. Lots of little shops – and a nice market on a Saturday.'

There were swathes of yellowing grass on the other side of the highway, stretching to distant mountains that clung to the horizon.

'What's that place you're staying?' Lori asked.

'I found it on Airbnb. The guy who owns the house built a smaller one at the back, by the lake. He said he hires it out through the summer. There's a deck and a really great view. He was telling me about the fruit trees and saying I could pick what I wanted.'

Melody sighed a little, wanting to share those things with

Evan. She wanted to tell him that she was fairly sure she'd been offered magic mushrooms but was too courteous to ask. He'd have found her politeness hilarious.

'What's the name of the guy?' Lori asked.

'Harrison-something.'

There was a momentary pause and then: 'Harrison *Dewar...*?'

The hesitation didn't sound like a positive thing. 'Do you know him?' Melody asked.

'Maybe not *Harrison*. But everyone knows his son...'

It was impossible not to notice the menaced undertone.

'Rick...?' Melody said.

'You've met him then...?'

'Briefly.'

Lori let out a long breath as she checked her mirror and then slowed to let a truck join from a slip road.

'There was a beach cookout thing a summer or two back,' Lori said, half an eye still on her mirror. 'It was at the park just down from the village centre and quite a lot of people were there. I think there might've been a band. That sort of community thing. Rick got in a fight with his wife and punched her. Can you believe that? There are videos of it online, which is why he got done by the police. His wife didn't want to press charges.'

She let that sit as Melody thought on Harrison telling her that Rick had run-ins with the police. That was one way of putting it.

'The worst thing was,' Lori added, 'it was in front of everyone's kids, including their own. I think their son was only three or four. You've just gotta hope he doesn't remember seeing it.'

Melody wasn't sure what to say. She obviously knew violence existed, though had never particularly experienced it. Her parents rarely argued, let alone fought. She'd had the odd play scrap with her sister when they were young but that was about it. The idea of one partner punching another was so far from her own life.

Lori must've sensed it, because she added: 'Don't let it put you off the area. You get people like that everywhere, right?'

Melody figured it was true enough, especially with cameras on everybody's phones. Not only were there people like that all over – but more of their actions were recorded to be shared.

The traffic slowed as they reached a large farm market on the outskirts of town. Cars stopped and started as they edged their way across a narrow bridge. A hotel was on the right, next to a large cannabis shop. Melody was partially distracted by how in the open that was, compared to the way it was banned at home. She also noticed the posters taped to the telegraph posts lining the highway. There were some advertising gardening services, or garbage removal: the sort of thing that felt universal. Others had faces of men or women, with 'MISSING' in large letters. As Lori stopped at a set of traffic lights, Melody took in the pair of posters on the nearest post. Neither was for Evan.

'I can't believe so many people are missing around here,' she said.

'Not all of these are new,' Lori replied, although it didn't feel particularly comforting.

Melody watched as Lori made her way across lanes. They'd barely moved in ten minutes, with a series of junctions in rapid succession, as if nobody had ever heard of a roundabout. There was no air con in Lori's car and, with the windows open, the heat stung Melody's arm.

Lori turned left at a spot where there were gas stations on three of the four corners. They continued a short distance, until turning onto a narrower street with a strip of grass along the middle. It was only as they were parking that Melody realised a train track was cutting through the green.

Once she'd stopped, Lori buzzed up the windows and locked the car as they got out. The heat was like a wall as

Melody gathered herself. None of the buildings were more than two storeys, leaving no shade, aside from underneath the smattering of trees.

Melody had her phone out, re-reading the email she'd received less than an hour ago. She was about to ask Lori what it meant by the 'totem by the station' when she realised she was looking at it. It was almost dwarfed by the trees but a wooden totem was standing across the park, painted red, yellow and green. Melody thought she might have seen something similar in a museum at some point, but couldn't particularly remember any details.

The carvings were intricate, not that anyone was paying it any attention. Half a dozen people were sheltering under the nearby bus stop, while other shoppers passed back and forth, looking at their phones.

Melody showed her own device to Lori. 'Do you think that's the totem?' she asked.

Lori pointed to the low red-brick building a short distance from the totem. 'That's the old station,' she said. 'It's a museum now, so I guess that's what she means.'

The email was from someone named Collette. She said she'd be waiting on a bench near the totem.

Melody headed slowly across the park. There were benches on the far side, but only one close to the museum. A woman was sitting on it, facing the other way, twisting from side to side. As Melody got nearer, she noticed the paper in the woman's hand, feeling a surge of hope as she spotted Evan's face.

It was the first time Melody had seen the actual poster Lori had created. It contained a cropped photo of Evan at some work function the previous summer, when he and his colleagues had shown a complete inability to dress down. Despite it being a picnic in the scorching heat, they'd still all shown up in suits and shirts. Except Evan had been smiling in the picture, and – unlike some of the images in Melody's gallery – it actually looked like him. Not posed, not smiling because someone had told him to, but a moment of unawares as they chatted together. It had been taken by the wife of one of his workmates, who'd sent it across with the single caption 'cute'. And it was.

Melody's heart was thumping now. She could feel it rattling in her chest as she turned in a circle, expecting Evan to be somewhere near.

A man was leaning on the bus stop – but he was too short and carrying a rucksack. Somebody else was walking past at pace, half dragging his girlfriend along with him. Melody scanned their faces – but none of them was Evan.

A slow, creeping worry began to seep through her.

'Are you Collette?' she asked as she reached the bench. The woman who'd been sitting leapt up and began pulling at her top. Her shoulders were pointy, arms bone thin.

'Melanie?' she said.

'Yes,' Melody replied, figuring it wasn't worth correcting her. She pointed to the poster still in the other woman's hand. 'You said you were looking at him...?'

Collette was nodding quickly as she turned and pointed towards the museum, and the bench at its side. 'Right there,' she said. 'He was sat right there.'

ELEVEN

Evan was not on the bench. Instead, a boy was cradling a skateboard while scrolling on his phone.

'Where did he go?' Melody asked.

'I'll show you.'

Collette didn't wait for a reply as she bounded around Melody, heading for the road. They passed a large purple shield that looked like a football crest, with 'Station Street' written on it, then continued over the crossing, past a bank, and along the road. Melody was struggling to keep up, with Lori another pace behind, as Collette strode at near running pace.

They crossed another road, this time Collette holding up a hand as if waving an invisible lollipop stick to stop the traffic. A man was dragging a rickety trolley full of empty cans and bottles in the opposite direction. One of the wheels was missing, though he appeared not to have noticed as the metal squealed on the pavement. Collette paid him no attention, weaving expertly around him as Melody skipped to keep pace.

Melody didn't know the difference between dry heat and whatever the other one was. She did know that sweat was stinging her eyes as she tried to wipe it from her brow. Her top was clinging to her back and her arms prickled.

They'd only been walking for three or four minutes, yet it looked as if they were almost out of town already. They passed a café with a green awning, then a clothes store, until Collette stopped at an empty bike rack.

She turned towards a bollard that was blocking an alley. 'This way,' she said, galloping into the space between two shops.

Melody was almost behind her until Lori grabbed her arm and pulled her back. When she turned, Lori released her, though offered a gentle shake of the head.

'What?' Melody asked, not knowing why Lori had stopped her. The other woman's features were scrunched, lips tight, as if asking Melody a silent question. She almost felt it pressing on her.

Really...?

Collette had noticed that she was now alone, halfway into the shadowed alley as she turned to look back at Melody. Suddenly the bright sun was dark.

'It's this way,' Collette called – though Lori had suddenly taken over. She stepped in front of Melody protectively.

'Where are you taking us?' she asked.

Collette spun in half a circle. The poster was still in her hand. 'To where he went,' she replied.

'But how do you know he went here?' Lori asked.

Collette was again pulling at the strap of her top. 'Followed him.'

'So you followed him this way, then went back to wait for us?'

'Um... yeah...?'

It sounded more like a question – and Melody knew. She should've known before.

'How do you know he's still here?' Lori asked.

There was a man now, idling out from behind a large wheelie bin. He was skinny like Collette, wearing trousers with more holes than material. He yanked them up, even as they instantly slipped to his hips.

Collette turned and eyed him, then started walking back along the alley towards Lori and Melody. She had a slight limp that Melody hadn't noticed before.

'We should go,' Lori said firmly – although it took a second for Melody to realise she was talking to her.

'Right, um...'

Collette spoke next. She was within half a dozen paces of them, relentlessly tugging on her top. 'You got cash?' she asked. Something had shifted in her tone as she faltered the words. 'I'll take you to him.'

Lori was still between Melody and Collette. 'We should go,' she repeated.

Melody saw it now. It was impossible not to – and yet a part of her still believed Evan had been sitting on the bench by the old train station. She had no idea how he could have got there, let alone why he wouldn't have been in contact – and yet she *wanted* it to be him. And perhaps he *had* wandered off, and Collette *had* followed, and she *had* emailed Melody to be helpful, and—

'It's a scam,' Lori said firmly – and Melody knew.

'Fifty?' Collette said, hopefully.

Lori moved to the side, not quite tugging on Melody's wrist, but reaching for it. 'Come on.'

'Thirty?' Collette added.

Lori had taken a small step away, as Collette edged closer. The man at the back of the alley was bobbing from foot to foot, making some sort of squeaking noise.

'Is she OK?' Melody asked, as Collette started to scratch her arm.

Melody didn't think Lori actually touched her, though the other woman shuffled her to the front as they started to walk back the way they'd come. When they reached the green awning, Melody checked over her shoulder, to where Collette was standing at the entrance to the alley. The man was there, too, shouting something Melody couldn't make out.

The two women hurried over the crossing, past the bank, and back to the totem by the train tracks. Lori slowed, waiting for Melody to slot in at her side as they walked across the park. People were picnicking on the grass and Melody turned from side to side, a part of her still believing Evan had been there.

'Do you want something to drink? Lori asked.

The idea hadn't occurred to Melody until it was mentioned. She felt drained from the heat and disappointment. She had gone from being convinced she was about to see Evan, to knowing he hadn't been there.

Her throat was dry and gasped a 'yes'.

Lori led them into the museum, which sat on the edge of the tracks. There were photos of old locomotives and what was probably the town as it had once been. There was also a large vending machine close to the door – and Lori tapped her phone on the panel. She asked what Melody wanted and then bought a pair of Diet Cokes, which thumped into the chute one after the other.

Melody devoured half of hers in one and then rubbed the chilled can along her arms. They were standing in a reception area, a few steps from a counter, behind which a man in a waistcoat was talking to a couple about a brochure.

'Was she going to rob us?' Melody asked. The threat suddenly felt more serious now she'd said it out loud.

It took Lori a couple of seconds to reply. 'Maybe,' she said, carefully. She was rubbing her own can along the back of her neck. 'She probably didn't expect two people to show up.'

'What if she did see Evan?' Melody replied, knowing it sounded desperate. The heat of outside had been replaced by a steady gust of air conditioning. Maybe it was because of that, but Melody found herself blinking rapidly, trying to gulp away tears that felt as if they might erupt. If she'd been by herself, Melody would've let them – but not here.

Lori must have noticed, because she moved sideways to stand in front of Melody, sandwiching her between the vending machines. It was subtle, but Melody recognised the inherent kindness. It only lasted a few seconds and then Melody whispered, 'I'm OK.'

The moment passed as Lori nodded to the counter. The couple had moved into the museum itself and the man in the waistcoat was looking to them expectantly. Lori fiddled with her phone and then approached the desk, Melody a step behind.

'Have you seen this man today?' Lori asked. She offered the man her phone, on which was the photo of Evan Melody had emailed.

The man squinted at the screen, moving it slightly further away as he pursed his lips. 'Has he been in today?' he asked.

'Maybe,' Lori replied. 'He was spotted in the area.'

The guy behind the counter made a 'hrmmmm' and then looked over his shoulder, calling across a woman who wore glasses on a chain.

'Have you seen this man today?' he asked her.

The woman peered through the glasses and mirrored her colleague by pursing her lips. 'I don't think so,' she said.

The man handed Lori back her phone, with an apologetic smile. 'I don't think I have, either. Sorry about that.'

Lori thanked him for the help and then shuffled back towards the vending machine. 'Do you want to go back?' she asked. 'We can hang around for a bit, if you want...?'

Melody didn't want. The image of Collette scratching while the man emerged from behind the bins was too close.

They headed outside, where the sun continued to sting. The sky was so blue.

'You get used to the false hope,' Lori said quietly, not unkindly – but with the sense of a person who really knew.

The problem was that Melody didn't want to get used to it.

TWELVE

Lori drove Melody back to the lake, and the camp, where they picked up Alice and Sam. The two children were three years apart and had been split between different areas of the camp – not that either minded being on the same back seat. Lori had said that Alice was twelve going on thirty – and she had been content to swipe away at her phone as Sam excitedly told them about his day. His group had gone on a treasure hunt through the trees, before playing a version of water polo in the lake. There had been painting in the afternoon, and then some sort of capture the flag game. It sounded as if he'd made friends with about a dozen other boys, as he told them what he was looking forward to the following day.

After everything from the past day, Melody had to bite her bottom lip to stop it wobbling. *This* was the experience she had desperately wanted him to have. The feeling of being liked and wanted. The same thing she had hung onto for so long. The fact he'd had such a terrific day was justification that she wasn't some mad woman clinging onto a childish memory.

Lori drove them back to the lake house, telling Melody to call if she needed anything in the coming days. They stood on the side of the road, watching the car pull away as Sam waved, even though he couldn't have known who she was.

At the lake house itself, Nina and Thomas were lying on towels at the edge of the water. Melody told Sam to go inside and have a shower. His protestations of 'being in the water all day' were half-hearted as he relented after a single gripe.

Melody headed down to where Thomas was on his back, in a pair of board shorts, holding up a book to block the sun. Nina was face-down in an orange bikini, though pushed herself up when she realised her sister was there. She sat cross-legged and straightened her top, shading her eyes with a hand.

'Any news?' she asked.

Thomas lowered his book and squinted towards Melody.

'Nothing,' Melody replied, not wanting to go into detail about Collette, or the blood on the car.

'Have you heard from the police?'

'Sort of. They were at camp this morning, asking people if they'd seen anything. They also took the car. I texted you about that.'

'Is there anything I can do?' Nina asked.

Melody had been thinking on that. 'Can you figure out a second car?' she asked. 'I don't think the police are bringing back the other one any time soon, and we're going to need something else with five of us here.'

Thomas had lifted his book back up, probably knowing what was coming. 'Can you sort that?' Nina asked him.

He sighed momentarily, though quickly stopped himself, probably remembering the reason why they needed two vehicles. He said he'd see what he could find and then pushed himself up from the towel, asking if the laptop was under the bed. After being told it was, he strolled towards the house in his flip-flops, shirt draped over his shoulder.

Nina patted the now empty towel and Melody sat, pulling

her knees to her chest. It had been a long day and she fought away a yawn.

'We picked up a massive bulk salad from a farm stand,' Nina said. 'Dad said he was going to fry the salmon we got from a different stall. The guy said it had been fished out of the ocean this morning.'

'Who'd have thought you could buy dinner off the side of the road?'

Nina laughed: 'That's what I said to Thomas. I guess if we all wake up with food poisoning, we'll have to think of something else for tomorrow.'

Melody lay on the towel and scrunched her eyes closed. The sun needled softly on her skin. 'Did you have a good day?' she asked.

'I suppose,' her sister replied. 'I was thinking of you. And Evan. And feeling guilty about it all.'

Melody considered her reply. She wavered from feeling angry her sister hadn't been around, to figuring Nina couldn't have done much anyway. Plus, not everything was about her. 'What was the bridge like?' she managed.

'Better than I thought. I'd never heard the word "trestle" but it's this massive wooden bridge that's out in the woods. It used to be for trains but you can walk over it, then go down underneath to the river. We sat in the sun for a bit by the water, then came back up. I didn't realise you'd messaged me 'til I got back to the car. There's no reception out there but I took a load of photos.'

Melody screwed her eyes tighter. It was supposed to be one of the things she and Evan did as well. Melody craved a worriless day in the sun with her fiancé.

'Sam had a good day at camp,' she said instead, moving things away from herself. 'I knew he'd enjoy it, like we did.'

Melody sensed Nina shuffling at her side. When she opened her eyes, yellowy-green stars swam.

Nina was sitting cross-legged. 'Not everyone enjoyed their first visit here,' she said.

'What do you mean?' It was similar to what their dad had said earlier.

'I suppose—'

Nina didn't get any further because Sam appeared on the deck. His hair was wet and he was in the full Everton kit his dad had bought him the previous Christmas, knee socks and all.

'Granddad says tea's ready,' he called.

Nina pushed herself up and reached for her sandals. 'I hope this salmon's good,' she said.

The salmon *was* good, though – as with the salad – there was way too much of it. The tomatoes were so red and juicy, the fish meaty and filling. Food always tasted better on holiday – but this was beyond that.

Sam spent the meal telling everyone else about his day. It was the second time Melody had heard it, and she suspected there would be at least a third that evening. Not that she minded. Anything that took his mind off the fact his dad wasn't there. As he started to repeat himself about the water polo, the yawns began. He would insist he wasn't tired and there'd be a half-hour back-and-forth before he eventually admitted defeat.

Before that, Melody asked him to clear the table and stack the dishwasher, knowing full well her dad would redo it anyway. With that done, she said he should check the kit list for the following day, and lay out whatever he needed for morning.

Sam yawned his way towards the stairs and then tripped his way up. Melody used to nag him about picking up his feet but had long since given up.

As Melody's dad crouched to restack the dishwasher, Thomas took out his phone. 'I can get a car from Duncan,' he said. 'They're open 'til eight, so if I go up with someone now, we can bring back both.'

Melody and Nina exchanged a quick glance, but didn't need to say anything as their father piped up: 'I'll go.'

He spent another minute or so removing everything from the dishwasher, before putting it all back in again. He set it running and then found his shoes, before the two men headed off to get another vehicle.

The two sisters sat at the dining table, picking at a few left-over bits of fish, while Sam clattered around above them.

'You're taking it well,' Nina said quietly.

Melody laughed humourlessly. 'I'm not. I just don't know what else to do.' She nodded upwards. 'He was so excited after camp that he didn't even mention his dad. I don't know if that's a good thing.'

She did know.

Evan had missed a lot of things in his son's life. There'd been the parents' evenings to which Melody had gone by herself. The sports days. The art gallery event Sam's class had hosted. So many meals. The truth was, a son *should* miss his father. One of the major reasons Melody had been so looking forward to the holiday was the chance to spend time with her fiancé when he wasn't staring aimlessly at a wall, clearly thinking about work. She wanted to watch him play with Sam. For them to be a family together.

Time passed and the stomping from above had gone quiet, so Melody said she was going to check on Sam. She crept up the stairs, rounding the banisters to a wide-open bedroom door. She stood in the frame and watched Sam fast asleep in his Everton kit, lying on his back, chest slowly rising and falling.

How could she possibly tell him his dad was missing?

What if Evan's fate was the same as Brent's? A man who never came back? How could she explain that to their son? How could she handle that herself?

Melody wasn't sure how long she'd been standing but she was distracted by a creak on the landing. When she turned, Nina was at the top of the stairs.

'I'm going to take a shower,' she whispered. 'But when the others get back, there's something I really want you to see.'

THIRTEEN

The sun kissed the tops of the trees, sending a glorious orange spilling across the heavens. They were three for three with sunsets since arriving on Vancouver Island. It felt like a summer that would never end.

Melody and Nina had got out of the car at the same time – and they took a moment to rest on the bonnet and take in what looked like a watercolour.

'Thomas was talking about getting up one morning to drive out to a lookout point he found,' she said. 'He reckons it faces east, so we should be able to see the sun coming up over the ocean.'

'What did you say?'

'I asked him what time the sun came up.'

'And...?'

'There's a quarter-past-five in the evening and I refuse to believe there's another in the morning.'

Melody laughed, having already guessed her sister's reaction.

Nina had parked on a patch of gravel slightly off the road that looped the lake. They were on the east side, more or less opposite the camp. Nina led the way over the stones, squeezing herself into an overgrown hedge and around a metal gate. Melody copied, following her sister along a dusty path, lined by bushes. They'd only taken a few steps when the lane opened up to reveal an overgrown patch of grass, with a dilapidated shack in the middle.

'We drove past earlier,' Nina said, by way of explanation.

Because there it was: There was barely a roof, and one side of the hut was scorched black by fire – but it was undoubtedly the cabin in which they'd stayed thirty years before.

Giant boulders were beyond the gate, presumably blocking anyone from driving, and Nina perched herself on one. Melody continued past her sister, the long grass brushing her knees as she edged towards her past. The burned half of the cabin had collapsed inwards, with the remains of the roof sitting partly on top of the crumbling walls. The other side was more or less intact, though the wooden deck felt brittle as Melody stepped on it. She didn't dare rest on the rail.

'Do you remember the beanbags?' Nina called.

Melody hadn't, except, from nowhere, the memory was there. The two sisters lounging on giant beanbags on the deck, as their parents shared a bottle of wine. They were playing Uno, something like that, and ended up arguing, so their mum confiscated the cards.

The shiver shimmered from Melody's neck to the base of her back.

If she blinked, she would be back there. It was so close.

Nina was at her side now, the two sisters staring across the darkening water to the orangey dock lights on the far side.

'Come this way,' Nina said, taking her sister's hand and guiding her off the deck, around the rail and to a log that was sitting on the private beach. They'd built sandcastles so many years before and the tide had never come in far enough to wash them away.

They sat on the log as the sky started to turn purple. It had looked exactly the same the day before when Evan had called.

'What do you think happened to it?' Melody asked, talking about the cabin.

'Looks like it burned down,' Nina replied, deadpan, which made them both laugh. Not for long. Evan was never far from Melody's thoughts. The urge to drive to the other side of the lake and start walking through the woods calling his name was strong again. 'It's so quiet, isn't it?' Nina said, from nothing. 'I'd forgotten that. There's always so much noise at home. You can never get away from it.'

She was right. The sisters listened to the silence and it felt endless, almost otherworldly. It was so quiet that it was somehow loud at the same time. A booming, echoing nothing.

Before the trip, Melody and Evan had talked of getting away from their lives to enjoy the peace. To reset. Except the hush was also the reason why there was no mass of police officers checking through the woods, or diving into the lake. Why it seemed as if nothing was happening. Solitude came with a price – and Melody was paying it.

'Do you remember when Dad used the barbecue?' Nina asked.

It was another memory that swirled from nowhere until it was suddenly so clear. 'Didn't he cook steak every night?' Melody asked.

'He met some bloke who basically sold him half a cow. Something like that. There was so much food all the time. Mum kept telling him he had to eat *some* vegetables.'

It seemed so extravagant at the time. They'd lived in a small two-bedroom house in the UK: parents in one room, sisters in the other. Then they'd flown for what felt like ever and Melody had a room to herself. They had their own beach, their own garden, a massive living room, a lake in which to paddle, steak every night. They'd lived a fantasy for three weeks.

'I see why you wanted to come back,' Nina said quietly. 'I've been trying to tell Thomas what it meant to you. He thought we should've gone to Ibiza, somewhere like that.'

'Aren't you a bit old for that?'

'Not the dancey bit of the island.' A pause. 'But, yeah...'

The quiet was splintered by a motorboat chugging across the water, a white light flickering on the back as the silhouette hummed into the distance.

'Why do you keep talking about what it meant *to me?*' Melody asked. 'Wasn't it the same for you?'

Nina sighed as she reached to tug her hair into a ponytail. The warmth felt as if it was going to continue through the night.

'A bit,' Nina replied. 'You were nine or ten – but I was fourteen. I didn't mix as well at camp as you. A lot of the girls knew each other from school, so I didn't make friends like you did. Then you were like Sam tonight. You slept a lot in the evenings, while I'd sit around waiting to be tired. Or Mum and Dad would send me to read in bed because they wanted to be alone.'

Melody didn't remember any of that, not even the being tired part. She remembered playing Uno on the beanbags as a nightly thing, not a one-off.

'Do you remember the night you came into my room?' Nina asked.

Melody had been about to ask about something else but the question stopped her. She turned to look towards the cabin, realising that the nearest window was the one that had been her bedroom. The charcoaled frame a little further along had collapsed inwards. That had been Nina's.

'Someone dropped a glass...?' Melody said, although she wasn't sure.

'I don't think it was dropped,' Nina replied, and her haunting voice was almost lost to the lapping water.

Melody remembered. She hadn't but now she did.

The breaking glass had woken her up. She'd listened for a

minute, maybe two, and then quietly opened her door and crept into her older sister's room. The novelty of her own space had worn off the moment the shouting had started.

'What were they arguing about?' Melody asked.

Nina didn't reply at first – but Melody knew she was right. The glass had likely been thrown, not dropped. Especially as it had been one or two in the morning, and then immediately followed by screaming.

'I don't know,' Nina replied, although it sounded like she did.

'What happened?' Melody said, knowing she was repeating herself.

Nina let out a long breath. 'Do you really want to know?'

'I think so.'

Nina didn't answer straight away. The boat with the flashing light on the back was returning the way it had come. They watched it disappear into the dusk, leaving a swell of water behind.

'Mum was cheating on dad,' Nina said softly. 'Someone at her work, I can't remember his name. It had been going on a while.'

Melody felt her mouth hanging open. She'd known her parents had fallen out at various times. They'd argue now and then, they'd spend weekends not talking. Melody didn't realise it was anything more than a married couple having minor issues, let alone an actual affair.

'How'd you know?' Melody asked, wanting details, yet not.

'I heard Mum on the phone with him one time,' Nina said. 'She gave me money to keep quiet about it.'

Melody spluttered a gasp. She couldn't believe it, even though she didn't doubt her sister was telling the truth. Like finding out Santa wasn't real.

'How old were you?' Melody asked.

Another sigh. 'It was only a few weeks before we came here.

Mum told me she was going to break up with the guy. She said she didn't want to get a divorce and that it wouldn't be fair on you if I told Dad.'

That was the real shock. Melody stretched and grabbed her sister's arm, forcing her to turn and look at her. 'What do you mean?'

'Because you were younger. She said it would affect you more if they split up. She said she was finishing it with the other guy, then gave me twenty quid and said not to tell Dad.'

Melody didn't know what to say. She had got used to life without her mum and, though she had always been closer to her dad, that didn't mean she'd fallen out with her mother. It felt as if Nina was talking about somebody else. It wasn't even necessarily the affair, but how could somebody Melody thought she knew be so manipulative?

'I figured she was probably right,' Nina added. 'I didn't think life was going to be any better if one of them left, so I kept quiet.'

Melody wondered if she would have done the same when she'd been Nina's age. Probably.

'Anyway,' Nina added. 'We came here not long after and I think the night you came into my room was the night Dad found out. They'd been drinking and I think she must have told him – which is why one of them threw a glass, and then there was all the shouting.'

A pause.

'At least you didn't lose your luggage this time,' Nina added, after a while, trying to make light.

It took a moment for that memory to arrive: something Melody hadn't thought about in a long time. 'I never did find my backpack,' Melody replied, suddenly picturing her pink bag that had a pig snout on the back. It had been bought especially for the trip, though Melody had no idea where it had ended up. She'd been trying to remember why she never wrote to her friends from camp – but that was why. She had lost their addresses.

It didn't take her mind away from that memory of her arguing parents.

The lake was clear and Melody stared across the water that glistened white in the moon. The orange of the sky had given way to the darkest purple. It had been this time the night before that Melody and Thomas had been on the other side of the lake, finding Evan's abandoned car.

'My friend, Lori, put up missing posters,' Melody said. 'She's the one who took me to pick up Sam and dropped us off.'

'That was kind of her.'

'She took me to Duncan because someone emailed, saying they'd seen Evan. It was a scam. I think I'd have been robbed if I was on my own.'

Melody left out the part about the man hiding in the alley, but more or less explained the rest. Nina listened, mouth open.

'Why would someone do that?' she asked.

Melody didn't answer because the answer was obvious enough. People did things for money.

And then she was thinking about Evan again now. There had been an underlying assumption through the day that he would simply turn up with an innocent explanation for what had occurred. Now that hadn't happened, what was she supposed to do? What were the police doing? Should she expect regular updates? Should she call them, or would they call her? Melody wondered if she should be angrier about it all, though it was hard to feel much more than a desperate resignation. What was she supposed to do? It was all so helpless and hopeless.

'Did you check Evan's phone?' Nina asked after a while. It felt as if she was searching for something to say. 'Maybe there's something on there?'

'I don't know his code. I've left it charging.'

Nina let out a gentle 'Huh...' and then added: 'I check Thomas's all the time.'

Melody almost asked 'Why?' but just about stopped herself. Her sister's relationship was none of her business, though she wondered if it was a symptom of other issues. Or maybe it was normal? Perhaps her relationship with Evan was the outlier.

They sat together, watching the white of the moon catch the gentle waves. The distant sound of an engine hummed under the silence.

'I'm sure he'll turn up,' Nina said, though it sounded as if she was talking to herself. A comfort blanket of a statement for everyone except Melody, who didn't reply.

A few more minutes passed until Nina twisted back towards the road. 'It's a shame about the cabin, isn't it?'

Melody agreed that it was, though the visit had given some degree of closure. When she'd been searching various tourism websites for accommodation, her first thought had been to find the cabin. It was now clear why she'd been unable to. She wondered how long ago it had caught fire and how it happened.

Nina pushed herself up from the log and stretched her legs. She held her lower back and arced backwards, before rotating from side to side. Neither of them needed to say anything as they turned and headed back to the car.

Melody rested her head on the passenger side window as Nina drove them through the crossroads of the village centre, where the only lights belonged to the pizza shop and sushi place.

Intermittent vehicles shuttled back and forth, with kayaks or paddleboards on top, their day at the lake done. There seemed to be more traffic on the east road and Melody wondered if things would have been different had Evan driven up the other side. He would never have seen the girl in the road, would never have stopped.

It didn't take long to loop around the top of the lake and

pull around Harrison's house. A single light was on inside, with another on the porch. Nina parked and the sisters clambered out, which was when Melody noticed the man sitting on the terrace of the main house.

Rick was smoking or possibly vaping. The undercurrent of cannabis brought back memories of the bushes at the back of the school, though it had been a long time ago.

'Who's that?' Nina whispered.

'The owner's son.'

Nina waved, though ended up lowering her hand when the gesture went unreturned. Rick sat unmoving and impassive, acting as if they weren't there.

The two sisters turned and headed across the gravel towards the lake house.

'What's his problem?' Nina asked.

'I have no idea,' Melody replied.

FOURTEEN

Melody lay in the double bed, staring at the ceiling. It was little surprise she'd ended up on the same side she had in England. Whether they were at home or in a hotel, Evan always slept on Melody's left. They had once tried switching when staying over for a friend's wedding, but barely lasted fifteen minutes before deciding it wasn't for them.

As she rolled onto her right side, Melody anticipated the covers being tugged back in the other direction. She and Evan had an ongoing, largely playful, niggle over who fidgeted the most overnight, and who stole the most covers. It was definitely him, with his big feet and 3 a.m. trips to the toilet, though he insisted it was her.

Melody craved that sort of argument that was a joke but wasn't. The sort of minor coupley disagreement that would go on for years, unresolved because it didn't really matter – even if they both brought it up multiple times a week. It was the same with not putting shoes on the rack by the door properly, or leaving things at the bottom of the stairs.

The squeak began almost as soon as Melody closed her

eyes. A rhythmic *eeyore-eeyore-eeyore* from the other side of the wall.

Melody opened her eyes. It had been a long time since she'd shared a house with her sister. Back then, their issues had been largely about clothes being left on the floor – but this was an annoyance Melody hadn't predicted.

Eeyore-eeyore-eeyore went the bed springs.

Melody unwrapped herself from the bed. If Nina and Thomas had relationship issues in checking each other's phones, they didn't appear to be having problems in another area.

Evan's sports watch was sitting on the charger next to his phone, and hers, so Melody picked up all three items and headed onto the landing. The squeaking was seemingly only noticeable through the wall between rooms, which at least meant Sam and Melody's dad wouldn't be disturbed by it. The only thing worse than a sister overhearing married, um, relations was a parent.

Melody crept downstairs and unlocked the door, before padding onto the deck. She pressed into the recliner and put her feet up. The melting heat of the day had been replaced by a welcoming late-night hug. The sort of warmth that never seemed to come along in the UK. It could be hot and it could be cold – but Melody couldn't remember a time when she could sit outside at midnight and simply be comfortable.

Flies buzzed around the solar lights that were spiked into the ground at the water's edge. The moon had dipped out of sight, leaving the steady shift of the cool, black water beyond.

Melody put down the phones and watch on the table and then leaned back, staring up to the blanket of tossed diamonds scattered across the sky.

It had been the year before that Evan had suggested driving out to a secluded spot to watch the meteor shower which had been trailed on the news. He'd shown her a website with a map that offered the best sites for seeing the stars, free of light pollution. Melody had been broadly up for things, if it wasn't for the drive that would take more than an hour.

Now, the sky for which they'd been searching was more or less above.

If only Evan was with her to enjoy it.

It had been more than a day now, with little in the way of an answer as to what had happened. She thought of Lori's resignation at her own circumstance – and wondered how long it would be before she had the same cynicism. That little voice telling her Evan would be back with a reasonable explanation was already a little quieter than the night before.

Melody thought of her mum and how Nina had kept a thirty-plus-year secret of an affair.

Did it matter now? She'd still raised two daughters, she was still Melody's mum. Still the person who drove them to clubs and shops. The person who taught Melody how to save and budget.

She wondered if those old cabin memories were tainted now. It sounded like her dad had probably thrown something at her mum after finding out about the affair – and Melody didn't know how she felt about that. He was three decades older, an ageing man who liked his crosswords and routine.

Melody knew she would never ask him about it. A big part of her wished she didn't know any of what Nina had revealed.

Time passed.

Melody knew she should go back to bed. If Nina and Thomas were still at it, she would knock on the wall to let them know she could hear.

Except she didn't.

Melody couldn't see the main house, and wondered if Rick was still on the porch. He didn't even live there, though he seemed to be around a lot.

Rick Dewar was easily googlable – which wasn't good news

for him. The top link was a local news story about an assault at a picnic. It sounded like the thing Lori had described and, when Melody clicked on it, a shaky video was embedded at the top. It was confusingly out of focus, punctuated by a series of screams from off-camera. Melody needed three views to properly figure out what was happening.

The woman who was presumably Rick's wife put down a long-haired toddler on the grass and then turned to jab a finger at Rick. He was in all black, wearing a baseball cap, with a vest, plus shorts that stretched below his knees. Someone off-screen shouted 'no' but it was too late. Rick slapped away his wife's finger and, as she started to poke it towards him a second time, he reeled back and punched her on the nose.

At that point, the screaming really started. It was impossible to know how many people were shouting – but the voices came from men, women, and children.

Whoever was holding the phone almost dropped it as the image fizzed across the water and the grass, before steadying.

The woman's face was a crimson explosion as she grabbed for her child, sending a spray of blood across his T-shirt.

The video cut out at that point, though Melody didn't want to watch any more anyway. The article said the injured woman refused to cooperate with police, though Rick had been prosecuted anyway due to what sounded like public outrage. Melody wasn't quite sure of the punishment described, though it sounded like he'd got community service.

Harrison's description of his son having 'run-ins with the police' felt like quite the understatement.

Melody swiped backwards and tried one of the other links. She'd found an old Facebook post about the incident on some sort of community group. The type of page that was usually full of locals complaining about kids riding skateboards, or a stranger parking outside their house.

This post was far more sinister than all that. It was the same video as the one embedded on the news page – and Melody had no inclination to watch it again. She did read the comments, though – which were almost unanimous in calling Rick variations of a disgrace or a scumbag. What Melody hadn't expected was for 'Sherry Dewar', presumably Rick's wife, and the woman who'd been punched, to be in the comments telling people to mind their own business.

It didn't take long for Melody to figure she'd seen enough, and return to the search results. There were pages of articles and reaction to the punch video, though, beyond that, there were other stories about Rick. He'd been arrested for stealing a pair of dirt bikes and, underneath a Facebook link of the story, he'd spent days arguing with anyone who dared to comment. Some were saying the arrest was overdue, while he'd tell them to 'Go back to the mainland', whatever that meant. Someone called him a 'redneck hick', and he replied that they didn't have the balls to say that to his face.

Melody clicked his profile and, in the main photo, he was sitting on an ATV somewhere in the woods, smoking a cigar, surrounded by beer cans.

He didn't seem the sort of person with whom Melody would get on.

She put down her phone and picked up Evan's sports watch. She still wasn't quite sure how it had ended up in her bag. Whenever her fiancé started to bang on about his runs or rides, Melody would zone out. Now, she craved him telling her about some hike they could do, along with the boring minutiae of the distance, elevation, and whatever else he thought was interesting.

Melody considered putting the watch on her wrist, if only as a way to feel closer to Evan... except she doubted he'd have wanted that. He got a new sports watch each year or so, which always looked the same as the last. It was one of the few indulgences solely for him, even though he asked Melody every year whether she minded him spending the money.

She returned the watch to the table and picked up her phone again. There was another thing she'd meant to google, before events had overtaken her.

There were far fewer hits for 'Grace Dewar' than her brother. The top story was from the early 2010s, and the twentieth anniversary of Grace's death. There were photos from a memorial service at a local church, with Harrison looking wildly out of place in a suit that was too big for him. The ponytail and scruffy white beard gave him the look of a person who'd accidentally stumbled into the wrong wedding. There were nine or ten others in the images, but no sign of Rick.

The article said Grace had been ten years old when she was riding her bike close to her house on Shawnigan Lake. She was the victim of a hit-and-run, leaving behind her twin, Rick.

Melody read it twice, making sure she hadn't missed something. Harrison had told her that Rick's sister had died when he was young – but he hadn't said they were *twins*.

It was no excuse for the things she had seen Rick do in the video – but it was hard for Melody to imagine what he'd gone through as a boy. Occasionally, when she was by herself and her mind was wandering, Melody would imagine something terrible happening to Sam. It could feel so real that she would be racked by worry until she was certain he was safe.

Rick had been so young when that absolute worst thing had actually happened to him.

Melody watched the water and listened to the chirping cicadas hiccupping from what felt like all sides. Not for the first time, Melody felt as if she was in one of the movies she'd watched growing up. Small towns, big trucks, and the pulsing noise of insects after dark.

It took a few minutes for Melody to force away her darker

daydreams and return to the article – not that it provided much comfort.

Although it had initially been a hit-and-run, Grace's killer was soon found. A local named Joel Boyd had been arrested, tried, and convicted after he was turned in by his own daughter. Melody had to re-read that part a few times but Starla Boyd had contacted the police almost a week after Grace had been hit, telling them her father had been out that night and had driven while drunk and possibly high.

The article backed up what Lori had said about people walking on the verges and drink-driving being an issue.

Is that what had happened to Evan? He'd got out of the car to check on the girl – and then been hit by a passing vehicle?

Melody shivered at the thought – but wouldn't there have been blood on the road? There was the small speck on the silver car but would that have been enough?

The yawn rippled through Melody, eventually enveloping her entire body. Before she could move, a second erupted.

It was close to 1 a.m. and Melody knew she should be in bed. She had to be up for Sam in the morning, so picked up both phones and the watch, then headed back into the house. She put everything down on the island and then poured herself a cup of water from the jug in the fridge.

The liquid was so cold and Melody instantly realised it was probably going to wake her up when she wanted to be tired.

Bit late for that.

She grabbed the phones and headed up into a thankfully quiet bedroom. The squeaking from her sister's room had been replaced by a muffled grunt of what was probably Thomas snoring. Melody slipped under the covers and lay on her back, staring at the ceiling, listening to what sounded like an injured hog on the other side of the wall.

Did lots of couples check one another's phones in the way Nina had talked about? Melody picked up Evan's from the stand and stared at the lock screen. Could there really be some sort of explanation inside for where he was? Maybe she could ask the police if they could unlock it? Would they do that?

The light beamed into her face as Melody knew she wouldn't be falling asleep any time soon. How hard could it be to figure out his code? How about 1-2-3-4...?

FIFTEEN
TUESDAY

Melody yawned her way across the kitchen and onto the deck. For a moment, she thought she was the first up again – except her dad was sitting in one of the recliners, iPad on his lap. He was staring at that day's crossword and Melody was almost over him when he realised she was near. He jumped a little and then squinted up to her.

'You look tired,' he said, looking away from the screen.

Melody slipped into the chair at his side. 'Good morning to you, too,' she replied, with another yawn. She had spent most of the night calculating the maximum amount of rest she could have if she fell asleep at the exact moment she was doing the calculating. At most, she'd probably had four hours, punctuated by moments of waking up and reaching for Evan, then remembering he wasn't there.

Her father turned back to the iPad, though only for a moment. 'Nina brought back some fresh eggs yesterday,' he said.

It was fairly clear where things were heading.

'Did she?' Melody replied.

'I thought we could maybe have poached eggs for breakfast. There's some nice-looking bread in there too.'

Perhaps Melody was too cynical, or maybe she was too used to getting up and making sure Sam was ready for school. She expected her dad to ask if she'd cook but, instead, he pushed himself up.

'I was waiting for you to get up,' he said. 'Do you want anything else with it? We've got some spinach and tomatoes. There's a bit of salmon left as well.' He didn't give her a chance to answer, instead standing and squeezing her shoulder gently. 'He'll come back. You'll get through this, love.'

Melody found herself shrinking into the chair. She wasn't sure she would get through it. She felt as if she was holding on and couldn't face another day of chasing false leads into literal dark alleys.

'Thanks,' she managed.

Her father picked up his iPad and headed for the house, Melody a couple of steps behind. After he'd volunteered to cook, she suddenly had the urge to do it herself. It was some degree of control in a situation where she was increasingly worrying she had none.

Melody started taking pans from the cupboard, placing them on the counter when she stopped. Her father was slicing the bread when he realised she was watching him.

'Was anyone up before you?' Melody asked, knowing the answer.

'No.'

'Was there a watch on the island when you got up?' she asked. She suddenly remembered picking up the phones the night before but forgetting Evan's watch. She'd been so tired.

Melody's dad was slicing the bread on the exact spot she thought she'd left the watch. He looked up at her.

'What sort of watch?'

'I thought I'd left Evan's watch there last night?'

'I didn't see anything...' A pause. 'Why have you got Evan's watch?'

'I don't know. I must've picked it up while we were packing. I was looking at it last night and thought it was on the counter.'

Her dad moved the chopping board, as if it could somehow be underneath. 'I didn't see it.'

Melody said she'd be back and hurried upstairs to check the dresser and the table at the side of the bed. Evan's phone was there – but not the watch. The more she thought about it, the more she knew she'd left it out the night before.

Her first thought was that he'd be so upset that it was lost – but the immediate one beyond that was that this was another day he was missing. She would look for it properly later on.

Back downstairs, Melody did somehow end up making breakfast for everyone. Sam was soon up, telling everyone about what he was doing that day. He couldn't pronounce the name but he was going on a minibus trip to the Malahat Skywalk that offered a view over the ocean and surrounding islands.

It was another place on Melody and Evan's list of spots to go as a couple. She'd seen the incredible photos of the speckled mountains dotted across the endless ocean. It was one of the things she had most been looking forward to.

Sam also had more lake swimming, plus games in the water, which had Melody remembering she'd have to do a clothes wash that night.

As Lori said, life went on. Breakfasts still needed making. Clothes still needed washing. It was hard for Melody to get her head around being in the middle of the biggest thing that had happened in her life – and yet still having to put on a wash.

After he'd eaten, Melody sent Sam upstairs to brush his teeth. Nina and Thomas were still eating their eggs as Melody asked if they'd seen a watch. They both said they hadn't.

Nina helped clean up, though their father silently re-stacked the dishwasher after she'd had a go. The two sisters exchanged a silent smile at that. He'd been reordering crockery since the day they'd got a dishwasher and he'd read the entire manual, before laminating it with Sellotape.

'Is there anything we can do for you today?' Nina asked, talking to Melody.

A part of Melody desperately wanted to ask her sister to stay with her. They'd drop off Sam at camp and then sit on the water's edge, hoping for news. Or maybe they'd go on a two-woman mission to walk through the woods and look for clues of who knew what?

Except Melody was conscious this wasn't only her holiday. Thomas and Nina had taken their time off and spent their money. Why would they want to sit around all day, waiting for a call from the police that might never come?

Melody felt Thomas tense on the other side of the island, likely fearing that a polite question was about to be taken literally.

'I don't think so,' Melody replied, not reacting as Thomas let out a barely perceptible sigh of relief. 'What are your plans?' she added.

There was a short glance between Nina and Thomas as Melody realised they'd figured out their day while upstairs.

'We were going to drive down to Victoria,' Nina said. 'There's a big park down there I wanted to see, plus you can walk along the bay. We'll probably have a coffee somewhere, maybe check out the shops...' Nina tailed off as she realised Thomas was giving her a 'stop talking' stare.

Melody recognised the look, having received it from Evan on more than one occasion when she started oversharing. It was a bad habit that reared its head when she'd had a couple of drinks at a wedding, or party. She would tell people about everything from the struggles they'd had conceiving, to the acne on Evan's back. The backne, as she called it.

So she knew the look.

'It's OK,' she said, even though nobody had indicated it wasn't. It was hard not to think it was the holiday she should be having, with Sam enjoying camp while she and Evan had coffees after walking along the bay.

'What about you, Dad?' Nina asked, switching the attention from her.

'I'm happy here,' he replied. 'Got my crosswords. Will probably go for a walk but I can help if you need something?'

Melody wondered for a moment, except there really wasn't anything to actually do. What were the options, other than wait for someone from the police to get in touch?

She shook her head, leaving him to it. The sisters had wanted to take him away to get him out of the rut they believed him to be in. It perhaps said more about them than him that he'd simply developed a brand-new routine remarkably similar to his old one.

As soon as Melody started driving Sam to camp, he asked if she'd spoken to his dad the night before. Melody didn't like lying to her son, not explicitly anyway, so repeated that the time zones were creating problems and that he was still hoping to join them. Sam seemed contented by that, immediately returning to telling her what he was looking forward to that day.

Melody queued along the forest road to drop off Sam near the picnic tables, then looped back out of the park and returned to the house. She didn't know what to do with the day. Perhaps she could offer to take her dad somewhere – but what if the police needed her? A big part of Melody wanted to be by herself, while another considered messaging Lori to ask if she wanted to do something. There was a degree of comfort in being with someone who knew what it was like.

As Melody reached the house, the beaten-up white car was at the front once more, parked next to the silver vehicle. Melody drove along the gravel, heading towards the lake house, but stopped when she realised an RCMP car was parked outside the workshop, near the lake house.

Melody wondered if anyone had noticed that she'd made food for everyone else, while barely eating a slice of toast herself. She knew she should have more but couldn't force anything down. It was probably a good thing as she felt her stomach lurch. It was early and an in-person visit from the police surely wasn't good news.

While telling herself to keep cool, that it was procedural, Melody parked in the usual spot and checked the empty deck. Her father was nowhere to be seen, while the other vehicle was gone, meaning Nina and Thomas had left for the day.

It was going to be bad news and Melody was alone.

She took a breath and headed up the slope to where Constable Burgess was now standing outside of the car. The driver's door was open and a laptop was on a stand where the handbrake would usually be.

'Has something happened?' Melody asked. The forced cheeriness in her voice felt fake, even to her.

'It's about the blood on the car,' Burgess replied.

SIXTEEN

Melody waited. It was Evan's blood and they'd found more somewhere else. Maybe they'd found his body? He'd been hit and killed, just like Grace Dewar had been.

Except it wasn't that.

'The blood's from an animal,' Burgess said. 'That's why we've got the results so quickly. It would usually take days – but it's not human.'

Melody stared at him, waiting for a devastating follow-up that didn't come.

The officer seemed entirely unsurprised. 'Did you hit something while driving?'

'I don't think so,' Melody replied, before adding a quick: 'No.'

'What about your husband?'

Melody was getting tired of correcting people to fiancé. 'Maybe,' she replied. 'Not that he said. When we were talking, he said there was a girl on the side of the road. Nothing about an animal.'

'Hmmm...'

The officer crouched to look at something on the laptop, before closing the lid. Melody was finding it hard to read him.

'Do you know what kind of animal?' Melody asked.

'Once it was clear it wasn't your husband's blood, we decided not to bother with the further tests.'

'*Fiancé*,' Melody replied.

'Fiancé,' Burgess said. 'Anyway, I'm here to ask what you want us to do with the car. It's on a trailer at the moment. We can bring it back, or return it to the rental place, if you prefer.'

Melody took a second. She'd gone from thinking she was about to be told Evan was dead to being asked logistics questions about a car she hadn't even hired. Lori's 'life carries on' had been so prophetic.

'What happens now?' Melody asked, failing to hide the irritation.

If he noticed, Burgess didn't react. 'With the car? We—'

'Not the car! My fiancé's been missing for a day and a half – and you don't seem to have any updates.'

Melody only realised she was shouting when her voice echoed back at her. She half wondered if it was illegal to scream at a police officer, though Burgess still didn't react.

'A lot's going on behind the scenes,' he said calmly. 'We've spoken to property owners in the immediate area, asking if anyone saw anything, or if they have security cameras. Your fiancé's picture is on our website and Facebook, plus we've sent a release to the local media. We've been screening calls from people who think they might know something but, if I'm honest, not a lot has come from that.'

He paused for breath, as Melody recognised the loaded way he'd said it. Collette was likely not the only time-waster.

'As soon as it was light, a search was done of the immediate area in which the car was left, plus we checked with the airline to confirm he was on the flight, as well as the car rental company. There's footage of him leaving the airport and hiring the car, so we know the precise time he left. We found him on a couple of the highway cameras, so the times you gave us match. We've been checking reports of missing girls to try to corroborate what you said he told you on the phone. We've also checked in with the local homeowners for that, seeing if any of them had children who might've been out at that time. You saw me at camp, asking the same things.'

He paused for breath again, as Melody started to feel a little silly. It was suddenly clear that the police had done an awful lot in the previous twenty-four hours. The fact she hadn't witnessed it didn't mean it wasn't happening. She could hardly expect them to call and update her on every small detail. If anything, that would take them away from the actual work of finding him.

'Did you find anything?' Melody asked, quieter now.

That got a shake of the head. 'It would be an odd place for a child to be out by themselves. There aren't many properties right there – and of the ones we made contact with, none had young daughters. It is a popular place with tourists, as I'm sure you'll understand, so there are still a few more places we can try.'

He gave nothing away, speaking with the same tone as when he'd mentioned the animal blood.

'There is a fire hall a little up the road,' Burgess added. 'They were doing drills earlier in the evening, so I've spoken to most of those who were on duty, wondering if they saw anything. I've got a couple more to check in with – but nothing yet.'

Melody really wished she hadn't shouted. It was as pointless as the times Sam got irrationally angry about things like not having fish fingers for tea. When he calmed, Melody would explain that shouting didn't get people what they wanted – although it was becoming apparent where her son got it from.

'Sorry,' she said quietly.

'There's no problem. I thought someone was going to call you last night but I'd clocked off and I know there was a bit of confusion with the handover. We've got a couple of people on vacation at the moment. That's why I'm here now – partly to apologise, partly to update.'

Melody thanked him, then said she would appreciate it if they returned the other car to the rental place. It was back towards the airport, a good forty-five minutes away, and would save her a job.

'How much longer are you here?' he asked.

'A week Sunday.'

Burgess reached into a pocket and removed a pad, on which he scribbled a note. He had opened his mouth to say something when the back door of the main house banged open. It clattered off the frame and sprang into place, as Rick stormed through, whacking it to the side a second time.

He moved so quickly down the steps that he almost tripped – not that his stare ever left Constable Burgess. By the time he got to them, he was out of breath, pointing and raging.

'I hope you've got a warrant for being here,' he shouted.

Burgess remained unflappable. 'I'm not here for you,' he replied.

'I thought I told you never to come 'round my property again.'

'It's not your property, is it, Rick?'

It felt as if Burgess knew the effect that would have, because Rick pushed himself up onto his tiptoes. His cheeks were puffed, eyes bulging.

'Besides,' Burgess added, 'you can't tell the police where they can and can't go.'

Melody didn't know the two men, nor any history between them, though it was clear Burgess was deliberately riling the man who'd charged towards him. She took a small step back, half expecting a fight. She eyed the pistol on Burgess's belt, fearing the worst. That was the thing with police in the UK – at least they didn't have guns.

Just as it felt as if Rick was about to launch himself at the officer, he lowered himself and turned between Burgess and Melody. He was so angry he could barely get the words out.

'If you're not gone in ten seconds...'

'Do you want me to count you in?'

Melody took another step back. She knew enough about parenting that you didn't start counting to ten unless you had a plan of what to do when you got there. She'd thrown in a few 'nine and half's in her time, but doubted Burgess would do the same.

The two men stood staring to one another, until Burgess broke the impasse. He moved backwards, putting the car between himself and Rick, then turned to Melody.

'Is there anything else I can do at the moment?' he asked.

'I don't think so.'

Burgess was nodding. 'I'll call if something comes up.'

He started to get into the car, though with the haste of Sam at bedtime. The officer moved something from the passenger seat to the back seat, then checked his laptop, before taking an item out of the glovebox.

All the while, Rick glared at him. The count of ten would have been long gone. Nine and fifteen sixteenths and all that.

As soon as the door slammed shut, Rick moved towards the driver's side. 'Don't come back without a warrant,' he said, with no response.

A moment later and the police car sent a series of stones chittering as Burgess pulled around the main house, then onto the road. Melody was left, standing a few paces away from Rick. She couldn't look at him without picturing him in the video, when he punched his wife. If he'd done that in public, while being filmed, how many times would it have happened when doors were closed? She doubted it was a one-off.

Rick's eyes narrowed as he looked across at her and Melody took another step away from him. Just as things were feeling awkward, the back door of the main house sounded again. This time, Harrison emerged, limping down the steps until he was at his son's side. Rick didn't turn to acknowledge him, as his gaze had barely left Melody.

'Everything OK?' Harrison asked, talking to Melody.

'It's fine,' Rick replied.

'I wasn't asking you.'

The silence bordered between uncomfortable and dangerous, punctured only by the humming of a boat somewhere behind.

'It's fine,' Melody repeated, even though she wasn't sure it was.

Harrison nodded. 'Any sign of your fiancé?'

'No – but the police said they've been checking with neighbours and looking for camera footage. There was blood on the car but it belonged to an animal.'

Harrison was still nodding, Rick staring.

'I'm sure they're doing their best,' Harrison said, which got a snort from Rick. 'I thought you were going home,' the older man added.

'I am,' Rick replied, although he didn't move. It took a second or two and then he appeared to realise what going home actually meant. He reached into a pocket and tossed a set of keys from one hand to the other. After muttering something that might've been 'bye', he hurried up the drive, towards the road.

Harrison watched him go, then turned back to Melody. 'He's got a lot on his mind at the moment,' he said. 'He's always a bit, um... *off* when Cody's at his mum's.'

Melody could only picture that little boy on the ground as his mum dripped blood over him.

Harrison had a few choice turns of phrase when it came to

his son. 'Run-ins with the police' after he was filmed punching his wife. Being 'off' when he threatened a police officer. She understood being defensive when it came to a son – especially one who'd been through what Rick had – but Melody wasn't sure she liked being on the property when Rick was.

'Everything else OK with the house?' Harrison asked.

'All fine,' Melody replied.

He nodded slowly, looking past her towards the water, then back towards his own house. 'He's harmless really.'

Melody was about to ask 'Who?', except he could have only been talking about one person.

The older man turned and started to shuffle back towards his house, as Melody wondered if he'd seen the video of the punch. Because, if he had, there was no way Harrison would say his son was harmless.

SEVENTEEN

Melody found her dad sitting on the other side of the lake house, earphones in as he poked at his iPad screen. He jumped for the second time that morning as Melody appeared in front of him, pulling one of the buds out as he rubbed his eyes.

'Everything all right?' he asked, innocently enough. He'd apparently missed the police visit and Rick nearly causing a fight. It didn't feel worth telling him about it.

'I dropped Sam off,' Melody said. 'What are you listening to?'

'Cricket commentary. I didn't realise you could get it out here but it's on the internet. Everything's on there these days.'

Melody smiled at that. Her dad finding out things were on the internet never ceased to be amusing. He had discovered everything from recipes to liner notes for his favourite albums over the years. Each time, he would enthusiastically let her know that he was amazed by how much ended up on the internet. The 'these days' at the end always made her grin.

She asked about the score, though Melody didn't listen for the reply. Sports stuff was always background noise.

'There's about another hour of play,' her dad said. 'I was going to listen to the rest, then head out for a walk. You're welcome to come...?'

'You've got to be careful walking on the verges around here,' Melody said, which got a roll of the eyes. Her father wasn't the sort to listen to practical advice about such things as being careful not to get hit by cars. It was the same when they were younger. He'd say he was going to try something like waterskiing, then roll his eyes when their mum told him to be careful.

'What are you going to do?' he asked. 'You shouldn't wait around here all day by yourself.'

Melody didn't want to do that, yet she struggled to know what else to do with herself. She still wanted to talk to Lori, to ask what it was like on day two. Day three. Would the other woman remember? She was counting in years now, not days.

'I was going to go for a drive,' Melody replied – even though she'd made it up in the moment.

It was probably inadvertent, but Melody's dad touched his ear and let out a delighted 'ooh', which probably meant a wicket had fallen, something like that. She said she'd leave him to it and then, instead of returning to the house, got into the car instead. She really was going to go for a drive. At least she would feel like she was doing something.

Melody drove back around the lake towards the camp, keeping the water on her left. She passed the fire hall Constable Burgess had told her about, then, not long after, it was Sam's camp. A few more minutes along the road and the driveway entrances gave way to a long bank of hedges on one side, and rock on the other.

She'd not been planning on visiting the place from where Evan disappeared but, from nowhere, Melody felt the pull. She parked up in a gravelly spot, a little past the place where Evan's car had been left.

Melody got out and rested on the side of the car, looking up and down the empty road.

It looked so different in daylight.

Two nights before, as the trees swayed and the dark closed in, it had felt so menacing. Now, it was simply a row of trees, a bit of gravel, some dry dirt along the side of the road. There were country lanes not too far from Melody's house that were similar, though, if anything, they were narrower.

Melody walked in the direction of the camp, sticking close to the verge as a truck zipped past, sending a cloud of dust behind. There were no tyre marks on the road. No blood. No ragged clothes, torn and discarded in the bushes.

It was a normal stretch of road.

Melody headed back the way she'd come on foot, continuing away from where Evan's car had been left. The trees were too dense to see the water, though the lake felt near. On the other side, the bushes had been interrupted by a small cliff face, perhaps ten or twelve feet high. Yellowy-brown moss clung to the sides as Melody crossed the road to peer up in an attempt to see if there was anything on top.

There wasn't.

Past that, there was a small gap before the next row of trees. Melody walked around the rock, following the route into an overgrown field. The grass was yellow, probably closer to hay, and stretched into the distance until it was engulfed by more trees.

There were no tyre marks, though parts of the grass had been flattened by something that seemed fairly heavy. There was room for a vehicle to squeeze between the rock and the trees, which meant somebody could have been waiting out of sight as Evan passed.

Melody had been pushing away the thought and nobody had brought it up, not even the police.

Not yet.

They were the darkest thoughts that drifted into Melody's mind as she woke in the early hours. The ones she'd not dared to bring up with Constable Burgess.

Could it have been some sort of trap?

Perhaps the girl had been on the side of the road, waiting for an unsuspecting driver to stop? People could have been hiding and jumped out to... what?

If it was a robbery, they'd forgotten Evan's phone and left the car with the keys in it. His luggage was missing but it would be an odd thing to steal – especially given the set-up.

But if it wasn't a robbery, then what was it? When Melody had been young, there were stories on the news of hostages in Libya, places like that. She didn't know if kidnapping was still a thing. Surely, even if it was, it wouldn't happen in a cosy place like this? But, even if it was, where was the ransom? Where was any demand? She and Evan didn't have lots of money but there was a bit in their savings.

It would also be a massive gamble for any potential kidnappers to take someone based on a guess of how much money they had. This felt like an area in which locals mingled with tourists who *could* be rich... or not.

The police wouldn't be stupid and Melody assumed they'd noticed the same gap as her. The flattened grass might even be because they'd driven on it. Perhaps they'd done the sort of search she'd assumed they hadn't? The truth was, the trees were dense on one side, the bank was steep on the other, and the only gap had tall grass.

Melody also knew the police would have considered a robbery, or a kidnapping, even if they hadn't specifically spoken to her about it. Except, if that was the case, what sort of thief left the expensive things? What sort of kidnapper didn't want a ransom?

It had been a few minutes since the last vehicle had passed and Melody trailed the road back to her car. She wasn't sure she'd got anything from the visit, even though it looked a lot less imposing during the day. They were minutes from the camp in a car – and yet also in the middle of nowhere.

Melody considered driving back to the house and offering her dad a lift to the village. They could maybe have a coffee, or a walk, something like that. Except she didn't quite feel ready to leave. Instead, she continued walking. If Evan had done the same on the night he'd called her, perhaps there was an obvious spot he could've gone? Perhaps another bank that he had slipped off? Maybe he'd got spooked by a wild animal and ran into the trees, only to get lost?

It took Melody five minutes' on foot until she reached an opening for a driveway on the opposite side to the lake. A mailbox sat at the end of the drive, just off the road, with the word 'newspaper' written along the side. Having a paper delivered felt like quite the throwback considering even Melody's father knew all that was on the internet these days.

She turned towards the house, which was easily three times the size of Melody's back in England. A veranda stretched much of the width, with an old sofa sitting under one of the windows.

Constable Burgess said they'd already visited the nearest houses, which meant they'd have almost certainly been here to ask if the owner had seen anything. Melody considered knocking on the door anyway and perhaps leaving a phone number. It couldn't do any harm.

She stood at the end of the drive, wondering whether she should, when she noticed that the mailbox didn't only say 'newspaper'. There were smaller letters above and, as Melody approached, she realised she'd seen them before.

'BOYD'.

It took her a few seconds to remember from where she recognised it. It had been the night before, when she'd been struggling to stay awake that she'd first read the name 'Joel Boyd'.

He was the man who'd struck and killed Rick Dewar's sister in a hit-and-run. The man who'd been turned in to the police by his own daughter.

EIGHTEEN

The urge to see who was in the house was too much for Melody. It had been many years since the incident and, assuming the Canadian justice system was similar to the British, Joel would have been released from prison a while back. Nobody ever got a serious sentence for killing someone with a vehicle.

The wooden steps creaked ominously as Melody headed to the front door. The house and everything around it was seemingly made of wood. Paint was peeling from the window ledges and Melody shivered as a wind chime clanked from the other end of the deck. There was a sense of being watched, perhaps even by the house itself. The stairs buckled a fraction from her weight, each step sending a low warning *creaaaaak* across the yellow lawn of the front.

There was no bell and no letterbox, so Melody knocked on the panel of the door. She waited, trying not to move as every shift of weight sent more squeaks shuddering around the front of the house.

After a minute or so, Melody knocked again, harder second time around. There was a dimpled window to the side of the door and she pressed her face to it, using a hand to block the glare. The ripples in the glass made it impossible to see anything and it certainly didn't seem as if anyone was inside – except, when Melody pulled back, there was a figure standing just off the deck, behind a railing.

Melody jumped, letting out a small yelp of surprise, as a woman in dungarees and gardening gloves looked across to her.

'Can I help you?' she asked, looking on curiously.

She was a few years older than Melody, with curly gingery hair poking out from under a wide-brim hat.

Melody stumbled over her words, explaining that her husband had gone missing a couple of nights before and that his car was found abandoned just along the road. The woman nodded along as Melody spoke.

'The police have been around,' she said, somewhat curiously, probably wondering why a stranger was on her doorstep.

'Right...' Melody replied, unsure what to add. 'I suppose I just... don't know what to do.'

It sounded pathetic and defeated. Though Melody hadn't meant it to come out in such a way, there was an instant reaction. The woman took off her gloves and walked around the deck until she was at Melody's side.

'Of course,' she said sympathetically. 'I don't blame you for coming. Poor you.'

Melody hadn't been feeling particularly emotional until the empathy came.

The other woman gently touched a hand to Melody's shoulder. 'Why don't you come to the back of the house,' she added.

They'd come from nowhere but Melody was blinking away tears. Her throat was dry and it felt as if she was trying to swallow a whole apple. The woman must have noticed, though she said nothing, instead leading the way around the side of the house into what turned out to be a giant field. Greeny-yellow grass stretched towards a small orchard, where rows of tidy trees brimmed with apples and pears.

The woman walked to a table on the lawn that had a garden chair on either side and put down her gloves. She told Melody she'd be right back, before disappearing into the house.

Melody sat and rubbed her eyes, trying to get her breath.

She was calmed by the glorious simplicity of the garden. The grass must have been half the size of a football field, with the edges ringed by small berry bushes and vegetable boxes. The orchard was at the end, though it was hard to tell how far back the trees went. There was so much land and Melody found herself drifting, wondering how many houses would be crammed on such a patch back home. They'd probably build an entire estate.

Melody was brought back to the present as the woman reappeared, jug of water in one hand, pair of glasses in the other. She placed everything on the table and then wrestled with a parasol until they were in the shade. It was only then that Melody realised she had sweated through her top. She swished it in and out, suddenly desperate for the water that the woman was pouring.

'I'm Starla,' the woman said, offering Melody the glass, as ice cubes jangled.

Melody took the glass but almost immediately dropped it. Starla Boyd was the woman who'd turned in her father for the hit-and-run. Melody used her other hand to steady herself, then sipped the water. That became a full mouthful, before she ran the glass along the length of her arms.

It was hard for Melody not to let on that she knew who the woman was. She didn't think she was a great actor, nor liar. Her 'That's a nice name' sounded disingenuous, even if she hadn't meant it that way. She couldn't stop thinking of her own dad, wondering what it would take for her to turn him in. If Melody knew for an absolute fact that her father had killed someone, would she have it in her to call the police? She hoped so but it was hard to know for sure. Starla had lived that dilemma – and here she was, years after the event.

Not that Starla knew any of what was going on in Melody's thoughts. She took the 'nice name' as a compliment, replying with a 'thank you', before drinking from her own glass.

'The police were around yesterday morning,' Starla said, picking up the conversation as if the past couple of minutes hadn't happened. 'They asked if I'd seen anything the night before – which I hadn't – or if I had a camera at the front – which I do. I did check, just in case, but there was nothing weird on it.' She waited a moment, then added: 'Sorry, I know that's not what you want to hear.'

Melody nodded along, trying not to seem so disappointed. It was essentially what Constable Burgess had told her earlier.

'We also don't have children,' Starla added. 'They asked whether we had a daughter who might've been on the road.'

'My fiancé said he saw a girl in the road,' Melody replied. 'I was on the phone with him and that's why he stopped. The line went dead after that.'

Starla frowned a little, biting her bottom lip. 'Huh. I suppose that explains why they asked. How strange.'

Melody finished the glass of water, then asked if it was OK to pour another.

Starla laughed at that. 'Of course it's fine,' she replied.

Melody wasn't quite sure why she'd knocked on the door, other than curiosity over the name 'Boyd'. A part of her wanted to ask if Joel was still around, more out of nosiness than anything else. She knew she couldn't bring it up.

'Your garden's lovely,' she said instead.

'Thank you,' Starla replied. 'It's a lot of work.'

'Is it just you?' Melody asked, before realising it was a bit of an invasive question. They were strangers, after all. 'I didn't mean it like that,' she added. 'I meant that it's a lot of work for one person.'

Starla batted away the offence she hadn't taken. 'It's fine. My husband works in Victoria and his company made everyone go back to the office at the end of last year. He's down there five days a week, and it's about an hour each way on a good day. I'm supposed to be working from home but that means I end up doing a lot of cleaning or gardening instead.' She laughed at herself, then added: 'Procrastination, hey?'

'What do you do?' Melody asked.

'I'm a sculptor.'

Melody wasn't sure how to reply to that. A part of her had never escaped the way her parents wanted her to study 'real' subjects at school. The idea of having a career as a sculptor would have baffled her dad in the past, and possibly still in the present.

The yawn came from nowhere and, as Melody tried to apologise, another one ripped through her. She turned her head, wiping away the tears as a third forced its way upon her.

'Jet lag,' she said as an explanation when she finally had control of herself once more. 'I've only been here since Saturday.'

Starla had an amused look on her face. 'Would you like a coffee?'

'I don't want to—'

The other woman was already on her feet. 'It's no trouble. Do you want to come inside?'

It felt rude to say no, so Melody found herself following Starla onto another deck at the back of the house, and then into a kitchen.

From the scuffed wood of the outside, Melody had expected something rickety inside – but the opposite was true. The kitchen looked as if it had come directly from an advert. It was almost surgically white, with pans and utensils hanging from hooks above the spotlessly solid black countertops. There were no dishes in the sink and nothing on the draining board. Everything was so clean, it was as if it had all been put in the day before.

Starla crossed to a sparkling coffee machine that was so big it could have come from a shop. After asking what Melody wanted, she pressed a series of buttons and then leant on the counter.

'Where are you from?' she asked.

'England.'

That got a nod. 'I always mix up English accents with Australian.'

Melody explained how they were there on holiday and that Evan had been due a day later. It felt unbelievable, even as she said it.

Starla listened, nodding and frowning in equal measure. 'That's awful,' she said, arms crossed. 'I'm sure the police are doing their best.'

Melody couldn't quite work out if the final sentence was sarcastic. The 'awful' part sounded genuine but there was a bit of a kick to the sign-off.

A few minutes later and they were sitting back outside. The first few sips of coffee had an almost instant effect on Melody. The sun was brighter and warmer, the chirping of birds louder.

'It's so peaceful here,' Melody said. 'It's such a lovely house.'

'It was my dad's,' Starla replied – and there was something in the way she said it that made it sound as if she didn't mind the inevitable follow-up. She probably expected it from locals, though perhaps not from Melody.

But it was too late. 'I'm staying in a lake house at the back of Harrison Dewar's property,' Melody said, studiously avoiding eye contact. 'I kinda looked him up...' She took a breath, half wishing she'd shut up. The oversharing thing was true – but, this time, it had taken caffeine, not alcohol. 'I didn't know that when I knocked on your door,' Melody added, wanting to explain. 'I should've said something when you told me your name.'

Starla had been lifting her coffee cup but paused midway to her mouth. She was staring towards the orchard but then took a sip of the coffee, before returning the cup to the table. It felt as if she was about to tell Melody to leave.

'It's OK,' she said, a little more quietly than before. 'Everyone around here knows what happened. That's the thing with living on a lake. It's a small community and nobody really moves. Everyone you grow up with ends up living down the road and having their own kids. Nothing is ever forgotten.'

Melody could feel an invisible Evan giving her that *stop talking* stare but she was too far invested now. She thought of Rick's anger at the police not long before. It felt unlikely he'd left the Boyds alone, given they lived so close to one another.

'Do you have any problems with Harrison, or, um... Rick?'

Starla didn't move for a moment. She was pouting her lips, gazing into the distance. 'Sounds like you looked up Rick as well,' she said, not waiting for an answer. 'Rick used to come by sometimes and harass Dad after he got out of prison. He brought a truck around one time and did doughnuts on the front yard. We had a couple of windows bricked but I suppose we don't know for sure that was Rick. We didn't have cameras then.' She took a breath, then added a resigned: 'It was him, though.'

'How long ago was that?' Melody asked.

'It went on for years. When Dad was in prison, I lived here largely by myself. Then I met my husband and, when Dad was let out, he lived here on his own.'

She was still eyeing the trees at the end of the garden and it felt like a memory that had imprinted itself.

'I'd come over once or twice a week and there were those broken windows, or the tyre prints on the garden. It got to the point I was worried what might happen with him by himself.

Me and my husband moved back about eight or nine years ago – and the trouble stopped after that. It was a big enough house for all of us.'

Melody glanced to the house: 'Is your dad...?'

'He died five years ago.'

It *was* a big house but Melody wondered how a relationship could survive a daughter effectively putting her father in prison – regardless of what he'd done to warrant it.

When Melody turned back, she realised Starla was eyeing her curiously. Weighing her up.

Melody could almost hear the other woman's thoughts. They were strangers who lived a long way apart and were unlikely to stumble across one another again. There must be a lot Starla struggled to say over the years because the community was so entwined.

'Do you know it was me who turned him in?' Starla asked.

Melody nodded. 'It said that in the article I read.'

That got the resigned sigh of a person whose single decision had followed them for a lifetime.

They sat listening to the birds for a minute, maybe more, until Starla downed the rest of her coffee.

'Dad would go out pretty much every night,' she said. 'He'd be at one of his buddies' houses and they'd have a few drinks, then drive home. He did that when Mum was alive – and he definitely did it after she died. I didn't even realise you shouldn't drink-drive until I was thirteen or fourteen.'

She poured herself a glass of water and held the glass to her forehead. The ice from the jug had long since melted.

'He was out the night Grace was hit,' Starla continued – and Melody felt herself tense at the mention of the young girl's name. 'The poor girl was only nine or ten. This was back when they delivered papers every week and I still remember the photo of her mangled bike on the front.'

Starla stopped again and bit her lip. Her stare had barely left the orchard but Melody's was fixed on the other woman.

'I just knew,' she added. 'I knew it was him. It happened down the road, on the route he took back from his buddy's. It happened at the time I knew he was on his way back – and then there was a dent in the front bumper.' She took another breath and repeated: 'I just knew.'

Melody wanted to say something encouraging but the words wouldn't come. She was transfixed.

'I couldn't leave it and say nothing,' Starla added and then a thoughtful-sounding: 'I suppose I *did* say nothing for a few days. But then the paper arrived with her bike on the front.' She turned to look directly at Melody, staring into her, wanting her to understand. 'I think I was hoping he'd go to the police himself.'

'But he didn't?'

A shake of the head as Starla returned her attention to the trees.

'How old were you?' Melody asked.

'Twenty. Twenty-one. Something like that. A few nights passed and then he went out to one of his friends' houses as if nothing had happened. He always had the same routine – but it wasn't only him. There were six or seven of them. I called the police while he was out and they picked him up driving back while he was drunk. They impounded his car and I'd already told them about the dent in the bumper, plus that he was out the night Grace was hit. Everything spiralled from there. Next time I saw him was in the jail.'

She sighed and Melody didn't blame her. It was a lot for anyone, let alone a person barely out of their teenage years.

'Did he know it was you?' Melody asked.

'If he didn't, then I told him when I saw him. I think he knew anyway. It had already gone around because someone at the police had told a friend, something like that. They'd told someone else and then everyone knew. There are no secrets around here.'

Melody thought on that because, though it might feel true, whatever had happened to Evan felt as if it was being kept secret by at least one person. It also made Melody think the previous remark about the police 'doing their best' might have been sarcastic. Starla reporting her father must have been hard enough, without someone there telling the community it was her.

'Did your dad admit it was him?' Melody asked.

'He said he couldn't remember. I suppose I figured that was the best outcome. It would've been worse if he knew he did it and kept quiet.'

Melody could see why Starla would want to convince herself of that – but it felt like a cop-out. The fact they'd picked him up driving while drunk a few days after Grace had been killed was hardly the sign of a person taking responsibility.

'Dad never talked about what happened after he got out,' Starla said. 'Not to me anyway. After I moved back in, we all kind of acted as if there wasn't that big gap from when he was in prison.'

Melody's coffee had gone cold but she finished it anyway. It seemed as if Starla had finished talking, at least for now.

'Someone told me yesterday that native women go missing around here,' Melody said, picturing the red dress she'd seen hanging from the trees. She'd passed it a few times now.

'Sort of,' Starla replied. 'Not necessarily *right* here but there's definitely an issue with indigenous women disappearing. You never really hear about them being found.' She paused and then added: 'Sorry.'

Melody wasn't sure what to say to that. All these missing women wasn't quite the same as what was going on with Evan – but the fact people were disappearing without being found was hardly a positive. There were so many more people out there waiting for news, hoping for something positive. It felt like the sort of thing everyone should know, rather than this small, local, story almost buried away.

Starla was tapping her foot on the grass and then jumped up suddenly. 'There is something,' she said. 'Wait here.'

Melody wasn't sure what was happening, though Starla scooped up both their coffee cups and bounded up to the house. She disappeared inside and returned a few minutes later, laptop under her arm. She placed it on the table and lifted the lid, before adjusting the parasol to make sure it was in the shade.

'There are always reports of thefts around here,' she commented. 'It's usually minor stuff but we got a few cameras put in. There's one in the bushes, facing the road. You wouldn't see it, unless you were actually looking for it. When the police came, they asked if there were any vehicles passing between 8 and 10 p.m. There were, obviously, but nothing weird. I clipped up the video and emailed it to them. The guy said they were most interested in anything at around eight thirty.'

Starla started clicking something on the laptop, before loading a video. As it started to play, she pressed the space bar to stop it.

'I was thinking about it overnight, so had another look this morning. This went past on Saturday.'

Melody didn't think the video had started at first. It was a clear, empty road, with the merest hint of a leaf in the lower corner. In a flash, a yellow truck raced past, appearing in the shot and disappearing in barely a second. Starla started fiddling with the laptop, though Melody wasn't sure what she was supposed to have noticed.

'This was Friday night,' Starla said, before starting another video.

For a moment, Melody thought she was watching the same video. There was an empty road and then a yellow truck zipped past.

'And Thursday,' Starla added, before playing a third clip in which the same thing happened.

When it was finished, she clicked around the screen, before loading three screenshots that looked remarkably similar to each other. From the video, Melody thought the truck was yellow – but the grab made it appear more of a gold. The vehicle itself was boxy, although the number plate was a blur.

'Do you know much about trucks?' Starla asked.

'We don't really have them in England,' Melody replied.

'It's an eighth- or ninth-generation Ford F-series,' Starla said, pointing at the screen. 'You can tell because of the square edges. They were only made up 'til 96, so there's not loads of them about. The gold is a rare colour, too.'

Melody looked to the screen again. Starla must know a fair bit about trucks to have figured that out from a slightly out-of-focus screengrab.

'It went past the same time, three days in a row?' Melody asked.

'Exactly, always at eight-fifteen, give or take a minute. I looked through the other videos and it never went back the other way.' A shrug. 'Obviously, you can just loop around the lake but it's still odd.'

'Could it be someone going home from work?' Melody asked, not quite sure what she was being shown, or why. 'Or going *to* work?'

'I thought the same – but it's only those three nights. I looked the nights before, plus last night. I was thinking of sending it on to the police but the truck didn't go past on the night your fiancé disappeared. I know it's probably nothing, I just thought it was weird.'

It was a good choice of words and hard to rationalise. Something that looked normal but was also slightly off.

Melody asked if Starla could send her the screengrabs and, moments later, her phone pinged. If it had been a similar vehicle in the UK, it would have been so easy to find. Here, it seemed as if eighty per cent of the vehicles being driven were pickup trucks. She'd have to take Starla's word for it that the gold Ford was a rarity.

Starla finished off the water and closed the laptop lid. She picked up her gardening gloves for the first time since putting them down – and it felt as if the conversation had reached its end.

'It's been good meeting you,' Starla said, as she stood. 'I hope they find your fiancé.'

'Thanks for talking to me,' Melody replied, taking the hint and standing herself. The car had been left on the side of the road for too long anyway.

Starla was squeezing her hand into one of the gloves. 'Why did you come to Shawnigan Lake? It's a bit out of the way, isn't it?'

'I was here as a girl. Mum won a competition for a holiday and I ended up coming to the camp. I suppose I never forgot it. My son's at camp now.'

That got something of a blank look – which was understandable in that most locals didn't think of their own town as anything particularly special. Melody had been to Edinburgh and spoken to someone who had lived there for decades but had never visited the castle. People usually travelled to see the exceptional, which was difficult to recognise when it was over the road from where a person grew up.

'Don't you have camps in the UK?' Starla asked.

'I think so – but I suppose it's different when you're young and you have a different accent. I made friends so easily. It was before the internet and phones, all that. I guess now we'd just swap numbers.'

Melody still wasn't sure she knew how to explain the appeal. The reasoning felt so clear in her mind, yet so childish when she tried to tell others.

Not that Starla appeared to judge. She was wearing one of the gloves but making no attempt to put on the other. 'You know some of the friends you made are probably still around? Those camps are usually extensions of the schools. After they break up, parents still need somewhere to look after their kids over the summer. If you met Canadians back then, most of them probably lived around here, which means they *still* live here.'

Back when she'd been booking the trip, Melody had thought about looking up the girls she once knew. The problem was that she couldn't remember any of their last names, if she'd ever known them. There was so little to go on.

'Do you remember anyone's name?' Starla added.

'There was a girl named Heather. I don't know her surname.'

Starla paused for a beat: 'Heather Robinson?'

Suddenly, Melody *did* know the last name. It had been gone from her mind for the best part of thirty years, yet there it was.

'That's it,' Melody replied, barely believing it. 'Do you know her?'

That got a laugh. 'Not only do I know her,' Starla replied, 'I know where she'll be right now. Do you wanna go say hello?'

NINETEEN

Melody followed Starla's car around the lake, passing the camp, fire hall, and Harrison's place, before eventually ending up on the approach to the village in which she'd had coffee with Lori. She was on autopilot, hoping that going with the flow might somehow lead her to Evan. At least she was doing something, which felt better than sitting at the house.

As the crossroads were in sight, Starla indicated right and turned onto the road next to the police station. For a moment, Melody thought they were going *to* the station but, instead, Starla headed past and then parked in front of a wide, low building with a metal roof. It had the vibe of a slightly run-down British sports centre. The sort of place in which pensioners would do pilates classes at one end, while school-children swam in the pool.

The reality wasn't far off. 'This is the community centre,' Starla said, as they met at the back of Melody's car. She added a 'this way' – and then led Melody around the side and towards the back, where they ended up in a park that backed onto the lake. A series of tree-stump stools were arranged in front of a line of easels. The only person there was a woman standing with her back to them, painting on a canvas.

As Starla and Melody neared, the woman turned and blinked around to them. Her painting was of the corner of the lake, with a boat moored off to the side, dark trees in the distance, the mountain beyond.

She grinned across to Starla. 'I thought your sculpt class was tomorrow?' she said.

'It is,' Starla replied. 'I brought along someone who says they remember you...'

Heather was very different to the girl Melody remembered. It was little surprise considering thirty years had passed, but Heather had sleeves of tattoos on both arms, a nose ring, and lip ring. She was wearing a baseball cap, though her blonde hair had been replaced by something dyed a purply-red. It could be another person, except the birthmark still crested around the curve of her neck. She had the same eyes, too: a piercing, decisive blue.

Those blue eyes narrowed as Heather took in Melody carefully. Seconds passed until it became uncomfortable and Melody felt as if she'd been forgotten.

And then the slow, confused 'Mel...?' came.

'Hi,' Melody said, suddenly feeling it might have been a mistake to follow Starla. It was one thing to want to return to a place in which she'd been happy, another entirely to find a person she'd not seen in so many years.

'You *do* remember,' Starla replied, delighted. She turned to Melody. 'I've got to get back, so I'll leave you to it.' She took a step towards the car park and then paused. Melody had assumed she'd be staying but seemingly not. 'I hope everything works out. Come by any time you need.' She looked to Heather and said something about catching up the next week – and then she was gone, leaving Heather and Melody alone at the water's edge.

Heather was holding a paintbrush, still squinting as she stared at Melody. 'It's like seeing a ghost,' she said. 'What are you doing here? It's been, like, twenty years.'

'Thirty,' Melody replied, which got a snigger.

'Thirty?! I'm so old.' A pause. '*We're* so old.'

Melody smiled along, then realised she hadn't answered the question. 'I'm over with my family,' she said. 'My son's nine and I brought him over to go to camp. Then me and my fiancé were going to do the touristy things.'

It got something of a bemused look, very similar to the one Starla had given back at her house. 'Don't you have camps in the UK?'

'I guess. But I had such great fun here. I always wanted to come back but Mum and Dad didn't have the money, then I didn't have the money, then it was Covid. It's taken a while.'

'Right...'

Heather seemed more bewildered than excited by Melody's appearance. It had obviously come out of the blue, and had been a long time since they'd been anything close to friends, but Melody had thought she'd get a warmer hello.

'It's a shame we never had phones or the internet back then,' Melody said. 'I think we swapped addresses but I lost my bag on the way home and it was in there.'

Heather nodded along. 'It's probably a good job we never had phones when we were in school,' she replied. 'Everything gets filmed and put online nowadays.'

Melody sometimes thought the same – and she'd already had conversations with Evan about the best time to let Sam have his own phone. She wondered what it would be like for him and his friends to live their lives online in a way she never had.

An awkward few seconds passed until Heather placed her brush in a cup and wiped her hands on her apron. She sat on one of the stumps and Melody followed. 'So... how are you?' Heather asked, which left a lot to sum up.

The two women swapped details of their families. Heather was married with three children of her own. They were sixteen, eighteen and nineteen, which made it feel as if she'd had such a different life to Melody. While Melody was out enjoying her twenties, Heather was married and in the process of having three children.

She told Melody how her oldest was at university in Victoria, while another was considering going to Vancouver on the mainland. It was two hours on the ferry, apparently, or via a seaplane. 'Close but not too close,' she added. The sixteen-year-old was working for the summer as a camp counsellor at a different lake around half an hour away. Her husband worked from home.

Melody didn't feel quite able to explain that her fiancé was missing. Once they went down that wormhole, it would dominate any conversation. Instead, she fudged things, avoiding actual lies, though saying that Evan worked for a bank, while she'd been working in teaching. She didn't say she was currently working in a coffee shop, hoping to find something she preferred. Whereas Heather's life seemed to be stable and together, Melody didn't feel as if she could admit her career wasn't going as she wanted.

Instead, she said that she was staying in an Airbnb around the lake with her sister, brother-in-law, son, and father.

They'd reached the point where it felt as if neither of them had much else to say. It had been an underwhelming fifteen-minute catch-up thirty years in the making. Perhaps this was why Melody hadn't gone too far out of her way to look up anyone else from the camp? She'd been right the first time.

Heather had picked up her brush again and was rubbing the wet bristles against her apron. 'How did you meet Starla?' she asked.

Considering Melody had left out the part about Evan being missing, it would be hard to tell the full truth. 'She lives near Sam's camp,' she said, which was true. 'We got talking and I mentioned a Heather I used to know from camp. Turns out she knew you.'

Heather laughed at that. 'Starla and I are good friends. She's a great sculptor. We end up running a lot of the same events, plus we both host classes here.'

The conversation again felt as if it had run its course, except Heather was too polite to say goodbye.

'What are your plans for while you're here?' she added. 'Have you been to the trestle?'

'Not yet,' Melody replied. 'My sister went and liked it. Sam's going to the Skywalk with camp today.'

Heather nodded along. 'I've never been. I've heard the view's great – but there's also a pull-in off the highway a bit further down that gives a similar view for free.'

She stopped and gave a slim smile. Like a couple on a first date who've run out of things to talk about before the drinks have arrived. They'd been friends for three weeks as nine-year-olds and the idea they had anything still in common was wild.

Heather stood and angled towards her easel, continuing to dab her brush on her apron, before she sighed. When she turned back to Melody, it felt as if she was staring deep into her soul.

'I'm so surprised you came back,' she said.

'What do you mean?'

She chewed the inside of her mouth, weighing up how to phrase things, before coming out with it. 'Do you ever feel guilty about what we did?'

TWENTY

Heather was looking to the ground now, standing over Melody but unable to look at her. Melody couldn't figure out how to reply.

'What do you mean?' Melody managed.

'Don't you remember?'

Melody was standing in the open again, steaming under the sun. Everyone local – men, women, children – seemingly knew to wear hats – but it hadn't occurred to Melody to bring one. She wasn't sure she even owned a cap. She was sweating, fighting against the ever-present sun.

Heather put down her paintbrush and took off her cap. She ran a hand through her hair and retied her ponytail, before returning to sit on the stump.

'You, me, and a couple of the others bullied Shannon relentlessly,' she said, holding up her hands. 'Don't you remember?'

Melody didn't, except...

...She did. It was as it had been at the burned cabin the night before, when seeing a place, hearing a name, brought it all back. It wasn't a simple flash of a face, or a setting. Everything had returned in one go.

Surrounding a girl in the woods, pushing her back and forth between them, throwing a towel in the lake, repeating a name over and over. A frightened girl with freckles and gingery hair.

Shaaaaaaaaaaaaaaa-non.

Shaaaaaaaaaaaaaaa-non.

How could she have forgotten?

Melody looked up to Heather, who was again avoiding her stare – and, from nowhere, Melody knew why the conversation had been so awkward. It wasn't only that they were very different people compared to back then, it was that they had very different memories of that summer.

For Melody it was a few weeks in which she'd been popular and well-liked. Where she'd been the centre of attention, and other children wanted to be her, or be friends with her. But a part of that was because she'd been involved with the group who'd picked on other girls.

How could all that have fallen from her mind?

'Shannon was in the year below me at school,' Heather said. Her tone was quieter and the words came reluctantly. Melody couldn't stop picturing the freckly ginger girl, with the brown eyes. 'I used to see her a lot after that summer,' Heather added. 'She was really into orchestra but stopped playing for a while. Whenever she saw me, she used to hide, or walk the other way. It was like that for years.' Heather waited a moment, then said: 'I don't think I've ever forgotten it. Have you? Is that why you're back? To make up for it, or something?'

Melody wasn't sure how to say that she *had* forgotten it. That she was back because she wanted her son to have a similar experience to her own, plus she'd been looking forward to a relaxing, touristy couple of weeks next to a lake.

'Shannon still lives around here,' Heather continued. 'She has a daughter with Down's – Ella. She's about eleven or twelve and I see her sometimes picking flowers on the side of the road, which she sells in the village. Shannon and Ella are both in the local acting club. I saw the pair of them in a Christmas play last year. She's such a great mum – and her husband is a carpenter. He builds these amazing decks and boat launches for people. Huge projects. I see them around sometimes, this lovely little family, but I always remember the time we hid Shannon's shoes after we'd all been swimming.'

That lump was back in Melody's throat. She couldn't breathe. Five minutes ago, she wouldn't have thought anything of the name Shannon – but the shame now burned. Not only for what they'd done, which was bad enough, but the fact she'd forgotten.

'We threw the shoes in the bin,' Melody managed – and she could picture the can at the edge of the car park. They hadn't simply discarded them, they'd buried them under the rubbish already there, making them harder to find.

Heather wouldn't stop talking. 'Do you remember her walking across the parking lot in her bare feet? She was crying and had to tell her mum she'd lost her shoes? Her mum was really angry. She kept shouting, "How can you lose your shoes?" – and that made Shannon cry harder. But none of us said anything. We just came back the next day, as if nothing had happened.'

Melody wished she didn't remember, but she did. She didn't need to close her eyes to see the tears rolling down the poor girl's face. It felt like an image that might never leave.

Heather had slumped, her elbows on her knees, head dipped. 'Sorry,' she said. 'I just didn't expect to see you. It's that time of year.'

It *was* that time of year – which felt like a weight Heather had been carrying for a long time. She had sunk onto the stump herself, weighed down by regret and embarrassment.

The two women sat together for a few moments, neither able to speak.

'I know we had fun that summer,' Heather said. 'Do you remember the speedboat trip? And the zipline?'

Those were memories that Melody had brought with her. The group of girls from her camp had been split into two, and then taken it in turns to pile onto a speedboat. They'd raced from one end of the lake to the other, before tearing back. It had been thrilling to feel the warm wind in her hair and scream with delight. It had been the same on the ziplines days after. At that point, Melody had never been to a theme park. The closest she had come to a rollercoaster was the roundabout at the local park.

Was it normal for someone to reminisce about that thrill, yet forget the cruelty around it?

'Do you remember the Jeeps?' Heather asked.

'It was the first time I'd been in a car like that,' Melody replied. 'We went up into the back roads and everyone got bumped around.'

'I don't think they're allowed to do that trip any more. Someone dislocated their shoulder a few years after that and they had to stop.'

Melody wasn't surprised. She remembered bouncing off the ceiling of the Jeep as they thundered along dust roads. All those thoughts had stuck while anything around Shannon had been blocked out. Her camp memories weren't false, but they were incomplete. She saw the sunshine, not the shade.

There were a few more moments of silence and then Heather pushed herself up. She straightened her cap and picked up the paintbrush again. 'Sorry,' she repeated. 'It's been great to see you. I hope you son enjoys himself at camp.' She turned to indicate the lake beyond. 'It's a lovely little community and there's so much to do on the island. I'm glad you made it back.'

It was said with kindness, yet it was what Heather didn't say that struck Melody. No offer of coffee, or lunch. No mention that they should get their families together for a picnic. Not that Melody blamed her. Nice to see your face, nicer to never see it again. If she was honest, Melody felt the same way.

Melody heaved herself up from the stump, still burdened by shame that felt as if it might never go. Except the flood of memories had sent another spiralling to the front of her mind. A name that had felt familiar ever since she'd first read it.

'Was there a girl named Grace at our camp?' Melody asked.

Heather had again been wiping the brush on her apron. 'Grace Dewar? She was in the year above. We got mixed together sometimes for things like the speedboat trip.' She waited a beat, then added: 'Do you remember what happened to her?'

Melody didn't, but she knew now. 'The hit-and-run...' she replied.

'We had that service on the beach, where everyone lit candles. I always picture the burning boat they sent out on the water to remember her.'

From nowhere, Melody could see that as well. The flames dancing as the sky darkened, and the water rippled.

Melody's recollection from the time was of boat trips and Jeep tours. The picnics and being centre of attention. Spending all day playing and then getting back to the cabin to eat barbecue. She had somehow isolated that part of her life and revelled in it for years, while blocking out the rest. Both Nina and her dad had been right: They didn't all have the same holiday back then.

Because the article from a decade back had said that Grace Dewar had been killed twenty years before – which wasn't simply any summer.

It was the summer Melody had been at camp.

TWENTY-ONE

Melody couldn't face driving, so she walked towards the water and then followed the abandoned train tracks through the trees until she reached the park Lori had mentioned. A short bank of grass dipped down to a small grey beach, where the sand looked more like dust. She sat at the empty picnic table and cradled her head in her hands.

The other side of the lake felt close, with dotted houses sitting on the far bank, surrounded by trees. A run of mountains sat in the distance, the green of the forest interrupted by large brown rectangle scars, from where logging companies had gone in.

A couple were on paddleboards next to one another, each wearing big red life vests. Past them, someone in a motorboat was humming along the far shore.

Melody's memories were a lie. A fraud.

She had built a personality around a magical time in her life that didn't really exist. She had spent thirty years, first wanting to relive it in some way, then engineering a similar experience for her son.

But none of it was true. Her joy had been at the expense of others.

Shaaaaaaaaaaaaaaa-non.

Shaaaaaaaaaaaaaaa-non.

Time passed, though not enough. There wasn't a single part of this holiday that had gone as Melody wanted – and now her entire reason for coming was an invention.

When Melody's phone buzzed, she almost ignored it. She would've done if there wasn't a chance it was someone from the police with news.

It wasn't them. Lori had messaged to ask if there were any updates. She was another local who'd been enormously kind to her, even though Melody didn't feel she deserved any of it. Her only contribution to the area was bullying a good person and now using up police resources. Melody felt embarrassed to reply, but realised it wasn't all about her. She thanked Lori for the concern, then added that there was no news of Evan. The 'thinking of you' that came back didn't do much to make Melody feel better about the compassion she was being shown, compared to what she had to offer.

By the time Melody had driven herself back to the lake house, her father had gone out. Nina and Thomas were also still gone, so Melody sat by herself on the deck, watching the water. More time passed until it was time to pick up Sam.

Melody was on autopilot as she followed the road around the lake, before pulling into the camp. She trailed the other cars onto the one-way system and then parked in one of the bays that faced the water. Children were spilling away from the park, ducking into waiting vehicles, before being whisked away. Melody was about to get out of the car when she spotted Sam a little past the picnic tables, talking and laughing with a couple of the other boys. It was hard not to picture her younger self on a similar spot, with a similar group. She would have been laughing then, too.

Instead of interrupting, Melody left her son with his new friends – and headed to the counsellor who was standing at the top of the path with a clipboard. It was the girl who'd checked emergency contact details with Melody yesterday – and she beamed as Melody approached.

'How's it been going?' Melody asked.

'Great! Sam's fitted in really well. They all had a good time at the Skywalk today.'

Melody turned to look towards her son, who was still laughing with the others. 'Has he made friends?' she asked.

'Of course. It's a good bunch here.'

The counsellor stopped to tick someone off her list as another boy hopped into a waiting truck. He waved goodbye as the counsellor called back to say she'd see him in the morning.

'Is this your first year as a counsellor?' Melody asked. The young woman looked so young, but then Melody was at the age where everyone seemed like that.

'Second,' she replied. 'I really enjoyed it last year, and they said I could come back.'

Another mum was out of her car and hovering, so Melody thanked the counsellor for her time and then drifted off towards Sam and his friends. As soon as she got within shouting distance, they went quiet in the way children did when an adult showed up.

'Can I go to Liam's tonight?' Sam asked. 'He's got a slide and a pool in his back garden!'

Melody didn't know who Liam was, though assumed it was the boy to her son's side who was staring at his feet.

There was going to come a time, probably soon, that Melody had to tell Sam that his dad was missing. His life was going to change – and she wanted him to enjoy himself while he could. Back home, their garden was so small there was barely room for a slide, let alone a pool.

'If it's OK with Liam's mum, or dad, or—'

Melody didn't quite finish the sentence. There was a muffled 'This way!' and then the trio of boys hurtled off towards a glossy red pickup truck. It was one of the ones where the bonnet sat at neck height for an adult. The sort of thing that worried Melody, even though nobody else seemed to be bothered by how big they were.

Melody followed the boys to the driver's side, where the giant mirror was inches from her head. The woman inside seemed nice enough, in the same way everyone had been since Melody arrived. She told Liam and the other boy to take off their muddy shoes and then get in, adding that there were towels on the back seat. It sounded like she told them the same thing every day.

'You must be Melody,' the woman said. 'I'm Caitlin – Liam's mom. Nice to meet you.'

She spoke as if Melody knew their sons had become friends and it felt as if everything had already been agreed between the boys and Caitlin. Melody supposed that was the way when it came to things like sleepovers and going to friend's houses after school.

'Are you sure don't mind taking Sam?' Melody asked.

It got a dismissive wave as a reply. 'There's always kids at ours during the summer. The more, the merrier.' She reached for a phone from the dashboard. 'Where are you staying? I'll drop him back later.'

Melody had to check her own phone for the address but the two women swapped numbers and then Melody messaged the details of the lake house. It seemed like the sort of thing Caitlin had done many times before. A community parent for kids whose parents had to work late.

And that was it.

Sam needed to jump onto the step that got him into the back seat of the borderline tank. Melody moved away as Caitlin backed out of the space and then headed onto the one-way loop, before disappearing into the trees. It was only as Melody got back to the rental car that she realised she had no idea where the other woman lived. She didn't even know her last name – and had waved her son off with a relative stranger.

Melody pushed that thought away as she headed back to the lake house. Caitlin was local, was known to the camp. Her son was safe.

Nina and Thomas's car was still missing as she pulled in, while her dad was apparently still out on his walk. Melody thought about cooking for herself, though, without Sam to look after, she couldn't quite be bothered. Instead, she took one of the granola bars from the cupboard and sat on the deck with Evan's phone.

As she'd drifted to sleep the night before, Melody had tried a series of passcodes that felt as if they might work. 1-2-3-4 and 4-3-2-1 hadn't done much, neither had 1-1-1-1, or anything similarly straightforward.

Melody hadn't quite processed the fact her sister casually checked her husband's phone. She'd never before had the curiosity to get into Evan's and find out what he was doing. She assumed it was largely work stuff, or sorting out times for a squash court with his friends.

Except it had stuck that maybe there was some sort of clue to where he could have gone. Perhaps he'd snapped a photo as he'd stopped the car? It seemed grubby trying to hack into his phone, but then Melody felt grubby from the day as a whole. She deserved to be alone.

Melody tried the month and day of Sam's birthday, then hers, then Evan's. When none of those worked, she tried Evan's mum's birthday, then his dad's. After that, she reversed the numbers, trying day and month instead.

Nope.

Their first date had been on 4 April, when they went crazy golfing, so she tried 0404, which didn't work.

Melody wondered if she had a certain number of guesses before the phone locked itself, or reported itself missing. If it was a random collection of numbers, she would be there forever.

She put down the phone and stared across the lake for a while. The smell of barbecued meat was drifting from a nearby property, making her mouth water. From somewhere else, boys were bombing into the water and screaming with joy.

When she next picked up the phone, Melody typed 1983 into the screen. It was an afterthought, the year in which Evan had been born, and almost a disappointment when the page of apps appeared. She laughed humourlessly to herself at how route one it all was. It was also no surprise that Evan's apps were organised tidily into folders, on a single screen. Melody's were also in order – but only one she would recognise. Multiple podcast players were scattered across various pages, along with at least six weather apps, too many news providers to remember, plus everything in between. She had two different programs to identify plant types, neither of which she used. There were apps from six different banks, two of which she hadn't ever held an account with.

Melody tapped into Evan's 'essential' folder and loaded his calendar. The flight numbers and car rental details were all listed, along with various activities across the days. Today's was marked 'Victoria?', which made Melody think he must have shared the itinerary with Thomas.

Nothing particularly odd about that.

There were hundreds of new emails, which Melody ignored. If hers was anything to go by, it would be a multitude of companies desperately trying to sell a product they already had. Buy one mattress, and the seller was seemingly convinced you'd need a new one every other week.

The squalid sense of betrayal continued as Melody pressed into Evan's messages. She saw her own face pinned at the top, but the entry under that wasn't taken by a contact, it was an 07 British mobile number. Somebody not in Evan's contacts.

Melody froze as she read the most recent message.

Hello? x

The kiss meant it wouldn't have come from one of his work friends, nor his squash buddies. It had been sent sometime that morning, a full day and a half after he went missing. There were more before that, scattered through Monday.

Are you safe? x

Did you make it to the lake? x

Where are you? x

Melody kept scrolling, though every message had the same kiss at the end. All had been received after Evan had disappeared, all were unanswered.

Then there was ice in Melody's chest. The final text sent by Evan hadn't been to her, it was to the 07 number, not long after he'd arrived.

Landed safely. Can't wait to see you when I get home. Stay safe! x

TWENTY-TWO

There had to be an innocent explanation.

Had to be.

Melody continued scrolling, unable to stop herself. Not wanting to. There were hundreds of messages between Evan and the o7 number, in which they'd gone back and forth over places and times. They'd been meeting for months, including at an Italian restaurant at seven o'clock a couple of months back. Melody checked her own calendar, where it was marked that Evan was at squash.

It dawned slowly, and yet all at once. Almost all of Evan's squash games that Melody had added to her calendar had actually been him meeting the owner of the o7 number. As well as the logistics organising each meet, there were the messages afterwards. The 'Great seeing you! x'. The 'Had so much fun! x'. The kisses were ever-present.

Melody had to scroll all the way to the top to find the name of the person.

Hi! This is Chloe! x

Evan had replied to confirm she had the correct number.

Melody put down the phone, then picked it up again. Put it down, picked it up. She didn't want to read anymore, though it was impossible not to. Her fiancé had been having an affair with someone named Chloe for the best part of a year.

Melody's thumb hovered over the number, daring herself to call. She would have done if it wasn't two in the morning in the UK. It was unlikely to be answered and having an unanswered call appear on Chloe's phone could tip her off that something was up.

Was it better or worse that Melody didn't know a Chloe? If Evan was going to have an affair with anyone, it was probably better for it to be a stranger. What if it had been one of her friends? Worse, her *sister*.

Melody scrolled back to the most recent messages and took a tiny amount of pleasure that this Chloe was worrying about Evan. Just as Melody had gone to bed desperate to know what was up, the same was true of his mistress. Let her worry. Let her not know. The bitch. How *dare* she. Evan had a son with somebody else. He was supposed to be a dad.

How *dare* she.

Then Melody wondered if Chloe knew about her and Sam. Had Evan deceived her in the way he'd deceived Melody?

They were supposed to be getting married in December. The venue was booked and so were the caterers. Sam was excited to be his own father's best man and Melody couldn't wait to see the pair of them in their suits.

And now... what?

Evan was missing but, even if he came back, it was all over anyway.

Melody stared at the phone, then the lake, then the phone. She wanted to throw it into the water and never think of it again. She wanted to fly home and forget anything from the past week or so had happened.

Except she needed to know.

Melody loaded the photos app and scanned through. There were so many of Sam, including at least forty of him at Goodison Park, when Evan had taken him to watch his first Premier League game. There were pictures from Sam's most recent birthday party, more from Christmas Day, with the grandparents. Sam had tried Christmas pudding for the first time and decided he didn't like it, so had a bowl of ice cream instead. Meanwhile, Evan's dad ate as much Christmas pudding as the rest of them, and then spent half the night in the toilet.

Memories that were all tainted now.

There were occasional photos of Melody, or Evan himself. There were a couple of him on a squash court with a racquet, so not every match was invented.

Then there were the photos of them as a family. They'd been to Legoland at Windsor the year before, and there were so many photos with the three of them standing in front of towers of plastic.

That lump was back in Melody's throat again. It felt as if it might never go this time. She had scrolled back through two years of photos and there wasn't a single one of a mystery woman. Was that better or worse?

Melody put down the phone and then picked it up again. Up-down-up-down. It was half past two in the morning back in the UK and she wondered if Chloe would pick up. She'd think it was Evan calling. What would she say if Melody remained silent?

Instead, Melody returned to looking at the messages.

Did you make it to the lake? x

She had missed the significance before – but Chloe had known Evan was staying at a lake. Did she think he was travelling alone, or did she know he had a family? A son? A *fiancée*?

Melody returned to Evan's home screen and tapped into the social media folder. He only really used Facebook to keep an eye on his mum, who posted at least half a dozen times a day. By the time they were back from their cruise, there would be a couple of hundred new photos that all looked broadly the same. Melody ignored that, instead loading Instagram.

The first few photos on his feed were of various footballers in blue kit, then there was Melody's own post from Saturday, when they'd first arrived at the lake. It felt like a different life in which she'd posted a picture of the sun setting over the water, with the caption 'Back at last'. Everything felt tainted now, from her memories of the lake and childhood, through to her life with Evan.

Melody kept thumbing through his feed. Her fiancé had a thing about old games consoles, so there were plenty of images of stuff like that. More football, of course. A couple of photos of people playing squash, which stung because Melody was still not sure how often Evan played. There were pictures from the top of a mountain, taken by his work friend who'd gone camping a week or two back. More of someone's new puppy.

And then Melody saw it.

The first photo was of a bottle-blonde young woman who couldn't have been older than her early twenties, if that. She was at an outdoor gig or festival with a couple of other women her age. They all had an arm in the air, with big fixed smiles, and unicorn bands on their heads.

Chloe wasn't simply another woman, she was *a girl*.

There were photos somewhere of Melody in a similar position at a similar age. She had done festivals in her twenties.

Melody couldn't stop herself from pressing into Chloe's profile, which didn't make things any better.

She was a twenty-year-old nail technician.

Twenty.

She was half Evan's age.

Could it be a different Chloe? It had to be.

Melody put down the phone again, then instantly picked it up. It was like kicking herself in the shins over and over. She couldn't stop as she scrolled through Chloe's photos to find an otherwise normal young woman. She went to gigs, she had nights out with friends, she had watched *The Lion King* at the theatre the previous Christmas, she liked swimming.

Except she was *twenty*.

In the year before, she'd been doing her diploma as a nail technician. It seemed like she was barely out of school. Then she was at a different gig, pint in her hand.

Evan's comment underneath dispelled any doubts of this being the right Chloe.

Looking good!

She was with one of her friends, faces smushed, ice cream in hand – with Evan replying again.

Looks tasty! Hope you had a great time!

He'd gone crazy with the exclamation marks – and it wasn't only those photos. He commented on almost everything Chloe posted, each time offering praise with another exclamation mark.

The prick.

Melody used to know older men like that back when she went out in town. The blokes who'd hang around the pool tables, wanting to play winner stays on, or show them how to hold a cue. The weirdos who never moved from the bar, even as their stares endlessly wandered.

Melody put down the phone again, locked the screen, and left it.

Twenty.

She could almost process Evan having an affair with someone broadly their age. It wasn't as if she liked the idea, or would accept it – but she knew he wasn't the first and wouldn't be the last.

Except Chloe was *twenty*.

Melody's throat was dry again as her stomach thundered with fury.

What should she do? Call Constable Burgess and tell him not to bother searching for Evan? Let Chloe find him? Let Evan fend for himself?

Except she couldn't – because he was still Sam's father.

A phone buzzed and, for a second, Melody thought it was Evan's. That Chloe was calling to ask where he was. Melody would answer and tell this child exactly who he was and what he was up to.

Except it was Melody's own phone.

For a moment, she couldn't remember who 'Caitlin' was, until it dawned that it was Liam's mum. The woman looking after Sam.

Melody snatched her phone from the table and pressed to answer. Caitlin's wavering voice was a far cry from the confidence of earlier.

'Is that Melody?' she asked.

'That's me.'

'I think you might need to come pick up Sam.'

TWENTY-THREE

Caitlin was waiting at the front door as Melody pulled onto her drive. It had taken Melody twenty minutes to follow Apple Maps' route to the house, which was near the junction with the highway. If her phone hadn't told her where to pull in, there was a good chance Melody would have missed the driveway. It was another massive house, probably five or six bedrooms, set back from the road, hidden by trees.

'I'm so sorry,' Caitlin said, as Melody headed up the stairs. Melody went to step around her but Caitlin didn't move. 'He's out back if you want to head around the side but...' She stopped and then added: 'He's with Liam and the boys in the pool. I managed to calm him down. I didn't know whether to tell him you were coming.'

For an area in which there was little traffic, Melody had somehow managed to find a time of day in which every junction had involved waiting for someone else. She'd been thinking in fast-forward, even as she was forced to move at what felt like a deathly pace. From Evan missing, to memories of Shannon, to the discovery of Chloe – and now this.

'I'd seen it on Facebook,' Caitlin said. 'Someone had posted on the local group about a missing British man. I can't believe I did it but I didn't put two and two together. I knew you were here on vacation and wondered if you all knew each other. I asked Sam if he knew the man – but didn't realise it was his dad...'

It was such an obvious thing to have happened that Melody wasn't sure how she'd not considered it. She wanted Sam to have a good time at a friend's house and had somehow been oblivious to the fact that knowledge of Evan's disappearance was out in the community. Constable Burgess had told her his image and details had been shared but because Melody didn't watch the local news, or wasn't a member of the area's Facebook groups, she hadn't grasped what that meant.

Except, in a small community, people were obviously going to have heard about a missing man. That was the whole point.

'It's not your fault,' Melody replied. 'I wanted Sam to enjoy a few days at camp before telling him myself. I didn't realise...' The sentence fell away as Melody struggled to explain herself.

'Is there anything I can do?' Caitlin asked, with genuine concern.

'No, I'll talk to him now.'

Caitlin took Melody around the side of the house, passing rows of raspberry bushes brimming with fruit, and a stack of bikes and scooters. They soon emerged in an enormous back yard. A deck stretched from the back of the house, leading to a pool that was filled with inflatables. Beyond that, a vast expanse of lawn pushed towards a row of trees at the far end. Music was playing, something modern and autotuned to the point that it sounded like angry bees. Melody had once wondered why young people listened to such nonsense, before Evan had pointed out they'd grown up thinking it was normal.

Melody followed Caitlin past a slide, on which a boy was at the top. A different boy at the bottom counted him down and then he launched himself off the top, before hurtling down and landing in the pool with a splosh.

Sam was sitting on a lounger, on the other side of the slide. He had wet hair and had been playing cards or trumps with Liam. When he looked up to his mum, he was smiling, though not with his eyes.

'Do you want to come and help pack away dinner?' Caitlin said.

Liam was immediately on his feet, putting down his cards, heading back towards the house.

Sam dipped his head as Melody sat on the spot Liam had been sitting.

'Have you had a nice evening?' she asked.

'Yeah... Liam's dad cooked burgers for us. He's got a Play-Station *and* an Xbox.'

Melody laughed a little at that, remembering the months of deliberation Sam had made over which console he wanted the previous Christmas. He'd created a spreadsheet of pros and cons for each one, before telling them which he preferred.

'I should've told you about your dad,' Melody told him, watching as he slumped a fraction. Water dripped from his hair, across his shoulders. 'Dad did fly and make it to the island – but he didn't reach the house. I don't know where he is. The police are looking for him now – and his photo's been released, so others can call if they see him.'

As Melody shifted her weight, she realised the lounger was wet. Her bum was damp and she shuffled uncomfortably. Too late now.

'I'm sorry for keeping it from you,' Melody added. 'I wanted you to enjoy camp and make friends...'

Melody wasn't sure if he understood, nor if she'd made the right decision. She was so used to co-parenting, to talking things through with Evan, that making a big call by herself felt strange.

Sam asked a few questions about what had happened,

which Melody answered as best she could, considering she didn't know either. He was obviously worried. Devastated, really – but had taken the revelation as well as he could. He seemed comforted that the police were looking for his dad, and also that Liam's mum knew. If she'd seen it on Facebook, others would have done. People would be looking for the missing man.

All the while, Melody did her best to reassure her son while trying to force away the knowledge that Evan had been having an affair with a girl half his age. She kept seeing Chloe's smiling face, unable to know how they could have possibly got together. What could they have in common? What would they even talk about? Unless they didn't do much in the way of talking...

Melody pushed those thoughts away as she headed back towards the house with Sam. There were five other boys sitting on towels at the side of the pool, each with wet hair, all talking quickly and excitedly until they noticed Sam and Melody.

'Are you staying over?' Liam asked. 'Mum said it's all right.'

For a moment, Melody thought Sam was going to ask if he could sleep at Liam's that night. She'd have to say yes, even though – selfishly – she wanted to know he was sleeping across the hallway from her. As it was, Sam spoke for himself.

'Maybe another night?' he replied. 'All my stuff's at the lake.'

Melody knew her boy well enough to realise he was saying 'no' while not actually having to say it. Not that anyone minded. The boys immediately moved on to talking about seeing one another at camp the next morning.

As they rounded the house, Caitlin waved Melody across to the front door, forcing a giant punnet of raspberries into her hand. 'We have so many,' she said, then added: 'I'm so sorry about earlier.'

She said that Sam was welcome to come over any time after camp, and that Melody should message if she needed anything.

'If you need a night off, just say,' she added – and it was yet another person offering enormous kindness for no benefit to themselves.

Nina's car was parked on the gravel when Melody and Sam arrived back at the lake house. Sam led his mum around to the deck, where Melody's dad was sitting with his feet up, iPad on his lap. He was one of those people who looked at the sun and turned brown. When he smiled at his grandson, there was a moment in which Melody melted. He seemed so relaxed, for the first time in a long time – and Sam was instantly drawn as he went to sit on his granddad's knee.

'Getting a bit big for that,' Melody's father said, and it was only half in jest.

'Sam's a bit upset about his dad,' Melody said, waiting for her dad to catch her eye and then raising her eyebrows.

Her father didn't need it spelling out as he instantly shot into granddad mode, asking how Sam's day at camp had gone. He put down the iPad and listened to every word, cooing and oohing in all the right places, before Sam moved on to telling him about the scale of Liam's house.

Melody watched in silence, revelling in the relationship across the generations, trying not to think about Chloe, a little girl called Shannon, to whom she had once been so cruel, or anything else from the day.

It was impossible, of course.

Perhaps her dad saw that she needed to be by herself, or maybe he simply knew what Sam needed after his own traumatic evening. Either way, he was on his feet.

'I was talking to a man along the bank earlier – and he was saying he'd take me out on his boat to see the sunset. It's probably about time. I reckon he'd love to have a strong man like you along to help pull the motor cord.'

Sam beamed at the description, flexing his non-bicep.

'Go and change first,' Melody told him – and Sam only needed telling once. He tripped over the stairs as he ran into the house and then thundered through the door. Melody put down Caitlin's punnet of raspberries on the table and then father and daughter stood on the deck, watching as the sun started to dip below the trees.

'You look like you've had quite the day,' Melody's dad said. He reached for her and pulled her close, wrapping an arm around her shoulder as if she was Sam's age. She pressed into him, biting her bottom lip, not quite able to say what the day had actually brought. He didn't push further, simply holding her until elephants began stampeding through the house again.

Sam exploded through the back door, jumping to land on the deck, wearing a set of clean clothes. His hair was a mess and Melody resisted the urge to tell him to brush it.

'Ready!'

Melody's dad released her and then pointed along the shore. 'We'll have to walk on the road but it's only five minutes. Not even that.'

Melody told them to be careful as her dad replied, 'I'll get him back for bedtime.'

It was technically *already* his bedtime, not that Melody said so. At least one of them would sleep well that night.

She watched as her dad walked side by side with her son up the gravel, towards the road. It was no surprise her father had made friends with the locals. He was like that anywhere. There was no town or city on earth in which he wouldn't plonk himself on a bench and find someone to natter to.

Melody sat by herself for a few minutes, watching the water and darkening skies. Her thoughts drifted from Shannon's devastated face after finding out her shoes were missing all those years ago, to Chloe's grinning features on Evan's Instagram from last week. What was she supposed to do? Who could she talk to?

It wasn't long until Nina and Thomas emerged from the house. Melody's sister was giggling in a way she rarely did as the couple sat on the other side of the table, and started to sip some sort of slushy, icy, cocktail they'd made.

'Have you eaten?' Thomas asked. 'We brought back some leftovers if you want them.'

'I ate,' Melody lied. She feared anything that went down would instantly come back up. 'Have some raspberries,' she added, indicating the punnet and then taking one herself. There was the merest hint of bitterness, though it was so ripe, it was almost liquid. Perfect.

'Victoria was great,' Thomas said, nudging Nina, who simply giggled. She was gazing across the lake, eyelids drooping. 'We walked around the big park, then along the front. We had ice cream twice. We're going to go back again at some point.' He paused, probably remembering the situation. 'You're, um, welcome to come next time if, er, well you know. With Evan and that...'

Melody ignored him as Thomas faked a cough to get out of the conversation. Melody was more interested in her sister, who was still sniggering.

'Are you OK?' Melody asked.

'Isn't it amazing?' Nina said. 'The water. It's amazing, isn't it?'

Melody turned to follow her sister's stare that hadn't shifted since she'd sat. The lake was unquestionably beautiful – though it was no different than when they'd arrived three days before.

'Look at all the water,' Nina added. 'Look at it.'

Melody wondered if Nina was seeing something she wasn't. A paddleboarder was back, floating around close to the park in which she'd been earlier in the day. Then, as if Nina was living a few seconds in the future, a small motorboat emerged from a little along the bay. As it chugged towards the main part of the lake, Melody cupped her eyes to spot Sam sitting at the back of the boat. He was wearing a greeny-grey life jacket, waving enthusiastically.

'Is that Sam?' Thomas asked, standing and waving back.

'Dad met someone with a boat,' Melody replied. 'They're going out to watch the sunset.'

The sky was already a bright orange wash. It was almost underwhelming in the sense that Melody had seen the same thing every night since arriving.

Melody waved as well and could just about make out her son's smile.

Nina was on her feet now, also waving, though facing in slightly the wrong direction. She was cackling to herself. 'It's amazing, isn't it?' she said.

'What's amazing?' Melody asked.

'The water. All the water.'

The motorboat had floated its way deeper towards the centre of the lake – and Sam was now an ant.

'Are you all right?' Melody asked, talking to her sister.

Nobody answered, with Thomas feverishly typing something into his phone.

'Is she OK?' Melody asked, trying Thomas instead, who didn't reply.

'Nina...?'

Her sister's only response was to begin tugging at her top – and Melody gasped slightly as Nina pulled it over her head and dropped it on the floor.

'What are you doing?'

Nina wasn't listening. She'd kicked off her sandals and was pulling off her shorts.

Thomas was standing now, reaching for his wife, who was starting to walk barefoot towards the water, wearing only her underwear.

'Shall we go skinny dipping?' Nina said, without turning.

She was already struggling with her bra as Melody pushed herself up.

'Has she taken something?' Melody asked, talking to Thomas who was trying to catch his wife. Except he was too late. Nina was struggling across the gravel. She lurched to the side, still chortling as she wobbled and then flopped face-down onto the stones.

Thomas was there first, on his knees at his wife's side as Melody arrived. He turned her over – but there was no laughing now. Nina was moaning to herself as a flood of cherry red blood gushed from the chasm across her hairline.

TWENTY-FOUR

WEDNESDAY

The alarm clock at the side of Melody's bed read a minute past midnight. There was no chance of a squeaking bed on the other side of the wall that night, given Nina and Thomas's room was empty after she was rushed off in an ambulance.

Melody's dad had said that Sam had fallen asleep on the boat, not long after the sun had gone down. He'd been roused after they got back to shore and just about managed to walk back to the lake house, before falling asleep in his bed.

At least he was safe.

The only conversation Melody had with her son before he'd passed out was to ask whether he wanted to go to camp the next day. The answer had been an enthusiastic 'yes'. She thought he was very brave in the way he was taking his father's disappearance.

Melody blinked and it was 01:27.

She was thinking of Chloe. *Twenty*. She was *twenty* years old. How could Evan do such a thing at all? Let alone with someone so young.

Melody blinked and it was 01:56.

How could she forget being a bully? How could that look of despair on Shannon's face at losing her shoes have been discarded? That poor girl. Melody didn't want to admit why she'd been a part of things, though she knew the answer. She wanted to be liked – and picking on one girl had made her popular.

Melody blinked and it was 02:58.

Where was Evan? He'd been there and then he wasn't. People didn't just disappear. She was so furious at him, so unbelievably, ferociously, *angry* – and yet she wanted him to be safe. He was Sam's father.

A creak echoed up the stairs from the floor below. Melody lay still and listened, wondering if it was another part of her dreams. The house in which she'd grown up had groaning, moaning, pipes that she'd once thought meant a monster lived in the attic.

Creeeeeeeeeeeeeeeeeeeak.

There was definitely somebody moving around downstairs. It wouldn't be Nina or Thomas, and she doubted it was her dad – which meant it must be Sam.

Melody rolled herself out of bed, yawned, and then headed across the cool floor. She wondered if her son had woken up hungry and gone down to have a bowl of his cookie cereal.

It was quiet as Melody reached the bottom of the stairs and emerged into the kitchen. She half expected the light to be on and Sam to be sitting on one of the stools facing the island.

There was nobody there and the kitchen was empty. Melody stood still, listening to a faint scratching, coming from somewhere she couldn't quite work out. It felt near and yet there was no sign of anybody around.

Except there was.

Melody yelped as a shadow stepped out of the space behind the stairs. It wasn't only the shape of a person that made

Melody cry – it was what was being held. Despite the dark, the white of the moon spread across the kitchen floor, illuminating the gleaming barrel of what was unmistakeably a shotgun.

TWENTY-FIVE

'Shuuuuusssh,' said the shadow. A man's voice.

'I—'

'Bear,' the man said, using the barrel of the gun to indicate the window nearest the door. Melody couldn't move her feet, though didn't need to. The white of the moon was instantly obliterated by the hulking shape of something huge brushing against the glass.

She didn't know where to look. Monster on one side, stranger with a gun on the other.

The man took another step, leaving the darkest shadows as Melody suddenly realised it was Harrison. The homeowner was wearing a padded vest, with a baseball cap, eyes fixed on the window.

The scratching was loud now, alongside a booming, thunderous snuffle that filled the room. It felt as if the bear was going to fall through the door and suddenly be right there with them.

Harrison took another step ahead, shotgun raised. He nodded wordlessly and Melody took the hint as she edged behind him.

Time dragged. Probably seconds, maybe longer, maybe a lot

longer – and then the snorting dimmed as light returned to the kitchen. Melody was leaning on the island, holding a spatula that she didn't remember picking up, as Harrison crept to the window. Melody held her breath as he craned his neck to peer around the corner, before – eventually – lowering the gun.

And... breathe.

'What were you going to do with that?' he whispered, indicating the spatula.

Melody lowered it to the counter, slightly embarrassed. It didn't feel very funny.

'I didn't mean to startle you,' he added, waiting by the door. 'I heard noises. There are problems with thefts around here, so I grabbed the gun. When I got to the water, I realised the bear was between me and the house. I had the keys on my belt and couldn't think what else to do, other than lock myself in here.'

He reached for the door lock and clicked it open.

'Sorry...'

Melody told him it was OK, though her heart was racing.

Harrison had placed the shotgun on the table nearest the door and was waving her across. 'Look.'

Melody joined him at the door and peered through the side window, to where what looked like a giant dog was hunched over the water.

A *really* giant dog.

Melody had seen bears on nature documentaries but they hadn't prepared her for the scale of the hulking black mass. Huge, clawed paws dunked into the water and then bucketed liquid into the creature's mouth.

'Beautiful, isn't she?' Harrison whispered.

Melody had no idea whether the bear was female, or if Harrison was guessing, though she wasn't about to argue. She watched the animal sit back on the shale, legs stretched as it scratched its shoulder. There was undeniable beauty, even if it felt as if that beauty could rip off an arm if it felt like it.

They watched together for a minute or so, until Melody turned to the window that faced the porch. The upturned table should have been a clue, though the chewed cardboard punnet was a bigger one.

Melody gasped as she realised she'd left the tub of raspberries outside. The main thing she'd been warned not to do.

'You OK?' Harrison whispered. His gaze didn't wilt from the bear.

Melody told him she was, not quite able to admit she'd brought this on herself.

More time passed as the bear scratched some more, then had another drink. When it hunched forward onto all fours, Melody took a small step away from the door, convinced it was about to come for them. It raised its snout to the air and sniffed.

'Can it smell us?' Melody asked.

Harrison snorted quietly and kindly. 'They've got the best noses on earth. They can smell food from a kilometre away. More.'

Any thought that the bear's appearance might not be Melody's fault drifted as she glanced to the crushed punnet on the deck. As mistakes went, this was a big one. Thank goodness Sam hadn't woken up in the middle of the night.

'Did anyone tell you what to do if you see a bear?' Harrison whispered. His commitment to a stare that never left its target was incredible. His lips barely moved.

'At camp a long time ago,' Melody replied. She didn't remember and suddenly felt embarrassingly under-prepared. Whenever she went for walks in the UK, she didn't need to think about a massive creature that could smell food from a kilometre away.

'If you startle a bear, you get big,' Harrison said. 'Lift your arms up, shout and stamp. Make as much noise as you can. If it moves towards you, throw sticks or stones. Anything that's nearby.'

Melody watched the hairy behemoth sink back into a sitting position. As it twisted and turned, she could understand it in at least one way. The poor soul had an itchy back it couldn't quite reach.

'Bears are usually cowards,' Harrison added. 'We only have black bears around here but most aren't as big as this.'

'That makes it sound like there are other bears...'

Harrison gave another gentle chuckle at that, though his attention was still on the bear. The creature was now lying on the gravel, frantically rubbing its back.

'Grizzlies are much bigger,' Harrison said. 'They're brown, with humped backs. If you see them, you definitely don't make yourself big and attract attention.'

'What do you do?'

'Pray.' He sounded horrifyingly serious, before adding: 'Or fight. Use whatever's in front of you. Go for the eyes if you can reach.' He patted the gun. 'Or take one of these.'

Melody almost didn't dare to ask the next thing. 'Do you get grizzlies around here...?'

The pause lasted too long, even if it was barely a couple of seconds. 'No, only occasionally on the northern parts of the island. They aren't native. They swam over from the mainland.'

Melody tried to remember what little she knew of the area's geography. 'Isn't that, like, a hundred miles?'

'Not up north – but it's still a bit of a swim.'

The bear was again on all fours and Melody couldn't get over the size of its paws. It was like something walking around on four dustbin lids. The creature looked from side to side and then began ambling up the gravel drive, towards the main house – and, hopefully, the road beyond.

'We don't have bears in England,' Melody said.

'What do you have?'

'Nothing really. Deer.'

That got another snort. 'We have deer, too.'

The bear was taking its time in moving away and, as it continued to snuffle, Melody worried it might come back to see if it had missed any of the fruit.

'Do you remember you told me about the mushrooms?' Melody asked.

'Sure. Help yourself. Just, y'know, moderation and all that.'

He spoke as calmly as the first time. It was an attitude that Melody had never encountered before. If anyone so much as mentioned drugs in the UK, one of the frothing-mouthed *Daily Mail* columnists would put out their hips in a rush to get to a laptop and excrete out a column.

'It's just my sister didn't show much moderation,' Melody said.

Harrison shuffled for the first time in a while, glancing momentarily away from the bear to frown at her. Melody felt like the time she'd been caught snogging a boy by her dad.

'There was an ambulance here earlier,' Melody added. 'I didn't know if you'd seen it.'

Harrison returned his gaze to the bear, which was again trying to scratch its back. 'An ambulance...?'

'Nina wanted to try the mushrooms and, er... overdid it a bit. She fainted and is being kept in the hospital tonight.'

'Is she OK?'

'I think so. Her husband tried them too but it didn't have such an effect on him. He called before I went to bed and said she was being looked after. He was worried about the travel insurance and whether it would cover the hospital bills.'

Harrison didn't reply to that. Melody had forwarded her brother-in-law the insurance email and gone to bed. The fact Nina's overindulgence could cost them had seemingly sobered up Thomas in the hospital.

'I didn't notice an ambulance,' Harrison said quietly. 'The living room's at the front of the house, and I don't hear much that's happening from the back.' He waited a beat, then added:

'Hearing's going at my age, anyway. Rick's always saying I should get my ears tested.'

Melody allowed herself the slimmest of smiles at that. She and Evan always joked that his father's favourite word was 'What?' He insisted he wasn't going deaf, despite having his television volume at a level rivalling a volcanic eruption.

Evan...

Melody had gone a short time without thinking about him.

Or Chloe.

Or Shannon.

She watched the bear, a part of her wishing it would hang around if only to distract her from the horrid reality of what the holiday had become.

The bear was on its back again, using the gravel to rub the itchy part. It really needed one of those scratching sticks people sold for a couple of euros at market stalls on holiday.

And, suddenly, as she thought about the holiday she should have been having, Melody couldn't stop herself. 'I was really sorry to hear about what happened with your daughter,' she said. 'I read an article about it after you said.'

Harrison chewed on that. Melody watched his beard bob up and down as she regretted saying anything.

And then he replied to a sentence she hadn't spoken. 'Sorry about Rick,' he said. 'I know he's around a lot. You shouldn't have to deal with him. He doesn't live here but comes around a fair bit when Cody's at his mum's.'

'It's all right,' Melody managed. She wasn't quite sure for what he was apologising, then realised it was probably a way of expressing his own disappointment, without having to say that.

'He's made a few bad decisions but tends to blame others,' Harrison added.

Melody wasn't sure what to say. It wasn't a conversation she'd expected, especially at this time of night.

Or morning.

She thought of the twins Harrison would have once had, and how one hadn't made it – while the other had turned out to be Rick. There was no way a parent wouldn't wonder what might have been.

From her limited impression of the two men, they were a very different father and son.

'I'd say he's harmless,' Harrison added. 'But I've seen the videos. I'm assuming you have as well?'

Melody wasn't sure how he knew, other than that she'd mentioned looking up the article. It was probably a fair assumption.

She still didn't know how to reply. The bear was now on all fours, steadily making its way up the drive.

'Where will it go?' Melody asked.

'Probably cross the road and head up the bank. There are berries up there.'

Melody pictured the berries that had been on the porch.

'Do you see bears regularly?' she asked.

'Not really. Not down here. Maybe at the end of the season, when there's not much food left. They come down, looking for whatever they can find before they hibernate for the winter.'

The bear was in the shadows now, thumping its massive paws past the house, in the direction Harrison had said.

Finally, Harrison stepped away from the door. He picked up the shotgun, keeping it low to his side, the barrel facing away from them both.

'I'm sorry about invading your privacy,' he said. 'It won't happen again.'

Melody told him it was fine and that she understood. If anything, she was grateful he was there. She had no idea how she'd have handled things if she'd stumbled into the kitchen herself, wondering what the noise was.

'I'm going to head back now,' Harrison said, placing a hand on the door. 'Is that OK?'

It took Melody a moment to realise he was asking her if she felt safe.

'Yes,' she told him.

He opened the door and stepped through it, allowing a gust of cool air to billow into the kitchen.

'I hope things work out with your husband,' he said, before closing the door behind him.

Melody watched Harrison limp up the drive towards his house, shotgun dangling at his side.

'Fiancé,' she whispered to nobody in particular.

TWENTY-SIX

Melody crouched and held her hand over the enormous paw print in the dust.

'It's MASSIVE!' Sam said – and he sounded as excited as Melody had ever known.

The bear had looked big from the house, though Melody shivered as she looked upon the actual size of the creature's paws. Its individual claws had etched scratches into the dirt that looked like five individual knives. The paws themselves were frying pan-sized.

'You should've got me up,' Sam added.

'I was trying to stay very still and quiet,' Melody replied.

'Did it look at you?'

Melody tried to remember. The bear had definitely turned from side to side. 'Perhaps,' she replied. 'I don't know.'

'Do you reckon it has a big breakfast every day?' Sam asked. 'Like a whole box of cereal?'

'I don't think it eats cereal,' Melody replied.

'What does it eat?'

Melody glanced to the deck, where she'd righted the table, put the crushed punnet in the bin, and wiped up the berry juice. If Harrison had noticed her mistake, he hadn't said anything.

'Fruit,' she said.

Sam put his own palm in the bear print and was thoroughly delighted the claws were roughly the same size as his hand. 'It's so big!' he said. 'Wait 'til I tell everyone at camp.'

Melody suspected that by the time Sam got around to telling his version of events, he'd have not simply been sleeping as the bear came by. He was at the age where most things had a slightly exaggerated air about them. Give it a few days and he'd be telling people he was best friends with the bear.

Back on the deck, Melody sat and sipped her coffee. Sam was eating his cereal outside, though Melody was careful to ensure nothing he dropped was left. She had seen enough bears for one holiday, thank you very much.

After driving Sam to camp, Melody stopped to tell the counsellor that Sam's dad was missing but that he still wanted to come. If there were any problems, her phone was on. As with everything else, the girl took the news comfortably in her stride – which was likely why she was left to be in charge of a bunch of kids.

As Melody drove away, Sam was already in a group with Liam and the others, holding his hands high and no doubt explaining the size of the bear he hadn't seen.

Melody might usually correct his wilder exaggerations – but not now. The poor lad had been through enough.

Back at the lake house, Melody had only just parked when another car sent a spray of gravel tinkering across the top of the drive. She waited as Thomas pulled in alongside her – then gave the raised-eyebrow glance of a man who'd been up all night.

Nina was wearing sunglasses as she hauled herself out of the car. It was a sight at which Melody almost laughed. She'd seen her older sister drunk in the past – but this was right up there. Thomas rounded the car and hooked an arm underneath his wife's shoulders, before they started to the house.

'Are you all right?' Melody asked, talking to her sister.

Nina grunted something that sounded a bit like 'Yeah', before Thomas clarified.

'She needs a bit of a sleep,' he said, in the slurred manner of a man who also needed sleep. Lots of it.

Melody followed them into the kitchen, where Thomas waited at the bottom of the stairs, asking Nina if she was all right. She mumbled something Melody didn't catch and then stumbled her way upstairs. Moments later and there was a soft bump as she presumably dropped onto the bed above them.

Thomas opened the fridge and took out the container of orange juice. For a second, it looked as if he was going to drink directly from the carton, before remembering Melody was there. Instead, he grabbed a glass from the cupboard and filled it.

'The doctor says she'll be fine,' Thomas said, before taking a gulp of the juice. 'They pumped her stomach, so she's a bit tender for now.'

Melody suspected this moment might be raised in future years. The sort of thing a person never quite lived down. Their dad still went on about the time he'd found a hungover Nina sleeping on the stairs one morning after she'd been out. This surely trumped that?

'Mushrooms for tea later?' Melody asked.

Thomas didn't laugh. 'Any updates about—'

'No,' Melody replied.

Thomas downed the rest of his drink, then left the glass in the sink before catching himself. He rinsed it instead, then fed it to the dishwasher.

'I'm going for a shower, then a sleep,' he said.

Melody didn't stop him as he headed upstairs.

Once again, she was unsure what to do with her day.

Melody desperately wanted to know what had happened with Evan – but, failing that, she really needed a quiet day.

Not that it was going to happen.

A flash of something caught Melody's eye and she turned to watch as an RCMP car grumbled across the gravel towards the house.

Melody moved outside, rounding the house until she was next to the vehicle. Constable Burgess was inside but didn't waste any time in getting out. He smiled, though there was no humour there.

'I'm sorry to do this,' he said, as Melody's stomach sank. 'There's no easy way to say it but we've found a body.'

TWENTY-SEVEN

Melody had never been in a police car before. Constable Burgess said she could sit in the front, which gave her a strange sense of power. Or it might have done, were it not for the stinging in her stomach.

They'd found a body.

It didn't help that Melody figured out after fifteen minutes why Burgess told her he would drive. She had offered to follow him but now realised that, if the body was Evan's, the officer didn't believe she would be in a fit state to drive back. She should have probably got her dad out of bed but it was a bit late now.

Burgess drove steadily through the bumpy roads leading back to the highway as Melody pressed herself into the seat and closed her eyes. There was a laptop on the armrest between them and two phones in the gap by the gearstick. Melody kept her elbows close.

'The body was found in the lake last night,' Burgess said. 'Someone was walking their dog late and spotted it floating. It's an adult man, aged roughly between thirty and fifty. It's hard to know how long he was in the water.'

Melody managed an 'OK', though wasn't sure what else to say. She opened her eyes for long enough to recognise Burgess was heading in the same direction Lori had gone.

'Are we going to Duncan?' Melody asked, closing her eyes again.

'Nanaimo,' Burgess replied. 'It's about an hour from here – but the facilities are much better than anything we have. The autopsy's happening this morning but we're allowed to view the body as long as nobody touches anything. It might help if we can identify the person before, um...'

Melody didn't want him to finish, and he seemed to realise that. She was already picturing Evan's funeral, and having to organise it herself. She would have to tell everyone he was the love of her life, because that's what his parents would want. She could hardly say he was dead, then drop the added bombshell that he was a cheater. It wouldn't be fair to them, or Sam, to destroy his memory, regardless of who he actually was.

Then there was Chloe. Melody obviously wouldn't invite her – but what if that young face with the blonde hair turned up at the back anyway? She'd be wearing black, trying to hide among the crowd, but Melody would see her.

What would Melody say? Would she pretend she didn't know anything? Would she confront the younger woman?

Twenty.

Melody couldn't get past her fiancé sleeping with someone half her age. How was she supposed to cope with it?

As those thoughts brewed, Melody opened her eyes intermittently to watch the road. There were a lot of trees, then vast fields stretching to mountains on the horizon. Occasional glimpses of ocean on the other side were intermingled with blink-and-miss villages. They stopped at a crossroads with a McDonald's on one corner and a Dairy Queen on the other, then continued on past a small airport and rickety wooden roadside stands selling produce.

Everything felt so open, so big. Endless opportunity but endless places to disappear. How could any missing person ever be found?

Except Evan hadn't disappeared. He'd barely made it from the lake. He'd been right there all along.

Melody wondered what might have happened to him. Perhaps that girl was on the road because she'd been at the lake with someone who'd got into trouble? Evan had gone to help and somehow fallen into the water, and... who knew?

Her fiancé knew how to swim in the way most people got around in water. People learned at school, bobbed around on holiday, and that was about it. Evan ran and cycled but actual swimming had never been his thing.

The police car bumped over a pothole, bringing Melody back to the journey. There was a billboard for the zipline place Sam was going the next day, though Melody couldn't remember if it was the same one to which she'd been years before. Cows roamed a wide yellow field, then Burgess drove them up a hill to a row of four or five places, all selling diggers.

The officer had gone quiet, which was fine by Melody.

They passed a sign to turn off for the ferry to the mainland, then there was the sign for Nanaimo itself. There were more vehicles now, shuttling from traffic light to traffic light. Two lanes to everywhere but nobody moving.

Eventually, Burgess pulled into an unmarked car park at the back of an anonymous building. Moss was growing through the tarmac, with a bulging black bin bag dumped in a corner.

Burgess asked if Melody was OK and then he took her up a set of echoing metal steps to an unmarked back door, where he pressed a button and waited. Seconds later, there was a buzz and the door clicked open.

There was an air of disorder inside. First a waiting room of sorts, then someone in a suit, then a person in a white coat.

Burgess did the talking, showing his ID, as if the giant 'POLICE' on his vest didn't give the game away.

Burgess told her he was going to check everything was ready, before disappearing through a door.

This was it.

Thirteen years of being in a relationship had led Melody to sitting in a gloomy corridor a short distance from a humming vending machine. The chair was slightly too high, leaving her feet off the ground as she shuffled to get comfortable. She eyed the contents of the machine, wondering what a Mr Big chocolate bar was. There was something called a Caramilk, too. But thoughts of sweets led her to the Snickers bars that sat on the high shelf of the cupboard next to the fridge. It was Evan's emergency chocolate for when he'd been on a long run and needed a sugar hit. He'd put them up high to avoid Sam finding them.

And now... Melody was about to see him for the final time.

They'd met on an app, before *everyone* met on apps. It was such a new thing at the time that they'd been slightly embarrassed to tell others how it had happened. After messaging for a while, they had ended up playing crazy golf as a first date. That's how they told everyone they met. It was an accident, as they'd planned to watch a Sherlock Holmes movie at the cinema, only for a pipe to burst and the place to flood. They had wandered around the complex, and considered going ice skating. Crazy golf felt like a better idea, largely because the risk of falling on their arses as teenagers flew past was lower.

Melody didn't remember who won at golf, or even whether they bothered counting the score. Her biggest memory was how much they laughed. They took ages to go around, letting other groups play past them. Then, at the end, they ate terrible burgers in the attached café, filled with bolted-down plastic tables. They had eaten far better meals since, in far grander places, but they always made a point of playing crazy golf wherever they ended up visiting. Evan had already found one they could go to somewhere on the island, though Melody couldn't remember where it was.

And now... thirteen years of memories destroyed because Evan was the cliché she never thought he could be.

Chloe was *twenty*.

Melody could not get past that fact.

She wondered how Chloe would find out what had happened to Evan. There would probably be some sort of story back in the UK, but would the young woman be following the local news? Melody couldn't imagine a scenario in which she would call the other woman to tell her.

And how could Melody ever tell Sam that his dad was not only missing but that he was gone? Would she use the word 'dead'? Sam had been so young when Melody's mum, his grandmother, had died, that it hadn't affected him. He had barely known her, so hadn't grieved. This would be the first big death in his life – and he was at such a vulnerable age. This was to be his final year at primary school.

Then she would have to contact Evan's parents on their cruise. Should she wait until they were on land again? Or let them know as soon as possible? Either decision felt wrong.

How could Melody make all those decisions herself? There were so many people to tell – and that was before she had to contact the bank about their joint account and the mortgage. The thought had occurred before – but it felt so real now. So close. She would have to start that afternoon, while in a different country.

How did people do this sort of thing?

The door clicked and Melody stood as Constable Burgess emerged. 'We're all ready,' he said grimly. They waited together under the gloomy lighting for a moment as he blocked the door. 'Have you ever seen a body before?' he asked.

'No,' Melody replied.

It sounded as if he'd expected that. How many people would ever answer 'yes'?

'The room will be empty, other than us,' he explained. 'The body is on a table. All you have to do is walk in and say if it's Evan. You don't have to wait around if you don't want to. If you choose to leave, that doesn't have to be final. If you want to see the body again at a later day or time, that can be arranged.'

He spoke calmly, as if it had all been rehearsed – which it probably had.

'I get it,' Melody replied. From nowhere, a wave of calm had washed across her. She was ready to see Evan's body. At least there would be an answer for what had happened. Knowing was better than not.

'Are you ready?' Burgess asked.

'Yes,' Melody replied – and so the constable opened the door.

TWENTY-EIGHT

A red and white Canadian maple leaf flag hung limply against the pole as Melody sat on the bench underneath. There wasn't a lot of wind around, leaving the area baking from another day of unbroken sun.

Melody eyed the pagoda across the way, with its pointed tip and wooden beams. Shawnigan Community Cemetery was different from the moss-covered churchyards back at home. From certain angles, it looked like a large, empty, green field with the flag in the corner, and the pagoda somewhere near the middle. At a closer look, there were hundreds of gravestones – except they were all flat to the ground. Narrow gravel paths weaved around the stones, making it feel almost like a country house maze.

'Is this quiet enough?' Lori asked.

'It's so peaceful,' Melody replied.

She occasionally visited the grave of her mum, which was hidden among a mass of other stones at a church in her home-town. Neither Melody nor her mother had ever been religious, let alone regular church-goers, so it had cost a premium for the spot. Melody always felt out of place when visiting, as if her mum should have been buried somewhere relevant to her life. Not that she'd told her dad such a thing.

But this... was different. There was so much green and so much space. It didn't feel morbid at all.

'We can go somewhere else if you prefer?' Lori replied. 'Sometimes I come here when I need the quiet.'

Melody understood that. She could hear the gentlest hum of a boat from the lake – and that was about it.

'I found messages on Evan's phone,' Melody said. Lori waited, probably anticipating what was to come. 'He's been having an affair with a twenty-year-old.'

Lori let out a long breath. 'I'm so sorry to hear that,' she replied.

'I don't know who else to tell. My dad would hit the roof – and my sister's enjoying the holiday with her husband.'

'Enjoying' wasn't really the correct word for that *exact* moment, given her mushrooms-related come-down. It was more of a general point.

'Do you want to talk about it?' Lori asked.

'No.' Melody needed a moment, then: 'Maybe. Not today. I just wanted someone else to know.'

'I get that.'

They sat for a few moments, staring across the stones and the grass towards the fence on the furthest side. It felt as if they were the only two people anywhere nearby.

'I had to identify two bodies over the years,' Lori said. 'The first could've been Brent. It looked a bit like him. Same age, more or less. Same height and build. It turned out the guy had been trail running, then tripped and hit his head on a rock. He was found by a hiker and they had to airlift him off the mountain. That was about a month after Brent disappeared.'

'Did they find out who he was?'

'A tourist from the mainland. He was on a ten-day trip here

and his family didn't know he was missing until he'd already been dead a week.'

It was such a bleak picture.

'The other one was IDing clothes,' Lori added. 'The man had been in the woods for a long time and they said there wasn't much left of the body. That was another hiker. I think he was a tourist as well.'

That sounded even grimmer than the first account.

'I'd never seen a dead body before today,' Melody said. 'I'd sort of braced myself for it to be Evan – and then, when I got in there, it wasn't.'

She looked out at the gravestones again, not really seeing them.

'It was a man with dark hair and about the same height – but not him. The officer was like, "Do you recognise him?" and I almost said "Yes", because I'd been so ready for it.'

'How did you feel afterwards?' Lori asked.

'I don't know how to describe it. Kind of... disappointed, I suppose – but that's the wrong word. Maybe disappointed I still don't know what's going on? But also glad it wasn't him, because it means he's still out there somewhere. Sort of happy and sad...?'

'The Germans probably have a word for it,' Lori said.

They sat for another minute or so. A pair of birds were chirping to one another from different trees and Melody wondered why one didn't fly across to the other.

'Brent has a grave here,' Lori said, breaking the silence. 'There's no body but enough time had passed. I asked Alice what she wanted. One of her school friends has a grandparent buried here, so I think she had it in her head because of that. But it costs about six thousand dollars for a stone here. Can you believe that?'

She sounded outraged.

'How did you afford it?' Melody asked.

'Someone at the school set up a bottle drive and community yard sale. Everyone helped out here and there – plus we ended up getting a bit of a discount from the engravers.'

'Does Alice come often?'

'Maybe once a month? Sometimes, she asks if I'll bring her and then I wait while she sits by his stone and has a conversation.'

It was hard for Melody not to picture Sam as Lori said that. Is that how he would handle things if it came down to it? He'd sit next to his father's gravestone and tell him what he'd been getting up to at school? About who'd beaten Everton at the weekend?

Lori asked if Melody wanted a walk and, together, they ambled around the path. She pointed out Brent's stone – and it was as unremarkable as the others, except that the grass had been tidily clipped around the edges.

They were almost at the exit when Melody stopped and did a double take at the stone marked 'Grace Dewar'. It somehow felt wrong that the death of somebody so young could result in the same shape and size stone as everybody else. There was something comforting in the sense of everyone being equal, all lives being of uniform worth, and yet that poor girl had been so young.

Melody stopped and Lori almost bumped into her as the other woman turned to take in the stone.

'I met the hit-and-run driver's daughter by accident,' Melody said.

'Starla?'

It probably shouldn't have been a surprise that her name was known – but Melody still felt a judder of surprise at the way everyone knew everyone else.

'Did you know she called the police on her dad?' Lori asked.

'I read that.'

Lori gulped and then added: 'It really divided the community.'

'How?'

'It's hard to describe. Some people threw around the words "Grass" and "Rat". This was before Facebook, or anything like that – but you'd hear them talking.'

Melody didn't understand: 'But her dad killed a little girl...?'

'I think a lot of it was guilt. It wasn't only Starla's dad who zoomed around the roads, or drove after drinking too much. There were all his friends. Everyone knew they met up at each other's houses, had a few drinks, and then drove home. It's just they weren't the ones driving on the road where Grace was cycling. And it's not like they were the only ones. People would drive home from bars, or they'd go out on their boats with a few cans, then drive home. It was everywhere.' She stopped, perhaps thinking on the next bit, then adding: 'It still is to some degree.'

Melody wondered if it would be the same at home. If a drunk-driver had hit a child, she couldn't imagine an angry community calling someone a 'rat' or 'grass'. Perhaps she was sheltered from it all?

Perhaps she sensed those differences and the confusion, because Lori added: 'People hate being told what to do around here. There's a certain number of people who think, "My land, I can do what I want." There are water restrictions every summer, but somebody just *has* to wash their truck. And somebody else reports it, so there's a Facebook post asking "Who's the rat?"'

'But people can't have been annoyed at Starla?'

'You'd be surprised.'

Melody figured she probably *would* be surprised. She supposed there were selfish people everywhere and yet *surely* there wouldn't be a backlash to reporting a killer drink-driver where she lived?

They stood together for a moment until Melody couldn't look at Grace's name any longer. She'd unlocked the thought of that memorial on the lake, the burning boat, yet didn't think they'd ever interacted all those years before. They had been in different age groups at camp, so the most that could've happened would've been noticing one another.

'What are you going to do about the twenty-year-old?' Lori asked.

They were at the gates of the cemetery now, next to where they'd left their cars. It was around noon and the sun was cooking. Melody needed to buy a hat.

'I don't know,' Melody replied. 'I was thinking I should probably tell the police, just in case there's something in it. I didn't consider it this morning, because I thought I was going to see his body.'

Lori clucked her tongue, sounding decisive as she spoke: 'You don't owe her anything.'

'I know... it's just, it's not necessarily her fault if she doesn't know he's married.'

Lori smiled kindly, though it also felt a tad patronising. 'You're too nice for your own good.'

Melody was unsure how to reply. Was it a compliment? Perhaps that was true, perhaps it wasn't. She kept telling herself to be angry at the right person – which was Evan. He was the one with a fiancée and child. He was old enough to know better.

They walked to the cars as Melody said she'd seen a bear outside the lake house the night before. She'd expected a reaction, though Lori offered a verbal shrug. Bears were semi common in these parts, apparently. Melody's thoughts drifted to telling her friends at home about the bear she'd seen, and how their reaction would differ from Lori's. Amazement and intrigue, not a shrug.

Except, of course, there would be far bigger things to talk about.

'I've got to head back to the house,' Lori said, as they reached their cars. 'I've got a few things to do before picking up Alice. Do you need someone to pick up Sam, or...?'

'I'm OK.'

'Well, look after yourself. Thanks for the message. We should go out for a proper meal or something before you go.'

It was strange for Melody to want to do anything that didn't revolve around finding her fiancé and yet Lori's offer was the first thing since Evan had disappeared about which Melody felt a twinge of joy.

'I think I'd really like that,' she replied.

'Let's book it in then,' Lori said. 'Assuming nothing weird happens between now and then, how about dinner tomorrow? Can you get someone to look after Sam? You don't have to. I know how hard it is.'

Of everyone Melody knew, Lori *was* the person who knew how she was feeling. There was a uselessness in relying on the police for updates. A helplessness in not knowing what else could be done. A dread in that it seemed as if she was heading towards a disaster – but very slowly.

Going out for dinner with a new friend while her fiancé was missing didn't feel like the right thing to do – and yet Lori would understand all those things.

Not only that, Melody's memories of her time on the island had been shattered. The friends she thought she'd made were only there because they'd gone out of their way to pick on someone.

But, maybe, amid the chaos, she'd made a new friend.

'Let's do it,' Melody replied.

TWENTY-NINE

The lake house was empty when Melody got back. Thomas had messaged to say he and Nina had gone out to find 'bland food', while her father was presumably out on another walk. Or making more friends around the bay.

Even though Melody felt as if she'd gone through a full day already, it was still only half past one. She sat on the deck, bare legs stretched into the sun, listening to the sounds of the lake. Children were playing somewhere and the voices could even be drifting from Sam's camp. It sounded like they were having fun, which was one thing. There were odd boats as well, all intermingled with moments of breathless, whispering silence.

It was half nine in the UK. Late but not *super* late. Most adults would still be up. Melody held Evan's phone in one hand, her own in the other.

What are you going to do about the twenty-year-old? Lori had asked.

Melody didn't know, not really, except leaving it didn't feel like an option. Evan might have said something to Chloe, which could offer a clue to his whereabouts. If nothing else, Melody should pass Chloe's details on to the police. But then, did she really want *them* to speak to this mystery woman, instead of herself?

She loaded Evan's messages and then typed Chloe's number into her own phone. Could she really do it?

It took a few attempts, and a full five-minute back-and-forth hypothetical conversation in her head – but Melody eventually tapped to call.

Nothing happened for a few seconds and then there was a long, singular ringtone. Melody almost hung up – except she was too late. A curious-sounding 'Hello...?' came from the other end. A woman's voice.

A *young* woman's voice.

Melody started to say something, though it caught in her throat. She ended up coughing a fraction, before managing: 'Is that Chloe?'

A somewhat confused: 'That's me' came back, and then: 'Who's this?'

Melody hrmmed over a reply. She'd spent the past few minutes running through potential scenarios and yet she was still somehow stuck.

'My name's Melody Bryant,' she said, pausing for the stunned reply. Chloe was supposed to repeat her name in dumbfounded horror. That's how it had gone in Melody's imagination.

There was a perplexed silence and then: 'Sorry, Melody who?'

This young woman didn't know. Evan had lured her into some sort of relationship and the poor girl didn't know he had a family.

'Sorry about this,' Melody stumbled. 'But my fiancé is Evan Gallagher. We're in Canada and—'

'Oh!' came the interruption. 'You're Mel! I thought your name was Melanie. I didn't know it was Melody. That's such a cute name. I've heard so much about you.'

Melody's jaw hung. It wasn't that Chloe didn't know who she was. Evan had openly talked about Melody to this girl half his age – and she was *happy* about whatever this arrangement was. How could that be possible? Who was this person? And why did she sound so chirpy about things?

Melody couldn't help herself: 'What have you heard about me?'

'Oh, nothing bad! Ha! Just that Evan's looking forward to marrying you, that you're a great mum. All good stuff, I promise. I can't wait to meet you and Sam one day.'

Melody couldn't get her head around what was happening. What on earth had Evan been telling this child? Were they supposed to be one, big, happy, weird polygamous family?

The only word Melody could get out was a confused-sounding 'What...?'

Not that Chloe appeared to pick up on it. She was sounding as cheery as if Melody had called her to say she'd won the lottery.

'What time is it out there?' Chloe asked. 'One o'clock? Something like that? Two? It must be early afternoon.'

'Just after half one,' Melody found herself saying.

'I hope the jet lag hasn't been too bad. Evan said it's much harder coming this way than going the other. I've only ever been to Spain, so there's not much difference there.'

It was a one-sided chat between friends now, except this was the first time Melody had ever spoken to the other woman. A flittering thought occurred that perhaps this was what dementia was like. *Had* they met? What was going on?

'Evan was talking about us all meeting before the wedding. He said he'd bring it up while you were away. I assume that's why you're calling. Let me load my calendar. Hang on.'

There was a crackle of something on the line as Melody removed the device from her ear to stare at the screen. Was she being pranked? She tapped to put it on speaker, just as Chloe began talking again.

'OK, I've got my calendar up on my laptop. I hope you're having a great time, by the way. I've not been getting replies from Evan. I assumed it was a reception thing at his end.'

Melody could feel the eager anticipation from the other end of the call. Fingers hovering over a keyboard, ready to enter details into a calendar. She could have worked through ten thousand hypothetical conversations with Chloe and never got close to the one she was having.

'Um... sorry,' Melody said. 'What do you mean he wanted us all to meet? I don't understand what's happening. Who are you?'

There was a pause. A *long* pause. Melody watched the call timer on her phone continue to move. If it wasn't for that, she'd have thought the connection had dropped.

'You mean Evan hasn't told you about me...?' Chloe said.

Melody's mind was racing. She wanted to scream. Of course he hadn't told her about this twenty-year-old! Why would he tell his fiancée about his girlfriend?

But before she could say any of that, Chloe had continued. 'You know I'm his daughter, right?'

THIRTY

'You're his...?' Melody couldn't finish the sentence. Couldn't really finish the thought.

'I thought you knew,' Chloe replied, the chirpiness gone. 'I thought that's why you were calling. I'm really sorry.'

'I just, um... No. I didn't know.'

Melody couldn't get out any more than that. How could the man she was marrying have a twenty-year-old daughter that she knew nothing about?

Chloe must have picked up on the shock, though it was impossible not to. 'Evan was seeing my mum when they were both nineteen,' she said. 'My age, really. It was a holiday romance thing.'

Melody's brain started to click. 'The summer he worked as a redcoat?'

'That's what they said. Mum worked at the pool as a lifeguard and he was one of the entertainers. I thought you knew...?'

Melody mumbled that she *did* know.

Sort of.

Kind of.

She knew Evan had spent a summer working at a holiday resort. At the time, he'd thought that was what he wanted to do – but three months of dealing with the British public had soon changed his mind. He hated it and instead went to university to study accounting and finance. It was quite the switch.

'It wasn't Evan's fault,' Chloe said. 'Mum never told him she was pregnant. He didn't know he had a daughter until a few months back when I contacted him.'

The jigsaw pieces were dropping into their correct places after Melody had previously jammed them all together in the first order she came up with. A completely incorrect order.

Not a mistress.

He wasn't obsessed with some twenty-year-old, not in *that* way.

He'd still lied a fair bit over the past few months, though.

Evan had told her he'd had a semi-serious summer girlfriend at that holiday camp years before. He'd mentioned it a long time back, when they'd talked about first times. Chloe's mum was the person to whom he'd lost his virginity. There'd been no talk of a daughter.

Melody put down the phone and wiped the sweat from her eyebrows. The sun had shifted around the parasol but she couldn't make herself get up to move it again.

'Sorry, this is a lot,' Melody said. And it was.

Chloe replied with more or less the only thing she could – 'I thought you knew' – because of course she did.

'Where do you live?' Melody asked.

'Just outside Newcastle.'

'Whoa. That's a long way from us.'

Melody should have probably picked up on that from Chloe's Instagram photos, except she'd been more focused on the pretty young woman's face. The accent hadn't given it away, either, although maybe Melody hadn't been listening properly.

The dates in Evan's calendar hadn't just been squash

matches, they had been squash matches *after* work to cover up the fact he was travelling half the length of the country to see his daughter. He must have taken time off, then driven up first thing.

It also explained Evan's 'work conference' that meant he was gone for two days after Easter Monday. He'd travelled up on the bank holiday.

More jigsaw pieces slotted together.

'You call him Evan...?' Melody said.

'Because I have another dad. I thought it would be confusing to call them both "dad". Evan didn't mind. I've not properly got around to thinking of someone else as "dad" yet.'

It was the first time Melody really felt the things Chloe must have been feeling. She had lived for two decades before finding out there was another father she didn't know. It must be so hard for her.

And then there was Evan. Melody had been so quick to think badly of him – and yet it must have been the shock of his life to find out he had a grown-up child, about which he had no idea. Melody could kind of understand why he hadn't gone straight to her with it. He was probably still processing it himself.

'Mum's had cancer,' Chloe said, her voice fracturing momentarily. 'I think guilt got the best of her. She told me about Evan last Christmas. I spent a little while searching for him, then got up the courage to email. He said he had a son and that he was engaged.'

That was something, at least. Perhaps the main thing. Melody tried to think how she would have handled things if a twenty-year-old had contacted her and said they were related in some way.

'He did say he was going to talk to you on holiday,' Chloe added. 'I thought it was about me going to the wedding. I thought you already knew about me.' A pause. 'I suppose he never properly said that. Maybe I assumed...?'

She sounded unsure as Melody figured Evan probably *had* sown a bit of untruth between them. She could imagine him alluding to Chloe that his fiancée knew about her, but not exactly saying so.

He probably *would* have brought up the whole scenario with Melody at some point while they were relaxed around the lake. What better time?

'I don't really know what to say,' Melody managed.

There was another pause as the call timer continued to tick. It had been quite the phone call for the pair of them.

Chloe eventually broke the impasse. 'I suppose... if you didn't know who I was, then why did you call?'

There had been a moment in which Melody had forgotten about what had happened with Evan. She'd been so stuck in trying to get into her fiancé's thoughts that the key thing had passed her by. She could hardly say she'd called to confront this young woman about sleeping with the man who was actually her dad.

'This is kinda hard to say over the phone,' Melody began. 'But Evan is missing. He landed at the airport and picked up a hire car but never made it to the house. I have his phone and was contacting people to ask if anyone knew anything.'

There was a momentary silence. 'He's... *missing?*'

'I'm sorry you had to find out this way – but yes.' Melody wondered if she should have said anything – but it was a bit late now.

'Do you know what happened? Was it a car crash?'

'Not a crash. We found the car but he wasn't in it. The police are looking for him.'

Melody could feel her skin start to tingle from the sun, so picked up the phone and walked into the house, explaining what had happened in greater depth to an increasingly upset Chloe. She found herself trying to comfort someone she didn't know and who, barely half an hour before, she'd thought she hated.

It had been an odd day. Bears, bodies, daughters.

As they talked, Melody flitted around the house, remembering that she was supposed to have washed some clothes the night before. She had forgotten that once Nina had collapsed. Her fiancé was missing and she'd just found out he had an adult daughter – and yet, as Lori had said, life carried on. Sam needed things for the camp the next day.

Melody took the hamper filled with her own clothes from her room and headed into Sam's. Considering his age, and some of the issues she heard from other parents, her son kept his room at home in a decent state. Only minor nagging was required for him to pick up his things. His holiday room was largely the same. He'd laid a towel in the corner and piled his dirty clothes there – which made it easy enough for Melody to dump the lot in the hamper.

The bed was slightly messy, so Melody cradled the phone to her ear as she straightened the quilt and then sat on the corner.

'Is there anything I can do?' Chloe asked.

'I don't think so.'

'You must be worried sick. How's Sam taking it?'

Melody needed a moment. She eyed the woollen footballer in the blue knitted kit next to her son's pillow. Melody and Evan had found it in a charity shop when she was pregnant. Evan had insisted on buying it – and their son had slept with it more or less every night since they'd taken him home. It felt so strange to hear her son's name in the mouth of this person she didn't know. It was only then it dawned on her that Chloe and Sam were sister and brother. At some point, she would have to explain that to Sam as well. She suspected he would love the idea of an older sister.

'He's taking it well for now,' Melody said, and she could

hear the tiredness in her voice. 'He's made friends at camp, so that helps. It's easier for him while he's keeping busy.'

'What happens now?'

'It's hard to know. The police have been in touch each day but there's a lot of wilderness out here. I think it's just waiting.'

Chloe was quiet for a moment as Melody realised it was a lot for her, too. She'd not long found her father after twenty years – and now she was being told by a stranger that he was missing.

'I'll let you know if anything happens,' Melody said. 'You're in my phone now.'

Chloe thanked her – though the yawn said plenty, too. It was after ten in the UK and Melody assumed the other woman had work in the morning. She said she'd let her go and they said their goodbyes, before Melody pressed to end the call.

She sat on her son's bed, staring around his room, trying to figure out what to do next. She wondered if Evan's parents knew about their secret granddaughter? If not, it was definitely a thing *he* should tell them, not Melody. That was if he ever turned up.

He wasn't a cheat.

A part of Melody never thought he was, except another part had. Perhaps it wasn't about him? Some of her friends had already married and divorced, precisely because one or both partners had moved on to other people. Someone from her school had already been married three times. It was only days before that Nina had told Melody about their own mother's affair.

Melody read back through the messages between Chloe and Evan – and she could see it now. In the wrong context, his affection *did* seem romantic. Those Instagram comments came from a father telling a lost daughter that he hoped she was having a good time. That she was looking good. The exclamation marks were overkill – but it was all innocent in the context of her being his daughter. It was so strange how the exact same words felt so different. And that those kisses in messages meant different things to different people. Not necessarily a romantic thing, especially for those who were younger.

She *really* wanted to talk to Evan about Chloe.

There was a tinge of annoyance about the lies over his whereabouts from the past few months but also a grain of understanding.

Conversations for another day.

Melody grabbed the hamper and left the room. She wasn't sure about doing her sister's washing – but a poke of the head around the door made up her mind. There were so many clothes on the floor that Melody could barely see the polished wooden boards underneath. It was the old argument they used to have when they shared a room. Nina was the messy sister, Melody the tidier one. She didn't necessarily mind doing her sister's washing – but she definitely wasn't picking up after her.

Into her dad's room and Melody had a sense of full circle. Children had their parents to do their washing for them, to feed them, look after them – and then, at some point in life, children would do the same for their parents.

They weren't *quite* there yet – but the time would come.

She smiled at the similarity between her son and her father in that both of them had created a tidy pile of dirty washing in the corner. Within an hour of arriving at the lake house, her dad had fully unpacked. His empty suitcase had been pressed into the wardrobe and his clothes tidily hung, or folded away. Melody's mum used to complain about that exact thing, back when they were taking caravan holidays. *Can we just settle for a minute,* she'd say.

Except, now, his suitcase wasn't tidily packed away. It was sitting on the floor, next to the dresser, a folded towel on top. Melody cleared the dirty clothes into the hamper and then eyed the towel, partly wondering if it needed to be washed, but more struck by how out of place it seemed. Her father wasn't the sort to leave things lying around, when he could find a drawer to tuck them away. The bedsheets were folded with military precision, the pillow directly in the centre, everything else put away. But not this.

Melody picked up the dry towel, but, as she did something dropped out from the folds and landed on the suitcase. She recognised it immediately.

Evan's missing watch.

THIRTY-ONE

Melody was waiting on the deck as her dad wandered along the gravel drive a couple of hours later. His iPad was in his hand and he initially smiled when he saw her, until he must have noticed the expression on her face.

'What's wrong?' he asked.

Melody held up her fiancé's watch. 'Where did you get this?' she asked.

She immediately saw the horrified realisation in her father's face. He opened his mouth, then closed it. 'Um...'

'You stole Evan's watch from the kitchen – and when I asked if you'd seen it, you lied.'

He took a breath and there was a moment in which his knees wobbled and Melody thought he might faint. Instead, he swayed around her and flopped into the chair on which she'd been sitting. He was sweating from the walk and Melody grabbed the parasol to wrench it into position, putting him in the shade. He hadn't spoken since Melody had shown him the watch. The sudden worry at his condition had eclipsed her fury.

'I'll get you a drink,' she said, not waiting for a reply as she hurried into the house and filled a glass from the water in the fridge. When she got back outside, her father was sitting up straighter. He took the glass and glugged. Melody stood over him for a moment, before sitting in the chair across from him. The watch sat ominously between them on the table.

Melody's dad drank again and then put down the glass on the table, alongside his iPad. Only three or four minutes had passed since he'd got back but something had changed. The smile he'd given her had been replaced by sadness.

'You don't need this now,' he said – which was definitely true. And he didn't even know about Chloe.

'Why did you take it?' Melody asked.

He slumped in the seat, ran a hand across his head. 'I was going to sell it. I remember you saying that Evan gets a new one every year. I figured he'd just replace it.'

Melody stared at her father, who was looking at the ground. 'Why would you want to sell it?'

'Why do you think?'

There was only really one reason why a person might steal something to sell – but it took Melody a few seconds to say it.

'What about your investments? I thought you were drawing money each month?'

She knew the truth before her father said it out loud. The way his shoulders drooped was enough.

'They tanked about fifteen years back,' he said quietly. 'I could never tell your mum, so I let her think they were still earning. I'd do bits of overtime here and there – and was always able to move things around so it worked out. Then, after your mum passed, there was the funeral and the wake—'

'We offered to chip in.'

He ignored the interruption, talking over her. 'I wanted a proper party for her life, so there was that big do at the rugby club.'

It really had been a large party. They'd hired out the

banquet hall of the rugby club on a Sunday afternoon, booked a buffet for three hundred people, and invited more or less everyone she'd ever met. It wasn't a memorial, it was a celebration. The way she'd have wanted it.

Melody and Evan had offered to put money towards it, as had Nina and Thomas. Their father insisted he could pay for it. He'd also paid for his own flights to Canada, plus insisted on chipping in his own part of the accommodation. There was no point in questioning him on that. Paying his own way was how he'd been brought up, and how he'd raised his daughters.

Now the truth was out, his pride was already dented, perhaps irrevocably.

'Have you really been eating lunch out each day?' Melody asked, immediately wishing she hadn't.

He didn't reply, though he didn't need to.

Melody pushed back into her chair, watching her hunched father massage his temples with his thumbs.

'What have you been doing during the days?' Melody asked.

'Just walking around. I stop and have a chat now and then.'

'Oh, Dad...'

Melody wanted to hug her father, though knew he wouldn't want that. He'd never been massively touchy-feely, aside from the odd moment. Him holding her the night before, in this exact spot, had been the exception that made it so special. He suddenly looked so old in front of her and Melody felt an indelible sense of sadness at the idea of him sitting alone in his house, worrying about money. Worse still, worrying about money and *not telling anybody*.

She wanted to ask why he hadn't said something but the answer to that was pride again. No point in making him say it. She wondered if he'd been stealing things from other places to sell, or use. Melody didn't want to ask, not wanting to hear the answer, even as she suspected it. The iPad had been a

Christmas present from Evan, Melody and Sam the previous year. He was so careful about keeping it safe.

'I'm sorry,' he whispered, with a croaky, cracked voice.

Melody reached for him anyway now, first touching his knee, then standing behind him, crouching to wrap an arm around his shoulders. He clung onto her with one hand and she felt his chest begin to bob.

It was too much. He was right that she didn't need this now. Her fiancé was missing, he had a secret adult daughter, her sister was barely recovering from a mushrooms excursion, and Melody's own memories of the island weren't what she thought.

But she also couldn't leave him.

'I'm so sorry,' he sobbed, and Melody clasped her father tighter. They stayed like that for a minute or so until his breathing started to steady.

Melody returned to her chair and turned, knowing her dad wasn't going to look up when he could feel her watching him. He needed the privacy, even as his daughter sat on the other side of the table. Instead, she gazed across the water and it felt as if she'd been doing the same thing for days. The rippling tide stretched deep into the distance, with the narrow shore on either side. There was the distant sound of children laughing again, perhaps Sam, perhaps not.

'When Evan gets back, we'll fix all this,' Melody said, still watching the lake. They could only have this conversation if there was no eye contact. She felt her father sit up. 'The three of us will go through your accounts and whatever you have coming in and out. We'll figure out how to make it work. We don't have to tell Nina.'

That was the other thing Melody knew her father would be thinking. His pride was already bruised from one daughter knowing. He could probably handle Evan finding out – but not both of his children.

'OK...' he managed – and that was it. Melody knew they

wouldn't talk of it again until Evan was back and they were home. Whatever they had to do to solve the problem would have to happen in a single afternoon, or evening – and they would never speak of it again.

They spent an hour pretending nothing had happened. Melody returned the watch to her own case, and then her father helped her hang the wet clothes. There was a drier, though that felt like too much of an extravagance, given the heat of the day. Melody poured herself a drink of water in the kitchen and then, when she returned to the deck, her dad was doing a crossword on his iPad. This crisis had been postponed, in among the breadth of other crises with which Melody was dealing.

She had half an hour to herself, taking a shower and then sitting in the bedroom, wasting time on her phone, until she had to pick up Sam.

The route was familiar now, a short drive around the lake, before pulling onto the one-way system that fed through the trees.

Sam practically collapsed into the passenger seat, exhausted from the day of games. Melody was ready to leave except, before she could reverse, the enthusiastic counsellor waved her across.

As Melody approached the young woman with the clipboard, she immediately feared the worst. Sam had been bullying other children, history repeating itself. Or, worse, the kids had turned on him and he was victim.

'Is everything all right?' Melody asked, trying to dampen the sense of worry in her voice.

'Of course,' the counsellor said. 'The boys have had another good day. I think everyone should be tired tonight!' She laughed as she waved over Melody's shoulder towards one of the other parents, who was about to leave with their son. 'We're off to the ziplines tomorrow,' she added. 'Sometimes parents come with us. They help keep an eye on the children but can also go on the wires if they want. I thought, with you only being here for a couple of weeks, perhaps you might like to join us...?'

Melody's mind was so full of missing fiancés, secret daughters, and thieving fathers that she could only manage an 'Oh...'

'Lunch is provided at the centre. Sam said you might be interested, so I told him I'd ask.'

The glare was too great for Melody to see her son in the car – but the fact it was his idea did make her curious. The truth was, they hadn't spent a lot of time together since arriving on the island. Perhaps this was his way of telling her, without actually needing to do it? Besides, as she was repeatedly discovering, there wasn't a lot she could do directly about Evan being gone. It had only been a few hours before, she'd been picked up to identify a body. If the police had any further updates, they could call. She still felt slightly chastened after Constable Burgess had pointed out the long list of things they'd been doing to find Evan.

'That sounds good,' Melody said.

'Brilliant,' the girl replied. 'Just wear something comfortable. You can come on the bus, if you want – but it does get a bit loud, with all the boys. Some of the parents are driving themselves, so you can meet us there, or follow the bus if you're unsure of the way.'

The young woman ticked something on her clipboard and then looked up expectantly.

'I think I might cramp Sam's style if I come on the bus,' Melody replied.

She got a laugh in reply, as the counsellor wrote something on her page.

'We'll be leaving here at ten, so you can drop off Sam at the usual time and hang around – or come back later. It's entirely up to you.'

Another parent was hovering, so Melody thanked the counsellor for the offer and then headed back towards the cars. It felt odd to admit, given everything going on, but actually having something specifically to do gave Melody a jolt of something close to excitement. She had been zip-lining on the island thirty years before and, though she had little desire to do it again, at least she would get to watch her son enjoy it.

She was at the car, about to crouch and get in when she found herself staring at the man who was about to get into the small truck parked in the adjacent bay. He noticed her gawking, and frowned a fraction, no doubt wondering what she was looking at.

Except it wasn't exactly *him* at which Melody was gazing – it was the blue and white T-shirt he was wearing. Because Melody would recognise that shirt anywhere. The small rip on the sleeve gave it away.

It was Evan's.

THIRTY-TWO

Melody rounded the car and moved across to the man, who was now eyeing her curiously. As he probably should, given a total stranger had first been staring and was now striding towards him.

'Can I help?' he asked.

'Where did you get that top?' Melody blurted out.

He looked down to it, as if only just noticing what he was wearing. 'What do you mean?'

Melody reached for him, tugging on the sleeve until the small rip separated further. He garbled a 'What are you—?' before Melody cut him off.

'That's my fiancé's T-shirt,' Melody said. 'I was there when it he caught it on a branch and it ripped. I bet if you turn it inside out, the label will be neatly cut.'

Another of Evan's traits: the first thing he did before putting on a new item of clothing was to snip away any labels. The T-shirt itself was plain enough – royal blue, with white stripes along the sides and shoulders. Perhaps not completely distinctive but also not common. Evan had two of them, in slightly different shades of blue. Always with the blue.

The man was pressed against the side of his truck, unable to open the door as Melody was blocking it. He was stumbling over a reply.

'Where did you get it?' Melody asked.

'It's mine.'

'No it's not. My fiancé is missing and so is his luggage. I can call the police if you want...?'

Melody raised the phone in her hand, which was enough to make the man hold up a hand. 'No!' he said quickly. 'Look, I found it. I can show you where. I thought it had been dumped.'

'Where?'

'It's not far. You can follow.'

Melody half feared he'd drive off and lose her, but she knew what he looked like, knew the colour and shape of his truck, and that he had a child at the camp. If he did hurtle away, she'd call the police.

She told him she'd follow and then got back into the car, where Sam lifted a sleepy head. 'What's going on?' he asked.

'This man's got something to show me,' Melody replied, indicating the truck that was now reversing behind her.

'What?' came the inevitable response.

'We'll see when we get there.'

Sam grumbled a little, though was too tired to put up much of a fight.

As Melody followed the other vehicle out onto the road, tiny crinkles of doubt started to creep into her thoughts. Perhaps the other man was simply playing along when he said he'd show her? Perhaps it *was* his T-shirt, he'd ripped it himself, and he'd said anything to get the crazy lady out of his face. Or, worse, he knew what had happened to Evan and was leading her into some sort of trap, all while she had Sam in the car.

Melody didn't know what to do. As she tried to come up with reasons why it couldn't be, she was so certain it was Evan's shirt. He'd torn it on a Sunday when they were on a towpath not long after Sam had learned to ride a bike. Sam was pedalling ahead and stopping as they walked to catch up. Then Evan had snagged his arm on an overhanging branch and the top had torn. He'd continued wearing it after that, saying it felt a bit more comfortable on his arms anyway. Melody teased that he didn't have the biceps to pull it off.

Except there it now was, being worn by somebody else. Evan's favourite blue.

The other driver led them first back towards the lake house but then, instead of turning right to follow the road around the lake, he turned left. The route quickly became a bumpy pothole-ridden stretch of tarmac, with signs for the trestle bridge. They had only been on it a minute when the wall of trees swallowed the gentle stretch of houses. From nowhere, it suddenly felt very remote.

Melody's edging sense of worry continued as the road split and, instead of continuing on the rumbling tarmac, the vehicle in front indicated and turned onto what was very much a dirt track. Yellow signs urged caution, and Melody heard that little voice in her head telling her to turn back. This was the part of the horror movie where every sane person changed their mind and backed away. Except she was already too deep, following the man wearing her fiancé's top.

In seconds, the track was only wide enough for a single vehicle. The truck in front had slowed as it bumped and bounded over the divots – though Melody's car fared worse. She vaguely remembered something in the rental agreement about not taking it off road, though it was a bit late now.

'Where are we going?' Sam asked, his voice a mix of curious concern.

'This man's helping us,' Melody said.

'What with?'

She didn't answer that, though Sam didn't sink back into the seat. He pressed against the seatbelt, looking from side to side as overhanging branches and bushes smacked both sides of the car.

Melody worried for Sam but told herself the man in front also had a child in his vehicle. Wherever they were going couldn't be too dangerous. Couldn't be a trap.

Could it?

She carried on anyway. They jumbled past pull-in points, riding the rollercoaster of the dirt trail.

'How far is it?' Sam asked.

'I don't know.'

The worry in his voice was obvious. Her neck was sore from the jolting vehicle and, in front, she couldn't see much more than the dusty fog being sprayed.

Sam bounced around, coughing and grunting with each movement. Melody eased off the accelerator, allowing the truck to put a bit of distance between them, before worrying that she'd lose him. She had no idea where they were.

And then, as tiny rocks dinked off the paintwork, as the haze of dirt from the truck up ahead spread wider and taller, the other driver pulled into one of the passing points. The film of clamouring sand was so thick that Melody was almost past the vehicle when she realised he'd stopped, quickly braking and sliding in behind. It took a few seconds for the fog to settle, for the stones to stop pinging. Spindly, needled branches scratched at the passenger-side window, separated from Sam's face only by the glass.

Melody could barely see much of anything before, suddenly, the man in the blue T-shirt was at the side of her car. Except he wasn't wearing the top any longer. He was shirtless, offering the balled-up garment to her as Melody climbed out of the car. She almost stepped away, baffled by the gesture.

He nodded past where they'd stopped, onwards along the

trail. 'There's a dirt bike rental place up there,' he said, not meeting Melody's eye. 'You'll see the sign. Instead of turning into the bike place on your left, look to your right. You'll see it.'

'See what?'

The man tossed the shirt onto Melody's driver's seat and turned to go.

'You'll see it,' he repeated, not waiting around for the conversation.

His truck was still idling – and Melody turned her head as he crunched it around in a semicircle. Dust started to rise as she slipped back into the car and slammed the door, watching as he turned around in three attempts. A moment later and he hurtled out of sight, heading back the way they'd come.

Sam had the T-shirt in his hands, turning it over and over. 'Is this Dad's?' he asked.

'I think so.'

'Why did that man have it?' His confusion was impossible to miss.

'I don't know. That's hopefully what we're going to find out.'

Sam strained against his seatbelt, trying to look in the direction the truck had headed.

Melody checked her phone and the zero bars of reception. They hadn't been driving for *too* long but it was enough for the isolation to have set in. Without the truck in front, it was suddenly very, very quiet.

'Where are we?' Sam asked.

Melody hesitated, largely because she wasn't sure what to say. 'Not far from camp,' she replied – which was kind of true in the sense they were maybe fifteen minutes away. Also not true.

She continued along the sand trail, taking it slower and trying to avoid the worst of the holes. Melody had no idea what she'd do if something bigger barrelled the other way, though hoped they'd be taking it as steadily as she was.

With no cloud of dust in front, Melody felt slightly more comfortable. It was still a driving experience she'd never had before; one she wasn't keen to have again. Branches continued to scrape at the body work as the sun almost disappeared behind the overgrown trees.

It was another minute until Melody spotted the small sign that read a simple 'x-bikes', with an arrow pointing left. It had been painted on a square of rotting plywood that was resting against a tree a fraction off the trail. She pulled to the side, squeezing into the verge and leaving just about room for someone to pass, before stopping the car.

'Wait here,' she told Sam, ignoring his protest as she climbed out of the car and onto the trail. Her legs were filthy with yellowy-grey dust and, as Melody rested on the side of the car, she could hear... nothing.

Nobody knew where they were and she had no phone reception.

Melody shivered, even though the heat still baked. Trees and bushes overhung the path, their branches lanky and exposed from the drought. Her top instantly stuck to her back.

Silence.

This was Melody's first proper experience of what Lori had told her. Of what Constable Burgess had said. When people went missing they could be anywhere. A few minutes and there were no people, no phones, no anything. She could walk into the woods and, within a minute, she'd be lost.

Melody stepped around the car, her sandals sinking into the sand. It felt as if there was dust everywhere and she could taste the cloying powder on her tongue as she tried to swallow.

The sign for the dirt bike place pointed left and the man had said to look right – except, when Melody did, all she could see was a mangled spaghetti of tree branches. Was it really Evan's top? Had that man led her out here to stop the crazy, angry lady from getting in his face? Melody wondered if he'd be back at camp the next morning and then...

There was something off the trail on the right. A flash of blue on the bank, hidden among the frail, wilting branches.

Evan's suitcase.

THIRTY-THREE

Melody waited outside the car, next to the yellow sign that urged caution for drivers who wanted to continue. She had already driven back along the dust path once, dropped Sam at the lake house, called the police, and then returned to wait.

It was almost half an hour until Constable Burgess pulled up in an RCMP cruiser. He apologised for taking so long, though did so with the look of a man who desperately needed a good yawn.

'Do you want to get in?' he asked, an offer Melody didn't think too much about before accepting. At least she didn't have to drive along the trail again.

Burgess checked they were heading in the correct direction, and then started bumping towards the dirt bike place, going a lot more slowly than the truck had gone.

'We identified that body from this morning,' he said. 'Sorry you had to see it.'

So much had happened with Chloe, her father, and then following the man in the blue T-shirt, that Melody had almost forgotten she'd travelled to identify a body hours before.

'Who was it?' Melody asked.

'Someone from Ladysmith who'd gone paddleboarding by himself. He was single and lived with his mum. He goes out by himself all the time, so wasn't reported missing until we already had the body. We found his car and board as well.'

Melody wasn't sure what more to say, other than 'Oh...' At least it hadn't been Evan – but somewhere, a mother was now grieving her son.

She thought on that as Burgess continued along the trail.

The route was a lot smoother in his vehicle than hers and it wasn't long until she told him to pull in next to the turn for the dirt bike place. For a moment, she thought someone might have come and taken the blue case while she was away – which made it a relief as she got out and pointed the officer towards the flash of blue, just past the treeline.

'I didn't touch it,' she assured him.

Burgess snapped on a pair of gloves and crossed the trail, then flattened down an overgrown bush with his heavy-looking boots. The sort of shoes her dad would've called 'clodhoppers' back in the day. The officer trampled and stamped, creating a path for Melody. She figured he must lose so much weight every day, lugging around such a heavy uniform in the heat.

'Are you certain that's your fiancé's?' Burgess asked, pointing at the blue case.

'Definitely. He supports a football team who wears blue – that's why so much of his stuff is that colour.'

That got the gentlest of laughs as the officer reached and opened the unzipped flap on top of the case. 'You definitely didn't move anything?'

'No – but somebody has. I saw a man wearing one of Evan's tops. That's how I ended up here. I don't really know why he took anything out.'

It certainly felt odd, though everything inside of Evan's was clean and newish. Or, it had been.

The case was still largely full of clothes, though nothing was as neatly folded as it would have been when Evan packed it. Melody watched the officer finger through the shorts and tops, before stopping as he reached a pile of underwear.

'Do you know what would've been in the case, other than clothes?' he asked.

He was likely making the same assumptions Melody had – that someone had gone through it looking for anything valuable, then dumped the rest. Presumably, with little else of real value, that bloke had settled for a top he liked.

'Not really,' Melody replied. 'He packed his own case.'

'Do you recognise the clothes?' Burgess asked.

Melody couldn't stop the merest of grins at that. They had planned to go somewhere fancy one night for a meal. Evan had teased that he'd bring his 'upmarket' tie, which was an obnoxious light blue monstrosity, with a cartoon pink panther in the centre. It had been a Christmas gift from his mum a couple of years back and had turned into a running joke. Melody told him that if he ever wore it, the wedding was off.

The tie was sitting on top of the pile of clothes and Melody had to stop herself from reaching for it. For the first time, the idea of heading somewhere fancy with Evan wearing that tie appealed. She smiled at the idea someone had gone through his things but left the tie. It wasn't even worth stealing.

'They're his,' Melody said.

Burgess stood up straighter and stepped away from the case. He turned to look in the area around the case, probably checking to see if there were other clues nearby. When he moved back onto the trail, Melody followed. They stood together in the shade, listening to the obliterating silence.

'A couple of the neighbours sent us through security camera footage,' he said. 'We've been going through everything we can today and I wish I had a better update.'

'Do you think Evan was here?'

Burgess glanced to the case, then back to her. 'I'll be honest, this area is rife with dumping. People leave couches, fridges, all sorts along here. It costs to get rid of it otherwise. I wouldn't be surprised if someone found it by the side of the road, took what they wanted, and left it here.'

Melody wasn't entirely surprised. There was a country park near her house where people were constantly tipping fridges and the like.

Burgess crouched to look at something on the ground, before dismissing it as nothing and standing again. 'I'll take any details of the man you saw wearing your fiancé's clothes – and we'll look into it. It seems like a few different people have gone through the bag.'

Melody told the officer what she'd seen at the camp, plus gave him the licence plate of the truck. He wrote everything down, then said he would drop her at her car, before returning to wait for somebody else to come and pick up the case.

Melody found herself wondering about the girl in the road Evan had spoken of, wondering if she had gone through the case herself. Wondering if she existed, or who she was. Was it all a theft gone wrong?

It was a quiet trip along the bumpy dust track, hopefully for the last time. Melody didn't ever want to travel on it again. She wasn't sure how she felt about the discovery of the case. It was perhaps one step closer to Evan but its location did feel as if someone had spotted it on the side of the road somewhere, taken it, gone through it, and then dumped it somewhere else. They were a few miles away from where Evan had disappeared and Melody couldn't imagine him carrying his case this far, along roads with no pavements.

Burgess left Melody at the junction to the dirt road, next to the yellow warning sign. He repeated that he'd be in contact and then headed back along the dust path, leaving her on the empty road with the rental car. She sat for a minute, wondering if they really were any closer to finding her fiancé. Despite everything from the past few days, it didn't feel like it. They'd found his phone, his car, his luggage. Everything but him.

She set off, driving back to the house. The roads were beginning to feel familiar, with the large gaps between houses and the almost hidden driveways that looped behind the trees. Every bus stop seemed to have an abandoned garden chair underneath, with handmade stalls every couple of hundred metres, selling eggs, flowers, and fruit. There were signs for kindling, with Melody assuming that meant a decent number of places were heated by fire.

It was an area that somehow felt modern, yet entrenched in the past. Where brand-new motorboats mixed with rickety wooden contraptions that looked like they'd sink if it rained.

Melody was on autopilot, thinking about what she'd do with the rest of the evening. Sam would be asleep before long but at least she had the ziplines to look forward to the next day. She'd have some time with her son, even if her fiancé was still missing.

There was nobody behind and Melody slowed instinctively as she neared the crossroads, giving way as a truck turned ahead of her. She was almost past when she stamped on the brake and turned to get a closer look at the vehicle. It was grumbling into the distance, easing around the bend and almost out of sight – except Melody knew what she'd seen.

It was the truck Starla had described. The one that had passed the spot where Evan disappeared three nights in a row at the same time.

A boxy, faded-gold truck.

Not only that, there had been movement from the back seat. A swish of golden hair as someone turned to look in her direction.

Not just someone. Not even an adult.

A girl.

THIRTY-FOUR

The wheels spun as Melody wrenched the car around the corner and accelerated after the truck. She was driving stupidly but instinctively, and caught the truck at the next bend. The driver in front was going a fraction under the limit – so Melody slotted in at a distance, trying to keep calm. She was close enough to see the Ford badge on the back and tried to remember what Starla had said about it. Something about it being from the nineties.

Melody didn't know cars, let alone trucks, though the gold one in front certainly looked as if it was thirty years old. There was a dent in the bumper, plus scuffs along the flap that came down from the flatbed.

Other than that, the main thing she noticed was how sensible the driver appeared to be. Whoever it was never went above the limit – and slowed at every bend. It was a big difference from the usual level of driving around the lake, where everyone seemed to fly around the narrow roads with absolute abandon. Not that it was different to drivers at home. Locals always tore around the routes familiar to them, while complaining about how bad everyone else was at driving.

The truck passed the fire hall and the camp, with Melody a fraction further back. Minutes later and they went past Starla's house, then the spot Evan's car was found. Melody thought about Starla's camera, and how it would have captured the gold truck once more. It was a little earlier in the day than the other occasions.

She strained to get a glimpse of the child on the back seat, though there was nothing other than glare from the window. If this was the truck that had been in the area close to where Evan disappeared, perhaps this was the girl he'd seen?

They continued on, tracing the route of the water until reaching a crossroads at the south end. Left would take them towards the village centre – a route Melody knew – but the truck rolled through a stop sign and turned right.

Melody's phone had fallen into the well at the front of the passenger seat – and hadn't been plugged in. She considered calling to let someone know where she was but would have to stretch to grab it. Her dad was at the house with Sam and would likely be wondering what had happened. The last she'd told him, she was heading back to meet Constable Burgess. That was around an hour before. It wouldn't be long until he would start to worry.

She was stuck, following a truck on a route she didn't know, while unable to let anyone know what she was doing.

They continued on for a mile or so, until they reached the wide, open junction with the highway. The truck merged right, which the green sign in front said was the way to Victoria. Melody at least felt some comfort with that. They were on the way to somewhere she knew. It was where Nina and Thomas had gone the previous day.

Still no clear sign of the girl in the back seat. Melody's only glimpse had been from the side but she'd been behind for a while, with no easy way of seeing inside.

There was a steady stream of vehicles on the highway and

Melody slotted in one back from the truck, wondering if the person in front knew they were being followed. She figured it hadn't been an intricate route from the lake to the highway and if a person was heading towards Victoria, there was only one way to go.

The truck led Melody past a lodge, then a campground, before dipping down a large hill and back up a bigger one. The road had seemingly been carved from a cliff, with a wall of towering rock sitting barely inches from the highway. The shadows were deep, the verges narrow. It was a long way from any motorway on which Melody had ever driven – except as quickly as they'd entered it, they were out again. A retail park appeared, with a giant Tim Hortons sign, and then the truck continued up the banking turn.

Melody was wondering how far they could be going. It was already eight o'clock and dusk would be on its way. She didn't much fancy driving at night, let alone any sort of distance. She couldn't even quite say why she was still following. The gold truck, or one very like it, had driven past the spot where Evan had disappeared on the three nights before. Did that mean anything? And, even if it did, was that worth following it into the unknown?

She had been focusing on the road for so long that Melody almost missed the truck's indicator light as it slipped into the lane to turn off. She knew she was playing a silly game, that nobody knew where she was, that she could end up anywhere – but she was too far in to stop. It was the same feeling she'd had hours before, following a different truck to Evan's luggage. At least that person knew she was there.

Melody had been following the truck for around half an hour as the highway quickly became a smaller road. Then they were on the edge of a residential estate. It was like something from a brochure, with pretty white detached houses, large two-car garages, many flying red and white maple leaf flags outside.

Basketball hoops and small street hockey goals sat along the edges of the street and it looked like the sort of place in which nothing bad could happen.

Not that Melody really believed that. Every area had its secrets.

And then they were in a cul-de-sac. Melody realised a moment too late as the truck pulled onto a driveway outside a tidy white house. There were three others, apparently identical, dotted around the circle. Each had a truck in the drive – and Melody had nowhere to go, other than to stop in the middle of the tarmac.

It was a man who got out of the gold truck. He slammed the door behind him, then turned and stared at her. He might not have noticed her following while they were blended with highway traffic, but Melody had trailed him all the way to his front door. She couldn't be missed now.

He was wearing a grey baseball cap and a white T-shirt, plus a pair of jeans – and started to walk along his drive towards her.

Melody didn't know what to do. She could reverse and zoom away, though that defeated the point of following. All of a sudden, she couldn't figure out why she'd done it. A part of her probably felt the driver would lead her to Evan, even though, now, it was such a mad thing to believe.

There was no sign of the girl in the back seat. No sign of any movement.

The man in the cap was getting closer as Melody glanced down to realise she'd put the car in park without realising.

What should she do?

The man was nearly at her bonnet now, staring in a way Melody didn't particularly blame him. She was about to get out, to try to explain, when he reached into his back pocket. Melody blinked, gasped, and then stared as he rounded to face her – holding a pistol at arm's length.

THIRTY-FIVE

The engine was still chuntering but Melody's hands were off the steering wheel, as she instinctively started to raise them. She'd seen videos online of people pulling out guns after what felt like innocuous interactions – but figured that was an American thing, not Canadian. But now, here she was in a random cul-de-sac, staring down the barrel of... a phone.

Not a gun.

Melody wasn't quite sure how she'd mixed things up. The man was holding out his phone with both hands and taking photos of the car. Of her. Then he came around to the driver's window, arm still outstretched, taking her picture.

'Are you getting out, ma'am?' he asked, sounding ridiculously polite given the situation.

Melody blinked at him, at the camera, realising how badly she had messed up.

'I'm filming this, ma'am,' he added. 'I'm just asking why you followed me home.'

Oh, no. He wasn't simply taking photos – which was bad enough – he was recording her.

'Can you stop filming me, please?' Melody called, voice shaking.

'I can't do that, ma'am.'

The idea of escaping off the estate and pretending she'd never followed the man was gone now. If she did that, the man would likely contact the police, who would trace the plate to the car hire place, then back to her. Worse still, he could post it online, saying some mad Karen stalker was after him.

Melody didn't know what to do.

Still the man filmed, not that Melody blamed him... so she opened the door and clambered out. The man stepped away, still holding his phone in front of him.

'If you're police, you need to identify yourself, ma'am,' he said.

'I'm not. I'm a tourist. Can you please stop filming? I'll explain.'

He eyed her over the phone, perhaps weighing up the request. She half expected another 'I can't do that, ma'am' but then, slowly, he lowered his arm, before tapping something on the screen.

Melody suddenly realised how much hotter it was outside the car, away from the air con. The heat never seemed to disappear across the evening. Her mouth was dry and she struggled to get out the words.

'My fiancé's missing,' Melody managed, with a cough. 'He has been since Sunday.' The man continued staring, though his eyes were hidden by the shadowed brim of his cap. 'A truck like yours was seen in the area he disappeared.'

The man turned from Melody to his truck and back again. They were still in the middle of the cul-de-sac's tarmac circle. A basketball hoop sat at the end of the one of the driveways and Melody felt eyes upon her.

'I don't know what I was doing,' Melody added, stumbling. 'It's been a long week.'

The man hadn't spoken since she got out of the car, though he carefully and deliberately slipped his phone into his pocket, making sure she noticed. There was stubble on his chin, though the cap made it hard to see the rest of his features.

'Do you want to search my truck?' he asked. For a moment, Melody thought it was sarcastic but, when he pointed an arm towards his drive, it felt authentic. 'I live right there. My wife and daughters are inside but you can look around if it'll make you feel better...?'

It was only then that Melody realised she was crying. She couldn't figure out if it had come on suddenly, or if she'd been sobbing the entire time she'd been speaking. Her body was suddenly heavy, as if she couldn't quite keep herself up. She rested on the bonnet of the car, trying to gulp away the lump in her throat and pressure in her lungs.

It was so embarrassing.

'I've got tissues in the truck,' the man said suddenly, before striding off towards the vehicle.

Melody bowed her head, hoping nobody was filming, not entirely sure how she'd come to this. It was impossible to deny that she had made some bad decisions in recent days.

The man was back, seconds later, and thrust a crushed box of tissues into her hand. Melody took them and turned her back to blow her nose.

Embarrassing wasn't the word for it. It went so far beyond that.

'I don't know what I was doing,' Melody managed. 'I saw your truck and it was like the one that was in the area – and I just... I don't know.'

She felt the man's gaze on her. 'Is your fiancé the British guy who went missing by the lake?'

'Yeah.'

'I saw it on the news.' He understandably sounded baffled. 'I didn't know they were looking for my truck. I don't know anything about it. I was taking my dogs to the trestle. They love it out there.'

As he said that, Melody spotted what looked like a pair of golden retrievers in the cabin of his truck which she'd convinced herself was the girl Evan told her he'd seen.

'I tend to take them to the same place a few days in a row, then I move on,' the man added. 'I'd say they get bored but I think it's actually me.'

Melody wondered if that was why this truck had been spotted on Starla's security camera a few evenings in a row – but that was almost immediately shot down.

'This is the first time I've been up there in weeks,' the man added. 'All my walks are on my watch. I can show you. I had a heart murmur last year and the doctor told me I had to do more exercise. My wife checks my stats every week.'

He was raising his wrist to show Melody but she shook her head. She had made an enormous mistake – and was lucky this was yet another example of a kind and tolerant local.

'You don't have to show me,' Melody said.

'Do you know if the police are looking for my truck?'

He sounded worried – and Melody immediately tried to assure him, saying that it was her who had created the issue and that he didn't have to be concerned. She pictured his wife and daughters inside, the dogs in the car. A lovely little family, living on an idyllic estate. She had no right to put this man through what she had.

'Are you OK?' the man asked after she was done talking.

'I think so.'

The truth was that she felt mortified, though she couldn't tell him that. She expected he knew.

'Do you want a drink?' he asked. 'More tissues?'

'I think I'm just going to go.'

'OK. I hope you find your fiancé.'

She reached for the door handle but he cut her off.

'You said my truck was seen near where he disappeared?'

'I think so. A gold Ford from the nineties. I don't know much about trucks. I was told it's rare.'

The man was eyeing his vehicle, then focused back on her. 'I suppose it is a bit rare, because of the colour.' He paused, thinking a moment, then added: 'Thing is, I was at an owners' meet-up a few months back. It was up island, past Campbell River. There was a bunch of us there – and this other guy had a truck almost identical to mine.'

THIRTY-SIX

THURSDAY

Melody's father was already up when she entered the kitchen the next morning. His financial issues hadn't been mentioned since their conversation the previous day and Melody doubted it would come up again until they were all back in England – if then.

By the time Melody had got back the previous evening, the house was dark and quiet. Everyone had gone to bed, though the light was on in her father's room. He might not have waited up for her as such, but he'd been listening for her return.

'How was Sam last night?' she asked. Melody had checked in on her son when she got home last night, though he had been tucked in his bed, peacefully sleeping.

'He watched a few things on his tablet thing, then went to bed. Poor kid could barely keep his eyes open. They're really tiring him out at camp, aren't they?'

Melody agreed they were, not mentioning the post-camp off-road expedition, then added: 'How was Nina?'

That got a small grin. A parent's *I told you not to run on the stairs*-smile. 'She's keeping her head down,' he said. 'I guess they'll be staying away from the fruit and veg for a while.'

He laughed at himself, then asked if she wanted anything to eat. Melody told him she was going on the zipline trip with Sam and the camp – and that food was provided. He sneaked a couple of cookies from Sam's cereal and gave her a wink.

At that, and after filling a mug with coffee, Melody returned upstairs to figure out what to wear. With everything that had been going on, she'd spent the past few days picking whatever was on top of her case – except, if she was going to end up on a zipline, she needed something practical. She went for a pair of shorts that had pockets, plus a neutral top and enjoyed the moment of normality. She had lurched from crisis to crisis – but the morning with Sam and his friends would at least give her the slimmest of indications of what the holiday was supposed to have been. His dad might be missing but Sam deserved to have some normality.

When Sam got up, he filled a bowl with the cookie cereal, then Melody talked to him properly about the police finding his dad's luggage. He asked if it meant Evan had been in that area and Melody had to tell him nobody was sure. He thought on it, going quiet for a while, though didn't ask any follow-ups. Melody had no idea if they should be talking more or less about things. Whether her son putting it to one side and enjoying camp was a normal reaction, or some sort of bottling up that would end badly. How could she know?

She wondered what Lori would think, or do, but stopped herself from messaging to ask. It felt like an in-person question, which was when Melody remembered they had arranged to meet that evening. It wasn't *only* the zipline trip with Sam, it was dinner with a new friend after.

A normal day.

Which only made her feel more guilty. How could she carry on as normal when her fiancé had been missing for four days?

Sam went upstairs to brush his teeth, and Melody headed

out to the car to wait. She almost jumped when she unlocked it and looked up to realise she was being watched.

Rick was standing a little outside the main doors of the workshop, a wrench in one hand, phone in the other. He was wearing jeans, despite the early-morning heat. For a moment, it looked as if he was scowling – but then he waved with the wrench.

'Morning!'

It felt too rude to ignore him, so Melody crossed the gravel to where he was standing. She couldn't look at him without thinking of the video where he punched his wife. He was still smiling, though it seemed unnatural to him. A right-hander trying to draw with their left.

'Sorry about the other day,' he said.

Melody blinked at him, assuming his dad had said something about the rudeness. She hadn't expected an apology. 'It's fine,' she replied, being very British in waving everything off. The way he'd launched himself at Constable Burgess hadn't been 'fine' at the time and still didn't feel right.

'How is everything with the uh...' Rick nodded towards the lake house and, though Melody wasn't completely sure what he meant, she assumed he was talking about Evan's disappearance.

'Um... OK,' Melody replied. 'The police are still looking for him.'

As she spoke, there was a scrape behind her and she turned to see Sam emerging from the house, holding the bag he took to camp each day.

'Is that your boy?' Rick asked.

'Yes.'

'How's he taking things?'

Melody turned from Rick to Sam and back. It wasn't a question she felt like answering, not to this man in any case. 'OK, given the circumstances,' she said.

'How old is he?'

'Nine.'

'What's his name?'

'Sam.'

Rick suddenly started fiddling with his jeans, before focusing on his phone. Melody wasn't sure what he was doing as he started jabbing the screen, before spinning it around for her to see.

'That's Cody,' he said. 'He's my boy. Just turned five.'

The picture showed a youngster on the beach with shoulder-length hair and a baseball in his hand. The only other time Melody had seen him had been in the video, when his mother had dripped blood across him.

'Where is he?' Melody asked, instantly regretting it as she remembered what Harrison had told her.

Rick winced a little, though kept up what felt like the forced cheeriness. 'At his mum's. Dad dropped him off on Sunday, then he'll go back to get him on Saturday.'

Melody didn't want to hear too much more about the family dynamic. The fact Cody's grandfather had to drop him off and pick him up likely meant there was some sort of restraining order involved. She was about to say she had to go when Rick called past her.

'Sam! Come look at this.'

Melody wanted to say no – but it was too late. Her son was already hurrying towards them, as Rick pulled open the door to the workshop.

'How d'you like boats?' Rick asked, talking to Sam.

Melody knew her son well enough to know he was too shy to answer an adult directly. Instead, he stared up towards the boat that was on a trailer just inside the door. It filled much of the width of the workshop. Sam's eyes were wide with wonder.

'He was out on a boat the other night, watching the sunset,' Melody said.

'Were you now,' Rick replied, as if it was Sam who'd spoken. 'Did you enjoy it?'

Sam managed a 'yes', though his gaze never left the boat.

'We had a wind storm a couple of months back,' Rick said. 'Put a dent in the hull but I've been too busy to look at it until now. It's a shame you're only here another week or so. It'll probably take another two weeks to fix up. You could've come out with us otherwise.'

Melody was partly relieved by the timeframe, thinking the chances of her letting Sam on a boat with a man who'd punched his wife were slim.

'That's a shame,' Melody said, thinking it wasn't as Sam took a few steps into the workshop. The walls were lined with tools, paint cans, strips of wood, garden tools and everything else needed to look after a patch of land this size. The workshop was close to the size of the lower floor of Melody's entire house – and she was constantly marvelling at how much land everyone seemed to have.

The boat itself wasn't that long – and there was space for something else under a giant tarp towards the back of the workshop. Past that, on the wall, was a calendar with a mostly naked woman on the front.

'We have to get off,' Melody said, talking largely to her son.

Sam continued for a few more paces before turning and walking back to the exit.

Melody had turned to head to the car when Rick said her name. It sounded rotten in his mouth.

'I dunno if Dad told you,' he said. 'But it's bin day tomorrow. If you leave your trash at the front, it'll get taken. They're not normally around 'til two or three – so you don't need to rush.'

He smiled again and, despite everything, Melody thought there was something genuine there. He might well have been told to apologise by his dad – but he'd also tried to be kind to both Melody and Sam. She could really do without her nine-year-old taking too much interest in the porny calendar, though.

Melody thanked Rick and then said she had to take Sam to camp, before the pair of them headed to the car.

And from there, Melody's day was... good.

She waited around camp for a while, before following the buses up to the zipline place.

Melody found it hard to admit to herself, feeling as if she was cheating on her fiancé by occasionally enjoying herself while he was missing. He never quite left her thoughts, and, with the children around her having fun, it was hard to escape the way her own memories of camp now felt false. That bullying of Shannon meant she wasn't the person she once thought she was.

But she couldn't wallow too much in that as she spent part of the morning counting down to various boys hurtling along the ziplines. The soundtrack was laughter and Melody found herself watching Sam from a distance. She let him be himself and the truth was he wasn't like her. He didn't need to pick on other kids to make friends, he did that by being himself. There was a bit of showing off and egging on from the boys – but they were also supportive of one another. When one of their group was nervous about the height of one of the lines, they didn't call him chicken, or goad him into jumping. Instead, they told him he could do it. They said 'You've got this' and they were right. When the boy got off at the other end, he wanted to go again.

Everyone ate on the picnic tables underneath the trees. Lunch had been ordered from a local catering place – with trays of fruit, deli meat, bread and cheese spread across one of the tables. There was an orderly queue as everyone lined up with their paper plates.

It was fair to say the group of boys who'd been zooming around the trees all morning were hungry.

Melody took some banana and pineapple and sat on a table

with the counsellor she'd been talking to through the week. The girl was more than half her age – but spoke with the confidence and clarity of someone older. She also seemingly had eyes in the back of her head as her attention never left the children in her care.

Her name was Emilie, with an I-E. Her parents originally came from Quebec but had moved across the country when Emilie was a child. This summer of working as a counsellor was to earn some extra money before starting university.

Melody never quite immersed herself in the goings-on, as her mind constantly wandered to Evan. She couldn't force answers for what had happened and had no influence over any police investigation. The way she'd inserted herself the night before by chasing down the gold truck had been one of the most embarrassing moments of her life. She would be lucky if the footage the man had taken never ended up online.

As Emilie and the other counsellors started regrouping the boys, ready for the afternoon, Melody began clearing up the leftovers. Her mind was drifting as she half overheard one of the mums talking to another about a classic car meet-up they were going to that weekend. There was something about how they expected a big turn-out – but Melody had stopped listening. She had been so riddled with shame the night before that she'd tried to forget much of what had happened in the cul-de-sac. Except the man had mentioned something about a truck owners' meet-up.

Melody finished collecting the dirty plates and then found her phone. She typed 'Ford truck meet-up Vancouver Island' into Google.

There was a Facebook group with a similar title, so Melody clicked into it.

People *really* liked their trucks on Vancouver Island.

She did a lot of scrolling, skipping past seemingly thousands of more or less identical photos of people standing in front of gleaming vehicles.

Back and back until Melody found a gallery from some sort of meet-up they'd had in the spring. The truck owners had done something called a 'run' that looked a lot like 'going for a drive'.

And then she saw the man from the night before. He was wearing the same jeans, T-shirt and cap, giving the impression that he likely wore something similar every day. He was standing next to his gold truck, which was a lot cleaner in the photos than the present. As Melody looked at his smiling face, the wash of shame flowed again. It was the sort of incident a person never forgot.

On and on. There were so many photos of trucks, all looking broadly the same. Most of the trucks were red or white. There were a few browns and the odd green. All the men were in baseball caps and jeans, like some sort of unofficial uniform for people who liked giant vehicles. Melody felt her eyes glazing, her attention shifting, as one of the other mums filled a bin bag behind her.

There were no other gold vehicles... until there was.

Because there, almost at the bottom of the page of photos, standing next to a boxy gold truck... was Rick.

THIRTY-SEVEN

Melody sat on the deck outside the lake house, waiting. There were another couple of hours of daylight, though the sun still sparkled. The heat never seemed to go away: a summer that was a real summer.

At a little after six, Nina and Thomas had mumbled hello-goodbyes, before heading out in the other car to get dinner somewhere. Melody had barely seen her sister since the collapse. She had a black eye and flattened nose, though other than that was seemingly fine. Her embarrassment was under-standable, which left both sisters with something they'd rather they hadn't done.

Inside the house, Melody could hear her son and her dad watching something on the iPad. Her father had said Sam could choose to watch whatever he wanted, which was a dangerous offer. It sounded like they were enduring Everton's greatest-ever goals, which seemed to end up on repeat back in the UK.

Melody was waiting.

She'd looked through Rick's Facebook profile properly after getting back to the lake house earlier. There were a couple of older photos of him with the gold truck, though Melody didn't know what to make of it. She'd already been monumentally wrong the night before. If there were two thirty-year-old gold trucks in this area, there could be three. If there were three, there might be four. Melody didn't know enough about it – plus didn't know if it was anything worth taking to the police. It wasn't as if a gold truck had been seen in the area on the night Evan had disappeared, only the three before.

Plus she could hardly confront Rick head-on and accuse him of... what? She'd already seen his temper, plus it was hard to know what to say. Knowing he owned a truck like the one that had passed Starla's felt like something, but she wasn't sure what. And she didn't know who to ask. She also didn't know where Rick lived, other than that he turned up to his dad's house most days.

Then, as she was lost in her thoughts, the gravel crunched and Melody looked up to see Lori's beaten-up car bumbling across the surface. Melody headed up the drive to meet her friend, and Lori stretched across to open the passenger-side door.

'Do you like cider?' she asked, with a grin.

Melody slipped into the car and closed the door. 'I suppose so.'

'I know just the place.'

'Where?'

'There's a cidery called Merridale that's about fifteen minutes from here. They close at eight but don't mind you hanging around to finish up. The food's great – plus they do an apple pie with their own apples.'

That was enough for Melody. She'd barely been hungry in the four days since Evan had disappeared but, suddenly, all she wanted was dessert.

The two women chatted about nothing in particular as Lori took them through the anonymous narrow lanes, probably driving a bit fast. It wasn't long until they were sitting across from one another at the back of what was effectively an enormous wooden treehouse. The valley below was speckled with a kaleidoscopic forest of apple trees. A gentle breeze skimmed through the open window as sun dappled across the flittering quilt of leaves below.

'This is really nice,' Melody said – and it was.

The front of the cider farm had a polished lawn, interspersed with picnic benches and more trees. There were so many apples that the grass was dotted with fallen fruit – promising much of what was on offer.

Past the grass and trees was a grand wooden hall, filled with tables and chairs. All of that hidden down a single-track road that, at first glance, didn't appear to go anywhere.

'Wait until you try the drinks,' Lori replied.

There were menus with a good dozen types of cider, plus food. Melody wondered if she could get away with simply ordering apple pie.

'Who's going to drive back?' Melody asked.

'One of my friends works in the kitchen,' Lori said. 'She lives about four doors down, so she'll take us.'

'It sounds like you've done this before...?'

Lori grinned, which was enough of an answer.

'Where's Alice?' Melody asked.

'She's at her friend's, who lives a little up the road. She's probably there every other night – or her friend comes to us.'

Despite the wooded cabin feel, there was a cosiness as Melody took another moment to take in the view of the valley. It was hard to ignore the despondent sense of wanting to experience it with Evan. The cupboard under their stairs at home was filled with half a crate of cider that he'd picked up when it was three for a tenner at the local supermarket. On the warmer summer evenings, they would sit in their postage stamp back garden and get through a bottle of cider each, while listening to the engines, children, and random screeching that made up any estate.

This was his kind of place. Hers, too. The only noise was a rustle of the other customers sitting at their own tables and talking between themselves.

'You don't have to feel guilty,' Lori said quietly.

Melody turned away from the view, blinking around to the other woman.

'You can't help anything that's happened,' Lori added.

Melody was still clutching the menu, though hadn't looked much beyond dessert. 'I don't know how to feel. Sam's being really brave about his dad being gone but I'm still making breakfasts and lunches, still doing the washing. My sister messed up on magic mushrooms. I had a heart-to-heart with my dad. I can't get past what you said about life carrying on around you – because I figure almost all of that would've happened with or without Evan. And it's the not knowing.'

Melody paused a moment, wondering if she could say it out loud. The thing she couldn't tell anyone else. And then she did: 'When I went to see the body yesterday, a part of me wanted it to be him. I know that's awful. That he's Sam's dad – but I thought if it was him, at least I'd know. I could start figuring out what to do. I could give Sam an answer. But I don't know who to tell any of that to.'

Lori was smiling slimly, kindly. There was, of course, one person Melody could tell it to.

'How did you do it?' Melody asked. 'How did you figure out not knowing what happened to Brent, while keeping up with everything?'

'I don't know how to answer,' Lori replied. 'I just made sure Alice was always looked after. I tried to answer any questions she had, while being broadly honest. Sometimes you need to keep a few things back. It's a cliché but you take every day one at a time. You hope the police do their job, while trying to accept you can't do much about it. You can't search every piece of forest or lake. You can't go through everyone's house, or truck. You can't compare every footprint. You can only control yourself.'

Melody knew it was true.

She pressed back into the chair and again looked out across the sweeping vista of the orchard. It felt like every piece of self-help advice ever given: Only worry about the things you can control. Well, that and stop eating so much junk. Both great advice in theory, much harder in reality. Hearing it from Lori didn't make it any easier for Melody – especially when twenty-four hours before she'd been standing in a cul-de-sac having followed a man to his house because of the colour of his truck.

She wondered if things would feel different once they left the island. If Evan still hadn't returned, would the distance of being back in the UK help her to focus on controlling the things she could.

Then she thought of the empty seat next to her on the plane, where Evan should be sitting. It still didn't feel real.

The melancholy was interrupted by a server appearing to ask what they wanted. They ordered separate cider flights, ending up with eight small drinks between them to sample. Everything on the menu was made with fruit and vegetables grown on the farm. It all sounded great but Melody had barely had a proper meal since Evan disappeared. The only thing she wanted was the apple pie, though she and Lori agreed on a char-cuterie, which they picked at, while sipping the drinks.

Melody told the other woman about the mix-up with Chloe. Not a mistress, instead a daughter. Lori's 'Wow' was an under-statement.

Time passed and, in short bursts, they talked about more normal things. Lori had never visited the UK, though had always wanted to go. There were vague promises about her coming to visit, which they both knew wouldn't happen. Lori enjoyed hiking and talked about trekking through the woods a couple of times a week to seek out high points. They enjoyed the quiet and solitude, the silence and simplicity.

Melody tried to explain how she and Evan would go on walks sometimes, though it didn't quite feel like the same thing. Theirs would always need forty-five-minute drives to muddy car parks – and the constant threat of torrential showers. Lori would simply cross the road. But then Melody could live a practical life by being able to get everything she wanted on foot. Meanwhile, outside of those hikes, Lori was absolutely reliant on a vehicle.

They lived such different lives.

Melody checked her phone when it buzzed, hoping it might be Constable Burgess with news. Instead, it was her dad, telling her Sam was fine and that they were having another evening in his friend's boat, watching the sun set.

And the sun *was* setting – leaving the back of the cider farm showered in a scintillating orange glow that felt more like a hug.

Soon after, a message came through from Thomas, asking if Melody needed a lift. She figured her dad had made him send it. Melody told Lori that her brother-in-law could pick her up. Lori said her friend could drop them all back at Lori's house, she and Melody could have another drink or two there – and Thomas could come later in the evening.

Melody sent Lori's address to Thomas and asked if he could grab her at half ten. She got a thumbs-up in reply.

On a trip to the toilet, Melody stopped to flick through the tourist leaflets, each one a reminder of things she and Evan could have been doing. She picked up one for the Cowichan Valley Wine Run, and took it back to the table to show Lori.

'Did Brent ever do this?' she asked.

Lori skimmed the leaflet, though shook her head. 'I don't think so.'

'I think Evan would've been up for this if we were here at

the right time,' she said. From what she could tell, it was an eight-mile run in which competitors stopped at a series of vine-yards to drink a glass of wine, before continuing on their way.

Melody pushed it into her bag, wanting to show it to her fiancé if he came back. *When* he came back. The wine and the running combined two of his loves. She remembered all the times he'd bored her with talk of various time splits and wondered how the glasses of wine would interfere with all that.

Melody had her slice of pie, plus one glass of the Merri Berri cider – and it was everything she wanted. Still impossible to fully enjoy without thinking about how she and Evan would have shared it. Lori sank three glasses herself, hiccupping her way through the final one, while saying she didn't usually drink.

The restaurant started to wind down at eight. It seemed early but they were in the middle of nowhere – plus Lori had definitely had enough to drink. Lori's friend emerged smiling from the kitchen, asking if they'd enjoyed themselves, and then she drove Lori's car back through the dark lanes. The pair were chatty, both with children of a similar age, whom they seemed to shuttle around for one another. Lori laughed loudly at her friend's jokes and it felt as if she perhaps didn't get out as much as Melody had suggested.

Melody's head tickled from the alcohol. She wasn't drunk, though it was impossible to deny she was a fraction light-headed. As they careered over the bumps in the road, Melody was floating. It didn't help that she was in the back of the car, wedged behind Lori, not quite confident enough to ask her friend to slide the seat forward. As pins and needles spread through her foot, she twisted it from side to side under Lori's seat, trying to get feeling into her toes. Melody figured adults didn't usually sit in the back seat of this car.

She listened to the other women talk and laugh – but it was mainly Lori. She was a happy drunk and a cheap date. Not a bad combination.

There were no street lights, the lanes narrowed, the hedges climbed. It felt as if they were on the road to nowhere and Melody pushed back into the chair, closing her eyes and taking in the rhythm of the engine.

When Melody opened them again, the steady orange glow of street lights had returned. She must have dozed off for a minute, maybe more, but the car was slowing. Melody's ankle was sore from the lack of room but it seemed like they were nearly at Lori's place.

The driver eased the vehicle onto a driveway and pulled the handbrake. She twisted to face Melody through the gap, saying it was nice to meet her and that Melody should return to the cider place sometime. Melody agreed she should, knowing she wouldn't – not without Evan in any case. Lori and her friend then opened their doors, which allowed Melody to wriggle in the back seat and free her foot. She opened the door and almost spilled onto the drive, hearing something drop out as she kicked up her leg.

Lori and her friend were on the other side of the car saying goodbye as Melody crouched to see what she had accidentally knocked out of the car. It had been under the passenger seat and she expected it to be a toy, something like that. When he'd been younger, Sam had gone through a stage of needing something to play with before he'd settle in the car – but he was always dropping things into footwells, that would wedge under seats.

It wasn't a toy.

The face was scratched and there were flakes of dust and grime on the silicone strap – but Melody had seen enough of Evan's sports watches to know one when she saw it. She brushed away the flecks and turned the device over to look underneath. It was chunkier than anything Evan had used any time recently. The screen was blank, likely because it was out of battery. There was a 'TomTom' logo on the back, a brand from which Melody hadn't heard much in a while. She vaguely remembered her first satnav being a TomTom – but that was twenty or more years before.

When she looked up, Lori was heading back to the passenger side of the car. Her friend was on the pavement, heading up the street, under the orange glow of the street lights.

'Are you OK?' Lori asked. She giggled a fraction. 'We can go in if you want? I've got a few bottles of wine, or there might be some more of that cider.'

She took a step towards the house before noticing Melody had her arm outstretched. She asked what was being held, before taking the watch from her and holding it up to the light.

'Is it yours?' Melody asked.

'God, no! I don't run!' Lori laughed but then a cloud shifted across her features.

'So it must be Brent's...?' Melody replied. 'It was under the passenger seat.'

There was a pause that lasted a second too long. Sometimes that was all it took.

'The car's about fifteen years old, so it could be,' Lori said, clasping the watch in her hand and again taking a step towards the house. There was something about the way she spoke. Something about that pause, too. Melody could almost see the tipsiness clearing, replaced by a cautious clarity.

'But if it's Brent's, wouldn't it have been on him when he was running? When he disappeared?'

'I guess he left it behind,' Lori replied, taking another pace towards the house. 'Come on in.'

Melody was thinking of Evan. He only took off his watch because he had a more professional one for work. He never did any exercise without recording it. From what Lori had said of Brent it was one of the things their partners had in common.

But there was another thing. It had been stewing almost since their first conversation, and had been repeated through the others. Perhaps it took Melody's tingling head, the whisper of tipsiness, for it to come together.

Can you believe that?

She had heard Lori use the same phrase at least three times. There was the price of the stone at the cemetery, the description of Rick punching his wife – and then, the first occasion, when she'd talked about how long it took for a person to be declared dead. Each time, it had been used with incredulity and astonishment.

But that initial time felt out of place with the others.

Plus Lori had said, so specifically, that the gravestone was for Alice, not herself.

Melody knew she wouldn't be thinking what she was if not for the alcohol. It had been on an empty stomach, too. She knew that if Evan had been there, and they'd had a quiet evening as a trio with a new friend, the thought wouldn't have occurred.

Oh, she knew, she knew.

But it was in her head now – and she could see it in Lori's face.

Because nobody was as good at compartmentalising as Lori had made out. Nobody could simply carry on with their life while stuck not knowing what had happened to their partner. Melody was living it. She knew how little she ate and slept. She knew how she was crumbling. It had led her to following a stranger the night before.

She *knew* what it felt like to not know the truth about a missing partner. To be riddled with questions but no answers. To go through all that and be expected to carry on.

And, suddenly, she realised that Lori did not know what that felt like.

Which could only mean one thing.

'Did you kill your husband?' Melody asked.

THIRTY-EIGHT

Melody shouldn't have asked. She knew that as soon as she'd said it – but she still didn't regret it. Lori stood a fraction straighter, still clasping her former husband's running watch. She first turned to the house, then looked past Melody towards the street beyond. It was a small residential road, a short distance from the lake. Not exactly a housing estate as Melody knew it – but with rows of large, detached houses on both sides of the road and branching streets. A community.

'I've got to grab Alice from my neighbour's,' she said – and there was no hint of that tipsiness any longer. Instead, her tone was cold. 'You should call for that lift.'

Lori moved around the other side of the car, momentarily swallowed by the shadow, before reappearing at the back.

'Did you kill him?' Melody asked.

Lori stopped again, this time at the rear of the vehicle. The orange of the street light cast her face in shade as she twisted the watch in her hand. It sounded as if she was chewing and her jaw was slipping back and forth. It was only them in the night, nobody watching or listening. Melody could almost hear her newest friend thinking.

And then: 'When you were pregnant and you first told people,' Lori said. 'How did you do it?'

It wasn't what Melody had expected. 'What do you mean?' she asked, which got the merest of shrugs, and it felt like Lori wanted her answer. 'I suppose I just said I was having a baby,' Melody added. It was too simple – but it got a nod.

'Whenever *we* told anyone, Brent's parents, mine, friends, neighbours, he'd snake an arm around my waist and tell them "*We're* pregnant".'

She let that sit a moment, though the word 'snake' had cut across the space between them as if she'd thrown a pair of scissors. There was venom there.

Lori soon picked up where she'd left off: 'I'd think, "No, *I'm* pregnant" – and I know it doesn't sound like much. Couples say "We're having a baby" all the time. I get that. But it was me who painted the living room, so when he told his parents "we" did it, it kind of...'

She didn't finish the sentence, not with words, though the way she scratched her arms made Melody shiver.

'And it was me who planted the strawberry bushes, and the cucumbers, and the tomatoes. So when he told Alice's daycare that "we" did it, I just felt... y'know.' Lori was speaking so quickly now, each memory blurring into the next: 'And it was me who assembled the bookcases. And me who sorted the home insurance. And me who cleared the gutters. And me who gave up my job to look after our baby, even though he told his mum that *we* had been reading to Alice each night.'

A pause for breath, but barely: 'And I wouldn't mind but he made it clear to everyone *we* knew that *he* made more money and *he* paid more of the bills and *he* was keeping this family together. And, in *his* world – which meant the world of all our friends – there were the things *he* did, and the things *we* did. But never anything that *I* did. And I suppose... I think I've done all right over the last eight or nine years. You reckon?'

Lori was breathless now. She had never once raised her voice, even as the cadence increased – which only made her sound more furious. Not the loss of control that came with shouting or throwing things. The steady, rhythmic, righteous anger that was so much more terrifying. Melody couldn't quite see the other woman through the gloom but she could hear it. She could *feel* it, radiating like a fireball. That absolute, end-of-wits rage that made hairs stand up on the back of a person's neck.

They were standing up on Melody's.

The night was cold, even though it wasn't. It was an answer, even if it wasn't *the* answer, even if it kind of was.

The two women stood a couple of metres apart, though it felt like so much more. A moment passed – but it was enough.

'You should call for your lift,' Lori said. 'I'm going to get Alice. If you want to wait inside, you can. The back door's unlocked.'

Then she was off, bounding into the night, head high, shoulders set. Melody watched her go, then realised the watch was now on the back of the car, abandoned and unwanted.

Melody took out her phone and scrolled to find Thomas in her contacts. He would be ten minutes away, maybe fifteen if he took a few minutes to leave.

'She killed her husband,' Melody whispered to herself, knowing she'd never tell another soul. Not that anyone would believe her. It also gave her a new reason to find Evan. The things Lori had said of Brent were not true for Melody's fiancé. He didn't claim credit for the things she did and, if anything, gave her more than she deserved.

Two different women with two different relationships to two different men.

Melody had thought they had so much in common.

Except only one of them was a killer.

THIRTY-NINE

FRIDAY

By the time Melody got to the kitchen the next morning, Nina was in the process of cooking for everyone. She'd seemingly moved past the embarrassment stage after her mushroom-related mix-up and was in the guilt and restitution phase.

That was all well and good, but Nina had always been a shambles in the kitchen. She was the sort of person to make toast and somehow use three saucepans, two baking trays, fourteen plates, six forks, three spoons, no knives.

It was chaos, and not even organised.

But as the sink filled and the run-off pile of pans grew higher on the counter, she did eventually rustle up something close to a full English for them all.

Well, almost.

Their father's 'No mushrooms?' got the filthiest of looks and absolutely nothing close to a laugh.

But for the first time since arriving, the five of them ate together on the deck. Sam hadn't seen his aunt properly in a day and a bit – so he spent plenty of time asking how she'd got the black eye, what had happened to her nose, and then inquiring about the rainbow of bruises on her neck. Melody stopped him in the end, although she would have been lying if she said she didn't take at least a small amount of amusement from it.

With Sam quietened, Nina started to tell them about the meal they'd had the night before. It was something with fish, though Melody wasn't listening. She couldn't stop thinking of Lori's bitterness towards Brent, the way her words felt like icicles. Melody's own relationship with Evan was not like that. There wasn't a him versus her. They were a partnership. Even for this trip, he'd told people 'we booked the cars', even though he'd done it. 'We' also booked the flights, even though he'd done that too. If anything, she was the Brent. She'd found the Airbnb and told everyone about it.

Perhaps that put her in the wrong – but it didn't feel like the sort of thing to kill over.

And Melody couldn't quite get past that. She would never know what Brent had put his wife through, assuming Lori was telling the truth. Perhaps Lori was only scratching the surface with her fury, or maybe she was some sort of overreacting psycho. Melody had considered telling Constable Burgess but what would she say? She found a watch that she no longer had, and then had a bit of a feeling after she'd been drinking?

As Sam finished eating, Melody's mind wandered back to the present. She asked him to clear the table, even though Nina said she'd do it. Once done, he went upstairs to check his bag, ready for the day. There was a pizza party at camp to finish the week, so he didn't need any more food.

Thomas and Nina were off to hike up Mount Benson, saying it was around an hour away – and that, from the top, there were views of the entire bay. They had a mini bicker about what they should wear and which shoes were appropriate. They were very much back to normal.

As they stood, ready to head inside and sort themselves out to go, Nina asked if there was any news on Evan. She hadn't wanted to say anything in front of Sam. Melody said his luggage had been found – but that was it for now. She'd not heard from Constable Burgess since the evening before, and figured she should tell him about the gold truck.

It was as Melody was leaving to take Sam to camp that she spotted the bins on the side of the road and remembered Rick had told her they should put their trash out. In the whirlwind of the day before, she had forgotten.

She'd not forgotten about Rick and that gold truck, though.

Sam was quieter on the journey. Melody asked if he was OK and he said he was. She didn't know if she should push further, because there wasn't a lot she could do to reassure him about his dad.

'What are we doing tomorrow?' he asked, as Melody realised why he was concerned. There would be no camp for two days, which was when it would start to settle in properly that his dad wasn't there.

'We can go anywhere you want,' Melody said. 'I'll make a list of options today – and you can pick...?'

Melody figured it would give her something to do that didn't involve sitting around moping – or getting herself into trouble by following strangers. She needed a normal day, or one as normal as it was going to get.

Sam gave a neutral 'OK', so she told him they could do nothing and stay around the lake house if he preferred – although that got a glum 'No'.

She didn't know what else to do – other than spend a bit of time with him and try to be reassuring, even when she didn't feel assured herself.

Melody pulled into one of the waiting bays at the camp and let him out. She watched him head off to join his friends and was reversing out when she spotted Lori's car heading in. The other woman waited, wanting the spot, and there was a moment in which it felt as if their eyes met in Melody's mirror. A fraction of a second and it was gone. It didn't escape Melody that, platonically, they'd had a sort of whirlwind holiday relationship that was gone almost as soon as it had started. A part of her still wanted to believe they were the same and could be friends – but that moment in the shadows the night before had a finality that couldn't be forgotten.

Back at the lake house, everyone had gone out – which left Melody to grab a bin bag from under the sink and go room to room clearing up. Her father's and Sam's were easy enough as everything had been bagged neatly. Nina and Thomas's space was the bombshell Melody expected – and she left it as it was, aside from picking up the empty Mr Big chocolate bar wrapper from the dresser. At least someone on their trip had discovered what one was.

Melody finished putting it all into a bigger bag, tied the top, and then carried it up the driveway, towards the road.

It *really* wasn't feeling like a holiday.

There were two black bins at the front and Melody took off the lids to see if there was space for her bag. She was conditioned from the council leaflets at home, with separate spaces for papers, cans, bottles, and the like. Either things were different around the lake or Harrison was lazy, because on top of the first bin was a wedge of torn-up letters. They all seemed to be from a bank, or possibly a credit card company. Waffle was waffle, regardless of country. Melody figured it was none of her business and was about to dump the bag on top when she realised the name on the letter wasn't Harrison, it was Rick.

Which meant, for the first time, Melody knew where he lived.

FORTY

It was none of her business, Melody knew that. But she couldn't stop thinking of the gold truck on Starla's security footage. How Rick had one just like it, which was surely too much of a coincidence.

Melody also knew she'd embarrassed herself on one wild chase after a gold truck, so going after another was madness. But that didn't stop her either. It didn't even make her call Constable Burgess. This was something she wanted to see for herself.

She was wary of being back in Duncan after her previous visit had almost led to some sort of robbery. Melody still wasn't quite sure what had happened with that, and her memories of it were now tainted by Lori being there. Perhaps that woman taking them into the alley really *had* seen Evan.

It was a bit late now.

This time, Melody was a little further north of the town centre. She navigated the baffling array of traffic lights and the endless stop-starts, before finding herself on a quiet road, with trees running along one side. There were a few run-down houses on the other, as well as a block of flats. Even driving past, the area felt dank and bleak. The sort of place where people rented their first apartments, because nothing was affordable. Melody's own first flat had been in a similar-looking area, on the edge of a trading estate, at the back of a pizza shop. She would wake up to find drunk strangers sleeping in the stairs, because they'd got lost on the way back from the pub.

Melody had put Rick's address into her phone and it had brought her here, though she was struggling to find the exact place. Apple Maps seemed to believe Rick lived in a hedge next to a row of mailboxes, which felt unlikely. She parked and took her phone and the ripped letter with her, retyping the address into the app and hoping for a different result that didn't come.

Moss was growing through cracks in the pavement, as small piles of desert-dry leaves lined the edges of the road. Melody walked up and back, confused, until she spotted a woman with a pram heading towards her. As Melody started 'Do you know where—?', she could see hesitation in the other woman's features. As if being asked straightforward questions might not be common around here. There was such a difference from the lake community to the one a little further up the highway.

The woman didn't break her stride as Melody stepped out of her way – though she did point to the crumbling block of flats and say 'There', without turning back to see if Melody had heard.

Melody realised her mistake as soon as it was pointed out. She'd been looking for a road that didn't exist – because it was the name of the apartments. She was looking at a boxy yellow block: three storeys of small, cramped flats, with cluttered balconies that overlooked a massive bin. A mattress had been dumped on the brown lawn at the front, while a giant cock and balls had been graffitied on the wall above. At least some things were universal across all countries.

It was drab and desolate, not that similar places didn't exist where Melody came from. The type of place nobody wanted to live, except they were left with no choice. Melody could imagine the mould without ever having to step inside.

As she walked around the front of the building, Melody realised Rick's flat was on the second floor. She also noticed there were numbered bays across the car park, one for each apartment. She'd assumed Rick lived in a house and had been expecting to see a gold truck sitting on a driveway outside. Now, it felt so unlikely he'd keep such a vehicle in a place like this. She knew it was showing her prejudice – but it was little surprise to see a battered white car sitting in Rick's numbered spot. It was the one she'd seen parked outside Harrison's house, that she had wrongly assumed was his. Either that, or some sort of scrap vehicle ready to be picked up. In reality, it was Rick's.

And with the flat, the car best left for scrap, and this area in general, it left a dark picture of the man who'd tried to be nice to her and Sam the day before.

There could be no question he'd brought on much of his misfortune himself, especially considering the video of him punching his wife.

That didn't stop things being grim.

Melody could see why he ended up spending so much time at his father's place. Anywhere was better than here. It also wasn't hard to see why he was so angry about his life.

But still something rankled about the Facebook photos of Rick with that gold Ford. She wondered if he'd borrowed it – except he had seemed so proud in the photos. People didn't look like that for somebody else's things.

Either way, the truck wasn't at his flat, and Melody couldn't quite figure out why she'd come. It felt like another poor decision, albeit one that hadn't ended in rampant humiliation, as with the last time she'd gone with a hunch about a truck.

Melody thought for a moment, wondering what she was missing – if anything – before turning away from the block and walking back to the car.

She turned around in the empty road, heading back the way she'd come. She would return to the lake house and start that list of weekend things to do with Sam. There was definitely an email from Evan somewhere with a list of activities he'd found, so maybe she would hunt for that, too.

Melody slowed for a zebra crossing, watching as two women in leggings vaped their way across. She edged to go but then pushed hard on the brakes as someone stepped out from behind a lamp post and hurried onto the road. The man was already halfway across when Melody realised who it was. He was staring at his phone, head down, not looking to see who'd given way – which was probably a good thing as Melody didn't have a good reason for being outside his apartment.

Rick stumbled over the kerb as he finished crossing – but, by the time he'd turned around to curse at himself, Melody had already sped away.

FORTY-ONE

Melody was back in the kitchen of the lake house when she found the crisp packet hidden under the fruit bowl. She went to put it in the bin, before realising this was one she hadn't emptied earlier.

Lori had been right about the life continuing on thing. Melody thought the most traumatic thing to ever happen to her would involve significantly less clothes-washing and bin-emptying – but here she was.

For the second time that morning, she carried a tied bin bag up the drive and dropped it into the container. This time, she didn't bother hunting through the scraps of paper – which was partly because paint spray cans had been left on top.

Melody turned and started back to the lake house. She was at the corner of the main house, watching the trees sway at the far side of the property when she remembered Harrison had told her he was going to be trimming them at the weekend. The potential noise from that likely ruled out doing anything with Sam around the house itself.

But then he only had that silver car parked at the front, which wouldn't be enough to haul away large branches.

Hmmm.

Melody hurried back to the bin at the front for a third time – but this time she knew what she was looking for. She'd seen it moments before, though her brain hadn't quite processed things. It wasn't only that she had seen paint cans in the bin... it's that the colour on the lids was gold.

Back at the lake house and there was no gold truck. Melody would have seen it earlier in the week if there was. The workshop was taken up with the boat with which Sam had been so enthralled, yet, if Rick *did* have a pride and joy, wasn't this the best place for it? It couldn't be at his own place.

But Melody had seen something the day before. She'd thought nothing of it at the time, barely paying it any attention, because she was more focused on her son. She didn't mind him being interested in a boat, she sort of minded him seeing the calendar with the naked women, she *definitely* minded him being interested in Rick.

Melody stood in the middle of the gravel drive, turning slowly in a circle. There was nobody by the lake or on the deck. She couldn't see anyone at the main house, which wasn't a surprise. It was only the lights inside in the evening that let her know someone was home.

With no hint of movement, Melody moved across to the workshop. Since arriving on Saturday, she'd more or less ignored the structure, figuring it was nothing to do with her. Since Evan had disappeared, she'd had bigger things to worry about anyway.

Now, she creaked the large wooden door open and stepped inside. The boat still sat at the front, marooned on the trailer, with the thunderous dent clear on the side. Melody ignored that and continued towards the back where the calendar with the naked woman was pinned to the wall. In front of it sat something large, covered with the giant olive green tarp she'd seen the previous morning.

At the time, she'd been focused on Sam, now it was only her.

Near the doors, Melody hadn't noticed anything – but inside, the smell of paint was strong at the back of the workshop.

Melody knew what was under the tarp without having to look. If she had paid a little more attention the day before, she might have figured it out then. She moved to the furthest end of the workshop, where benches lined the far wall. Tools were hanging in meticulous order from hooks, and paint cans were stacked tidily in the corner, like a display of baked beans in a supermarket.

And there it was.

The tarp itself was only covering the front part of the truck, with the back exposed, the tailgate down, bed exposed. The smell of paint was stronger still, with a freshly sprayed golden patch on the back wing, near the Ford badge.

Rick had said the boat had been in the workshop for a couple of months, since a wind storm, but it was on a trailer. Easy enough to wheel back and forth to allow the truck to leave.

Melody thought on that – because they had been at the house on Sunday evening and not noticed a truck coming and going. Except, maybe the truck *hadn't* been in the workshop to begin with. It might have been put there while she and Thomas were out looking for Evan. Sam had been in bed, with her dad and Nina waiting for Melody to get back. Maybe they'd seen a truck being put in the workshop and thought nothing of it. Or not seen it at all if they were in a different part of the lake house? Or it had been put there at a time when everybody was out on the Monday?

There would have been plenty of opportunities for somebody to drive the truck away, and drive it back again, without any of them noticing.

Melody didn't know whether the truck was Harrison's or Rick's. It looked a lot like the one that had passed Starla's house the three nights before Evan had gone missing. But so did the other one Melody had followed. And did it mean anything anyway? It hadn't been spotted on the night Evan disappeared – and there was no evidence it had been anywhere other than the workshop the entire time they'd been at the lake house.

Except Melody had that same feeling as when she'd been looking at Lori, knowing what the other woman did. It was too much of a coincidence.

She could call the police, perhaps even the more direct number Constable Burgess had given her – but what would she say? As far as she knew, Starla hadn't passed on that footage of the gold truck.

Creeeeeeeeeeeeeeak.

The ground moaned as Melody moved around the truck towards the far wall. A large car dolly was at the side, speckled with grease and oil. One of its wheels was sitting on a grotty rug that reeked of petrol, and was covered in blobs of oil, paint, and who knew what else. Melody accidentally had half a foot on it. She was still wearing sandals and something wet touched her big toe. She reeled away but only succeeded in stepping backwards onto a second rug.

Creeeeeeeeeeeeeeak.

This time, Melody felt the merest give in the ground. The rest of the floor was covered in cement but there was something softer under the rug.

She stepped away from it, which left her pressed against the side of the gold truck. Melody turned towards the front of the workshop, where the door remained open. She should have closed it on the way in, though she could see the lake glimmering in the distance.

Melody crouched and had to fight the instinctive gag at the stench of petrol coming from the rug. She took a breath and tried again, reeling from the sliminess of the material as she slid away the mat and flipped it to the side.

She stared at the ground, to where there was a hatch in the floor.

It was maybe a metre square, made of what looked like heavy wood, with a pair of thick metal padlocks securing two of the corners.

Melody stood tall for a moment, turning again to look towards the lake. It was as silent as it had been since she'd arrived. No boaters, nobody driving past, no distant echo of children playing.

Silence.

Melody tapped the hatch, first with her foot, then her hand. She wasn't quite sure what she expected, though nothing happened. The wood really did feel heavy – and the padlocks were chunky and immovable.

The bench was covered with tubs on which were handwritten numbers. Melody wondered what they meant until she realised each tub was full of nails and screws. She was looking for a key to the locks and scanned the hooks above the bench, which were full of tools and implements. There were multiple types of different saws, plus hammers, pliers and screwdrivers.

No keys.

The other wall was lined with outdoor tools, with a spade, rake, and fork next to an axe – before a row of power tools, including a leaf blower, mower, and strimmer.

It was the sort of collection Melody could imagine a bloke in his seventies having. The types of things that got passed down and down until they invariably broke. Everything was in varying states of repair and cleanliness.

Still no keys.

Hmmmm.

The workshop hadn't been locked, even if it was hidden away from the road. Technically, anyone could walk along the side of the main house and let themselves in. Some of the tools would be valuable and they could walk off with any of them – except whatever was inside the hatch was worth locking away.

Melody turned and had another glance towards the front of the workshop and the lake beyond. There was still nobody in sight, although a gentle hum sat on the breeze. Someone mowing a lawn nearby. Maybe a boat?

A key could be anywhere, most likely on a ring with a bunch of other keys. It was probably in the main house, though Melody had never been inside and didn't fancy sneaking around any more than she already was.

She eyed the benches and the tools again, before making up her mind. What was one more bad decision on top of all the others?

Melody first tried to pick up the big axe, realised it was far too heavy, and settled on the smaller one. She'd never swung an axe in her life and was unsure if there was some sort of technique to it.

Bang!

The first of the padlocks disintegrated into two pieces. It happened so sweetly that Melody let out a perplexed laugh at herself. She couldn't quite believe she'd done it.

Bang!

She missed the second lock, embedding the blade in the wood and having to wriggle the tool to get it out again. Her shoulders ached and it had only been two swings.

Bang!

Another miss. Not so easy after all.

Melody left the axe in the wood and arched her back, taking a breath. The thuds had echoed around the workshop, no doubt making it outside, too. If Melody had been sitting on the deck of the lake house, she'd have heard it. She checked the door again, though there was nobody in sight.

Stop.

Breathe.

Bang!

The second lock fell apart as sweetly as the first. Melody wrestled the axe from the wood and put it back where she'd got it, before nudging the locks away with her foot. There was no specific handle, though a looped cord was flat against the hatch. Melody stretched to first pick it up and then pull. Her back cricked as, first, nothing happened, and then – as she strained harder – the door popped up so quickly that Melody found herself stumbling backwards. She only stayed on her feet because she fell into the bench behind, scrambling to hold on to it and keep her balance.

But the hatch was open. Thick carpet had been stapled to the underside of the wood and a flow of heat drifted up from the now open space. Melody couldn't see anything below, so picked up a fleck of gravel from near the truck and dropped it down. There was a way of being able to estimate height from the time it took to hear a noise from an object dropping. Melody couldn't remember the equation – but the click of gravel on something hard came very quickly. Not a big drop.

Melody peered directly down to the darkness. From somewhere off to the side was the faintest of lights. Without dropping herself down into the space, Melody couldn't crane herself around enough to see from where it was coming.

'Hello...?'

The croaky man's voice echoed up from the dark. Melody almost jumped as it appeared from nowhere. It was almost immediately followed by an inquisitive: 'Is someone there?'

Melody continued to stare into the gloom, not quite able to reply. She knew the voice.

'Evan...?'

FORTY-TWO

'Mel...?'

There was a scuttling of footsteps, a hint of movement, a flash of shadow – and then someone was directly under the hatch's opening. Melody still couldn't see much of anything, perhaps a shape, but the voice was unmistakable.

'What are you doing here?' Evan asked. There was a rasp to his voice and he sounded bewildered.

'What are *you* doing here?' Melody called down, not quite able to believe what she was hearing.

'I was on the phone with you, I saw a girl – and then I don't remember. I woke up here. I don't know where I am.'

'This is the lake house,' Melody replied. All this time worrying and wondering – and he was barely steps away.

'What lake house?'

She was still crouching but her back ached. There was no chance of her knees being able to handle the cement floor, so she sat and angled over the gap.

'The Airbnb. This is where we're staying.' She turned and glanced towards the water. 'I can see the house from here.'

A baffled 'What...?' reverberated up and then 'I don't understand.'

'Neither do I.'

They paused for a moment, metres apart, though it felt like so much more.

'Are you hurt?' Melody asked.

'No.' Evan sounded surprised himself. 'A man brings me food three times a day. He has a gun on him but he's never even threatened me. Just asks me to stand back while he puts down a tray.'

'What do you mean?'

'I don't know. I've asked what's going on but he never answers. I don't even know how long I've been down here.'

Melody needed a moment to think on it. She was still shouting into a hole for one thing – and started to look around for a ladder.

Meanwhile, Evan was still calling up: 'Everything's covered in carpet down here. It's sort of cold but gets hot sometimes. I shouted a lot when I got down here but it didn't feel like anyone could hear me. I sort of gave up.' The croakiness was stronger now, as if he hadn't said anything out loud for a while.

Melody eyed the carpet on the underside of the hatch. Then there was the fact the opening was at the back of an anonymous workshop, off the main road, behind another house. Even without the improvised soundproofing, it was no wonder Evan hadn't been heard by her.

Her mind was racing. How had her fiancé ended up in a hole not far from where she'd spent the past week? As she looked back to the lake house, she could see the window of the bedroom in which she'd been kept awake worrying about him.

'There's a telly down here,' Evan shouted.

'A TV?'

'Yeah. And a bed. There are pillows. He left me books. Even brought ice cream the other night.'

Ice cream?!

Melody could hardly believe what she was hearing. What was happening? If it was a kidnapping, where was the ransom? If it was some sort of random attack, why was this unknown man bringing Evan *ice cream?!* And who was it? Rick?

Melody was on her feet, not wanting to leave the hatch but desperately looking for a ladder. It felt as if there was every other sort of tool, though she couldn't see anything to help Evan get up. She returned to the opening and crouched once more.

'Does he come down from here?' Melody asked.

'No. I didn't even know there was another way out. There's a door down here. I don't know where it goes. It's made of metal. I tried it, obviously, but it's always locked. There are no windows down here.'

The thought struck that, until now, Evan hadn't seen any sort of daylight in five days.

Melody stood and stepped around the truck, still looking for a ladder. She remembered Rick standing next to this truck in the Facebook photo – plus the fact the vehicle had been close to where Evan had disappeared in the days before.

'Do you remember a gold truck?' Melody called.

'No.'

There was something about the reply that almost made Melody laugh. One word but so much past it. An implied: *Can we have this conversation another time?* – which was fair.

There were no ladders on the benches or, as far as Melody could tell, on the walls above. It felt strange that a space would be so filled with tools and yet something so common would be absent.

A minute passed, probably more. Melody could sense Evan waiting patiently below, knowing they were so close. She just needed a ladder!

And then she saw them. There were three stacked underneath the long bench that ran along the length of the workshop.

Melody pulled out the first, knowing immediately it would be far too heavy and wide to fit into the space.

The second was more of an option and, though Melody struggled to lift it, she dragged it around the workshop, wincing from the grinding scrapes on the ground. Melody fought it into position, realising quickly it wasn't going to fit widthways, trying diagonally, and then giving up on that as well. She dropped the ladder to the ground and the metal clanged loudly.

'Sorry,' she called.

Evan sounded cooler than her, replying with a steady, 'It's OK. You're doing great.'

Melody's shoulders burned, her back spasmed. She wasn't used to such physicality.

There was one final ladder that was a fair bit smaller than the other pair. She and Evan had a similar one in their garage at home and used it to replace light bulbs and the like. It wasn't tall.

Melody wrenched it out from under the bench, almost tripping over the largest ladder in the process. As she tried to right herself, the ladder she was holding folded into place, catching two of her fingers between the metal. She screeched with her mouth closed, freeing herself and swearing under her breath. This was full toe-stub territory when it came to pain.

With her teeth gritted, Melody carried the ladder across to the opening and positioned it diagonally.

'I'm gonna drop it,' she called, waiting a moment until Evan replied, 'I'm clear'.

The crash was like someone going berserk with a pair of cymbals. There was the initial clang and then a series of smaller ones until, eventually, a moment of silence.

'Got it,' Evan said. She could hear a scrabbling as he presumably tried to arrange the ladder under the opening. Melody wasn't sure if it would be tall enough – though they would soon find out.

'Sorry,' he called up, after another series of scratching. 'I'm just tired. It's hard to sleep.'

There was another scraping – but then a much louder *clank-clang* echoed up and around.

Evan's 'Oh' was enough to have Melody dropping to her knees, trying to figure out what was going on.

'Are you OK?' she asked – but there was no answer. Not at first, anyway. Instead, there were footsteps from below, the sound of more than one person moving around, and then a new voice. Not a British accent.

'Well,' the man said. 'I didn't expect to see you up there. I guess you should come on down, so we can have a bit of a talk.'

It wasn't Rick's voice. It probably wasn't Rick's truck, after all.

It was Harrison's.

FORTY-THREE

Melody hovered over the hatch as Evan's 'Just run!' bellowed up from above. She knew she could, possibly thought she would, except a second voice came right after the first.

'Remember that shotgun from the other night,' Harrison added. He sounded inexplicably calm – too much like the way Lori had listed her grievances. He wasn't even shouting.

'Run!' Evan insisted – and Melody thought about it. She'd grab the keys, get into the car, drive to camp, snatch Sam, then call the police. They would be safe... except she knew she wouldn't do that.

Couldn't.

She would barely be out of the workshop when the bang would come. She'd heard it in Harrison's voice.

'You can call the police if you want,' Harrison called, reading her thoughts. 'I'll be long dead by the time they get here.' A beat. 'But so will he.'

Melody lowered a leg into the gap, ignoring Evan's 'No!' as her foot landed on something broadly stable. The ladder wobbled slightly as she lowered her second foot – but the frame held firm.

Her fingers ached from being trapped as she continued down the ladder, rung by rung.

'Two more,' Harrison said, and Melody counted the steps until she ended on a carpeted floor. She was in a dark corner but turned towards a gloomy, yellowy light. Harrison was standing a short distance away, shotgun extended towards Evan, who had both hands up.

Evan looked thinner in the face than she remembered. He was wearing clothes far too big for him that she didn't recognise.

'Are you OK?' she asked him, which got a gentle nod in reply. She could see the disappointment in his face. He had wanted her to run and would have taken whatever happened to him.

Meanwhile, Harrison stood steady. He was so calm, so unmoved. Not a wide-eyed, gun-toting maniac. Just an old man.

An old man with a shotgun.

'I think you should both sit down,' he said.

Melody didn't need to ask where. The single bulb hung above a brown cord sofa that was across from a combined television-VCR. A microwave sat on top of a small, humming fridge – while a kettle rested on a square table next to a sink. In front of the sofa, a plastic fork sat by itself on a chipped coffee table.

It was so odd. Melody's first flat wasn't a million miles from this sort of thing – albeit there was a toilet as opposed to a bucket under the sink. Plus there wasn't carpet on the walls. It also had windows, and no big metal door at the far end.

Someone in London would still want four grand a month to rent out this sort of prison.

Melody moved across to the sofa and sat next to Evan. He touched her hand and there was a spark. He locked his fingers into hers and she squeezed him back.

'Are you really OK?' she asked.

'Why didn't you run?'

'I couldn't leave you.'

He smiled kindly and she saw the crinkles around his eyes. 'Oh, Mel...'

Harrison had shuffled a pace or two and lowered the gun, so the barrel was pointing to the ground.

'I suppose I knew it was a risk keeping you here,' Harrison said, presumably talking to Evan.

'I don't get what's happening,' Melody said.

That got something close to a shrug. 'No. You wouldn't. You're not supposed to. That's the point.'

There was a long, long silence. Melody realised Harrison was leaning on a bookcase that contained a pile of old VHS cases. She spotted *Ghostbusters* and *Back To The Future* among the titles. There were books as well, battered and well read. The sort of thing people sold for 10p at car boot sales.

'But you kidnapped him...?' Melody said.

That got a nod. 'You made it very easy.'

'Me?' Melody replied, which got another nod.

She didn't know what he was on about – and then she suddenly did, even before he explained.

'You told me so much,' Harrison added. 'About how you'd first visited in the nineties, when you were young. About the people coming with you now, about your wedding at Christmas, about your son. You really spilled your life in those messages.'

Melody let go of Evan's fingers, no longer able to feel him touching her. It was true. When she had been sorting the Airbnb, she had told Harrison she was booking the place for five people. That her son was signed up for the camp and her fiancé was going to be a day late. She'd asked about the best route to take from the airport and had even told Harrison the car Evan would be driving. At the time, she hadn't known whether there was limited parking, and he needed to know the car. She was trying to be practical.

No wonder Harrison knew so much. Melody was a chronic oversharer – just like Evan said she was.

She wanted the sofa to swallow her to protect her from the shame she felt sitting next to her fiancé. It was all her fault.

Harrison must have seen it. He was nodding slowly, though it felt like he was acknowledging the fact, not gloating.

'I went and waited,' he said. 'I wasn't sure how to get his car to stop. I thought about maybe faking a breakdown but not everyone would stop for that. I could've dropped nails on the road – but it could've got someone else, plus it would've been hard to clear up. Then I figured most people would stop for an upset child.'

Melody almost asked where the child came from – but then she knew. Harrison had told her himself. So had Rick.

'Cody,' she said quietly. 'You were taking him to his mum's?'
A nod.
'But he's a boy?'

That got a shrug. 'That confused me too, actually. I didn't know you'd be on the phone to each other – and then there was a police report about a potentially missing girl.'

Melody knew why: Rick had shown her the photo of Cody on his phone. His son had long hair and, in the flash of a moment of Evan seeing someone on the road, he'd assumed a girl.

'I don't remember,' Evan said quietly.

'You roped a four-year-old into this?' Melody said.

For the first time, Harrison's mask of cool slipped. His eyebrows dipped in annoyance. 'Of course not,' he snapped. 'He's a child. I told him it was a dressing-up game. Our little secret. I end up looking after him quite a bit and he always likes army games. I told him you were in on it.'

So there was a child in the road. Not a girl but easily mistaken.

Harrison flicked the barrel of the gun towards Evan, before lowering it again.

'I don't get it,' Evan said. 'Why me? Do you want money? We have money. Not loads but we can get some together.'

Melody and Evan looked hopefully as one to the man with the gun, who didn't react. If anything, he seemed weary of it all.

'I don't want your money,' he replied. 'I don't want anyone's money. I just want you to know what it feels like.'

There was a twinge of anger to Evan's voice now: 'To know what *what* feels like? Being in a prison?'

The momentary change of tone did nothing for Harrison. It almost felt as if he was stifling a yawn.

There was a time the previous Christmas when Melody had been out with some friends from a mums group she'd been in when Sam was born. They'd drifted between a handful of places, having a drink or two in each, before heading out to find a taxi home. In among that, Melody had somehow got separated from the others and found herself in an alley she didn't recognise. The shadows were long, the lights dim, and there was nobody in sight. Then a man had appeared from a doorway, hulking and massive. He had stared at her and Melody had felt an instant, wild, terror of isolation. Of being in a situation where nobody knew where she was – and this giant of a man could do anything while she wouldn't be able to stop him. It had lasted a second, perhaps less, and then he'd turned and walked off. Just a normal bloke looking for a bus or taxi home.

Melody knew fear – but this went so far beyond that. Harrison was letting them speak and not interrupting. He was answering their questions and managing their anger, all while barely blinking. She almost craved threats and fury, because she understood that. She didn't know what this was.

'I wasn't talking to you,' Harrison said gently.

Melody felt his gaze shift to her.

'I want *you* to know how it feels – and you have, haven't you? Only a few days but you felt it.'

The shiver took over Melody's entire body and couldn't be

forced away. Evan was holding her hand again but she didn't know when he'd taken it.

'Felt what?' she asked, not wanting the answer.

'The confusion of not knowing what's going on. The unanswered questions. You had no idea where he was, or why he'd gone, or if there was anyone else involved. I watched you from the house, rushing around, baffled by it all. That's what I wanted you to feel.'

Evan squeezed Melody's hand gently. He could feel it as well. It was impossible not to. The hairs on the back of Melody's neck were up like a dog's hackles.

'But why?' Melody asked. 'I don't know you.'

That got a nod and a bite of the bottom lip. 'I know,' Harrison replied steadily. 'It's unfair – but life's unfair. When someone drove into my little girl, I didn't know what had happened. Who'd done it. Whether it was an accident, or on purpose. I had no idea. There wasn't even really a body afterwards. She was hit so hard that the driver must have noticed. But the driver never waited around. Then, before we even buried her, my wife had a heart attack. *Bang-bang*, y'know? I had a wife and two children, then – barely a week later, just the one.'

More shivers. It was terrible. Genuinely one of the worst things Melody had ever heard and far too much to comprehend. Harrison had been living with that for decades. Despite the gun and the dungeon, despite the power he held over them, she could see that ache within him. It was in the way his body slumped slightly. The way his eyelids drooped.

It was him.

Melody almost felt sorry for him. Or maybe she did.

'Joel Boyd,' Melody said. The father Starla had reported to the police. There was a minuscule wince at the mention of the name.

But then a shake of the head. 'He didn't kill Grace,'

Harrison replied, dismissively. 'I could've spoken up – but everyone knew he'd drive around after drinking, so I figured he deserved what he got.'

Melody remembered Starla talking about her dad, and how torn up she'd been over what she had to do. How Lori had explained that the community was bafflingly split over what she'd done.

'How do you know it wasn't him?' Melody asked.

'Because I saw who it was.' A moment passed. 'Actually, that's not true. I saw a car. I was on a bike down the road and didn't see the hit. I *heard* it. I saw the car fly past without stopping.'

And Melody knew. She didn't need him to say it but he did anyway, right as he stared into her soul.

'It was a yellow Corvette,' he said.

FORTY-FOUR

Melody had never known the make or model of car they had hired thirty years back, not properly anyway. Her father had spelled it out days before of course. The yellow Corvette, like the one in *Cannonball Run*. A film Melody had never seen.

She could picture the car, though.

Melody felt Evan fidget at her side – but it was as if only she and Harrison existed. Harrison had seen it in her. Saw her very being twist in front of him. They both knew now.

'Why didn't you call the police?' Melody asked.

'That's a good question,' came the reply. 'But what state of mind do you think you'd be in if you'd been around the corner when someone ploughed into your boy? When you have to see... *that*.' He paused. 'Sam, isn't it?'

Evan's fingers tightened and it felt as if he might say something, so Melody *squeezed* him, telling him silently not to speak. Sam's name felt so wrong in this other man's voice – but the image of their son lying broken in the middle of a road was now at the front of both their thoughts.

For the first time, Harrison smiled a fraction. He saw the reaction.

'*That*'s what it would feel like,' he said. And then: 'When the police first got there, I couldn't really say anything. Couldn't *do* anything. I was there with what was left of little Gracie for half an hour. Imagine what that was like.'

Melody didn't want to imagine.

'It was a day later, maybe two, when I figured I'd find that yellow car,' Harrison said. 'There couldn't have been too many like that around the island – not that colour. I spent days going up and down the highway, looking for it. I'd have done that forever if I had to. And then, out of nowhere, this yellow car – *that* yellow car – went past. I remember following and having to force myself not to ram it. Not to smash it into the ditch. Then I saw these two kids in the back and realised it wasn't some crazed drunk-driver. It was this family. So I kept driving until you stopped at a McDonald's.'

As soon as he said it, Melody remembered. They had been on the way back to the airport – but she *really* needed the toilet, so they had stopped a little off the highway for her to go.

'I watched you all go inside,' Harrison continued. 'And I didn't know what to do. I didn't expect kids – but I knew your mum or dad had killed Gracie and I just... I didn't know what to do.'

'My backpack,' Melody said, which got a nod that felt almost kind.

'I've still got it somewhere,' Harrison said. 'It might be in the attic. I could probably dig it out but...' He tailed off and lifted the gun a fraction.

'I left it on the back seat,' Melody said.

'Right. But nobody locked the car, so I just picked it off. This pink thing with a pig snout. And you'd written "Property of Melody Bryant" on it. There was this little book inside, where you'd written all about your life. Your mum's name, your dad's, your sister's. You wrote all about their jobs and how you were into running and dancing and singing.' A pause. 'Bit like my Gracie.'

Melody could barely breathe. It felt like a violation. She had spent so long wondering what had happened to that bag. But she'd never imagined anything like this.

But Harrison wasn't done: 'I looked at that little bag, and your little book. I didn't know what I wanted to do about your parents – and I couldn't do it anyway, not with you there. So I just left.' He took a breath, chewed on nothing for a moment, before adding: 'But imagine what it was like when, all these years on, I got an Airbnb request from a Melody Bryant. And not *any* Melody, *the* Melody. Telling me all about how she wanted to come back and give her son the holiday she'd had.'

Oversharing.

Her name would have prickled Harrison's attention anyway – but Melody couldn't figure out why she'd felt the need to go into so much depth.

And that holiday all those years ago had been so far from the paradise she remembered. Not only the bullying of Shannon – but her parents had killed a child and not thought enough of it to stop. They'd let her go to camp and return to talk about the memorial they'd held for the girl who'd died, hit by an anonymous car, while never saying a word.

She realised she had even heard them arguing about it on the night she had gone into Nina's room. They weren't fighting about an affair, it was because one of them had hit Grace and continued driving. They had been arguing over what to do... and decided to do nothing.

Harrison had decided to do nothing as well – until Melody's name had popped up looking for a place to stay. Talking about the amazing holiday she'd had decades before. Like rubbing acid into a wound that had never healed.

The moment settled and Melody couldn't speak. What could she possibly say?

'I never wanted to kill anyone,' Harrison said, nodding at Evan. 'I looked after you, didn't I? Fed you, gave you books, videos, emptied your bucket. You'd have lived a decent life here.' He gulped, then added: 'Not your *old* life, of course. But decent.' Harrison turned to Melody and there was steel to his tone. 'But you'd have always been left not knowing. Weeks become month become years. And that's your whole life. The not knowing. That's what I've had. Not knowing how things would've been if your parents hadn't driven on. Not knowing what life Gracie would have had. Whether my wife would have lived. How it would have been different for Rick.'

'I was a kid,' Melody whispered.

'You're not now though. Why did you come back?'

'I didn't know.'

It got the merest nod of acknowledgement, though it didn't feel as if he cared much. Things had gone too far.

Harrison motioned towards the big door behind them. 'There's a tunnel there that goes to my house.' The gun flashed towards the hatch, in the other corner. 'I don't actually know what that's for but I think it was for dropping coal back in the day. How did you find it?'

Melody needed a moment to remember. It had been a lot to take in – and she had no idea what would happen next. No point in antagonising the man with the gun, though.

'The gold truck,' Melody said. 'It was spotted in the place Evan disappeared three nights in a row.'

That got a slightly confused *Hmmmm*. 'I'd had a few practices to figure out where best to wait. I guess someone was paying attention,' he said. 'There are always fire drills at the hall on Sunday nights, so I went the other way around the lake. Probably a good thing...'

He'd zoned out but only for a moment. As soon as Evan shifted, his focus returned.

'If you let us go, we won't say a word to anyone,' Melody

said. 'You deserve your anger but we'll book a plane and go today. You'll never hear from any of us again.'

Melody watched as Harrison tugged gently on his beard with his free hand. For a second, she thought he'd go for it.

But then he raised the gun and pointed it at them.

'I'm sorry,' he said.

FORTY-FIVE

The voice echoed from the hatch, bouncing around the gloom.

'Dad?'

It wasn't only a voice. Melody turned to see Rick's face in the gap of the hatch. He was staring puzzled towards them, eyes narrow, probably trying to adjust to the dark.

Harrison was suddenly concerned, stepping away from the sofa towards the ladder, then back again. He lowered the gun, then lifted it back up.

'Get out of here!' he shouted.

It was the first time that Melody knew Rick had no idea what had been going on – and he wasn't listening to his dad. He was already three steps down the ladder when his father managed an exasperated 'What are you doing?!'

Too late. Rick was at the bottom of the ladder, panting slightly as he turned to take in the bewildering sight of Melody and Evan on a sofa, while his father covered them with a shotgun.

'What's going on?' he asked, with a sense of bewilderment.

'I said get out of here!' Harrison shouted, the mask of calm gone. The gun was raised properly, wavering between Melody and Evan, as Harrison's attention slipped between them and his son. 'Get out of here!' he repeated – but his son was going nowhere. Melody couldn't quite see him through the shadows, but she felt him take a step forward.

'You're pointing a gun at two people, Dad. I'm not just going to leave.' He took another step ahead, the light creasing across his face as Melody saw him watching her. 'Who's that?' he asked, motioning to Evan.

'It doesn't matt—' his father started, though Evan got in next.

'I'm Evan,' he said.

Harrison was furious now. He lunged ahead, thrusting the weapon within an inch or three of Evan's head. 'Speak again,' he said harshly. 'Go on. Speak again and see what happens.'

Spit frothed from his mouth as Evan, sensibly, remained quiet. Melody eyed sideways towards the barrel, not daring to move. Barely daring to breathe.

'You're the missing husband,' Rick said – though nobody answered. 'What's going on, Dad?' Rick added.

Harrison moved away a fraction, though the gun remained at head height. 'It's them,' he said. 'They killed your sister. It was her mum and dad in the car. One of them was driving.'

'What are you on about?' There was a confused pause. 'Joel Boyd killed Grace.'

That got a frantic shake of the head. 'No he didn't.' The shotgun was thrust towards Melody now. 'Tell him. Go on: *tell him!*'

Melody hesitated but she was staring directly into the abyss. Her voice was a stumbling mess. 'I think it was my mum and dad,' she said. 'But I was only nine.'

She didn't dare turn away from the gun, let alone move – but she could feel Rick putting together pieces.

'Let them go, Dad,' he said.

'No.'

'You can't do this.'

'I can.' The barrel of the gun wobbled sideways as Harrison's hand shook. 'You should want this,' he added. 'Think of everything they took from you.'

That chill crept along Melody's back. It was right that Rick had lost as much as anyone.

'I *need* you,' Rick said breathily. It was barely a whisper as the pain filtered through him. 'I don't have anyone else, Dad. I messed up. Cody's always with his mum. Why do you think I'm here all the time? You can't do this.' He waited a second, and then added: 'I *need* you to not do this.'

Melody felt it as the barrel wobbled again. Harrison was wavering.

'So go then,' he said, talking to his son.

'I'm not leaving before they go,' Rick replied.

It happened quickly and, because Melody hadn't dared take her stare from the shotgun, it was more or less out of sight. But then Rick was in front of her, the gun between him and them. He moved forward, pressing his father and the weapon backwards. His hands were up.

'Let them go, Dad,' he said, before, without missing a beat, he spoke to them without looking behind. 'Get out of here,' he urged.

Evan rose first, stepping ahead of Melody so that there were now two men between her and Harrison's gun. Her knees were wobbly as she stood.

When Rick sidestepped towards the ladder, Evan and Melody moved with him. Together, they edged sideways, like some sort of human crab. It took seconds and they were at the bottom of the ladder, Rick still in front, shielding them.

'You go first,' Evan said, talking to Melody.

She hesitated, not wanting to argue but also unable to see anything past Evan's back. She had no idea whether Harrison was still pointing the gun. He'd not spoken in a while.

'It's OK,' Rick said, as if reading her thoughts.

So Melody did as she was told.

The ladder squeaked from her weight but one step became two, became four. Then she was at the top, reaching for hard ground as fresh air spilled into her lungs. She blinked at the light, gasping for a breath so wonderful she could never imagine such a thing. She stretched and lifted herself upwards, all the while half expecting a bang from below.

Nothing came.

She crawled and then stumbled away from the hatch, still blinking, still gasping, not quite able to understand all that had happened.

A moment later and Evan was there too, his alien clothes hanging from him. In the light, he looked so weak, so tired.

Still him, though.

He was also blinking, but reaching for her. 'You OK?' he asked.

'Yeah.'

Not really, though.

They moved as one, neither with a plan beyond getting away. They were out of the workshop now, stumbling towards the lake house and the car. Before anything, they had to get their son.

'Sam,' Evan said – and for the second time in as many minutes, it felt to Melody as if someone had read her thoughts.

'Sam,' she said.

She couldn't remember where the car keys were, though figured they'd be in the kitchen. She wanted to move quickly. To get off the property and never come back. But, as she stumbled towards the house, there was another crunch of gravel. She looked up to see Harrison emerging from the workshop, gun limp and loose in his grasp. He looked shattered, as if he couldn't hold up his own weight.

For the merest of seconds, it felt as if he would turn towards them. That the nightmare would continue – except he was done. His head was down and he started trudging back towards the main house. He had only taken a few steps when Rick flew out from the workshop.

His father had gone one way, while Melody and Evan had gone the other. Rick was in the middle and turned between the two sides. It felt as if he wanted to ask them to go but say nothing. To let this be the end of it. Melody had offered to do precisely that – and she'd do it again, even if it wasn't completely up to her. She would talk Evan into it. Make him understand that what he'd gone through was terrible but what Harrison had been through was worse. She would make it work. They'd fly home and never, ever talk about it again.

But then Evan grunted, and Rick turned towards the main gate at the side of the house. Melody was the last to see it – because ambling along the drive, iPad under his arm, was her father. He looked up to take in the man in front of him – but it was far too late for that. Melody saw what was going to happen before it did, not that she could do anything.

The gun fired and her father fell – and then there was only silence.

EPILOGUE

As airport waiting areas went, the one at Victoria certainly beat Heathrow's. The fact it was a fraction of the size probably helped. There was less of everything. Fewer screaming children, fewer people with speakers instead of headphones, not as many endless announcements.

Melody was staring across the hall when Sam appeared in front of her. 'Can I have money for the machine?' he asked.

'What machine?'

'They call it candy here.'

Melody opened her bag and dug out the leftover Canadian dollars, which she passed across.

Sam's eyes boggled at the amount of money. They hadn't needed much in the way of cash. 'Can I spend all of it?' he asked.

'As long as you don't *eat* all of it,' Melody replied.

Sam turned to move away and Thomas hopped up, saying he'd take him. Melody watched her brother-in-law and son disappear to the far end of the hall, and the vending machines beyond.

She, Nina and Evan sat in a row, hand luggage tucked

under their feet. Nobody spoke for a while, though Melody knew what her sister was going to say a moment before she did. It was probably the twentieth time she'd repeated the same thing.

'Do you think it was Mum or Dad driving?'

Melody didn't answer, she never had. Both parents had been in the car on the night Grace had been hit, so, in a lot of ways, it didn't matter. They were each responsible. Nina was desperate to know but Melody couldn't give the answer, even if she knew.

They were about to get on a plane in which there would be a body in the hold. Or what was left of one. Evan had said he'd arrange the funeral and Melody wasn't going to stop him.

'Can you give us a minute?' she asked, talking to her sister.

For a moment, it didn't feel as if Nina would move – but then she pushed herself up slowly, without speaking, and strode away.

The sisters were taking what happened in very different ways. Melody couldn't talk about any of it, Nina wanted to talk about *all* of it. They would probably have that conversation one day, but it wouldn't be in Canada.

They were in a lounge full of people and yet the noise blended into nothing. In that moment, Melody was sitting in silence with her fiancé. She took Evan's hand and clasped it. They hadn't had a lot of time for just the two of them. There had been all the police interviews, of course. The time together with Sam, then the admin that never ended. Talks with car rental companies, and airlines, and the like. Lori had been so right about life continuing. Melody knew she would never forget her – for more reasons than one.

Melody had hoped to find time to talk to Starla – though it had never come. She had no idea what the poor woman was going through, given her father hadn't been the one to hit Grace after all. He was a drink-driver but he hadn't been a killer. And having died years ago, he would never know the truth of what had really happened. Melody wondered if she might email the other woman one day, or find her on Facebook.

Or perhaps not.

Her family had done enough damage to this community.

'Did you talk to Chloe this morning?' Melody asked.

'Yeah,' Evan replied. 'She knows what time we're getting back and what happened.'

'It'll be nice to meet her,' Melody said – and it would. Getting home would feel like something of a new start – and that would involve having a twenty-year-old step-daughter of sorts. A strange situation for them all. Evan had apologised for not telling her but, as things went, Melody had far larger things that kept her awake. Sam didn't know about Chloe yet but they knew he'd be delighted about it all. They'd largely kept the brutality of what had happened to his grandfather from him but he'd gone through a lot. They all had and it was going to take a while for much of it to sink in. For now, Melody simply wanted to get home. It would be a new world without her father, though with the knowledge of what he'd done. She'd never get to ask him why.

Melody and Evan sat quietly, holding hands. She liked that. It was enough. She closed her eyes, breathed, and then opened them again. Two more hours and she'd be on a plane.

Across the aisle, a girl was going through a book filled with pictures of flowers. She would point to one, tell her mum what it was, be told 'That's nice', and then turn to the next page. Melody watched the routine happen a good dozen times, before the girl went back to the beginning of the book and started again, this time talking her father through the images.

Melody could feel the love between them all – and, as she watched the trio, it was one more thing she knew.

Heather had said that Shannon's daughter was named Ella and that she collected flowers to sell in the village centre.

Shaaaaaaaaaaaaaaa-non.

The voices from all those years ago hung in the airport rafters. The shame of everything Melody and her family had done.

She almost wanted to go and say sorry.

Almost.

She couldn't – because Shannon had moved on. They all had. Even if the other woman knew who Melody was, it wasn't as if an apology would change anything.

Suddenly, the girl turned sideways, noticing Melody had been staring. A smile spread across her face as she started to wave. Melody waved back as the girl's mother caught her eye.

There was no recognition there, simply the gentlest of nods and a smile to thank her for joining in.

The girl looked back to her book as Melody stopped staring.

'Has Sam been asking about that list of things to do?' Evan asked.

'Yeah.'

'You know he wants to come back...?'

Melody did know – mainly because her son had told her as much at least three times. In fairness, she had been the same at his age.

'What do you think?' Evan asked.

'I think I'm done with Vancouver Island,' Melody replied.

It got the softest of humourless laughs. 'I agree.'

PUBLISHING TEAM

Turning a manuscript into a book requires the efforts of many people. The publishing team at Bookouture would like to acknowledge everyone who contributed to this publication.

Audio
Alba Proko
Sinead O'Connor
Melissa Tran

Commercial
Lauren Morrissette
Hannah Richmond
Imogen Allport

Cover Design
The Brewster Project

Data and analysis
Mark Alder
Mohamed Bussuri

Editorial
Ellen Gleeson
Nadia Michael

Milton Keynes UK
Ingram Content Group UK Ltd.
UKHW012127110424
440929UK00004B/147

9 781835 254691